They'll Take Everything

C. H. Connor

SPECTRE
& GWIN
PUBLISHING

for Susan and James,

to whom I owe it all

CHAPTER 1

"It was when I looked over at her lying there, motionless, and I realised she was no longer breathing. That none of them were breathing." David looked to the ceiling and wiped away a single tear as his throat swallowed his words.

Allen's lips didn't move, and his expression didn't change, but his eyes flicked up at David.

"It doesn't matter what I do, or where I go," he continued, his voice fractured, "that moment, along with the seconds that led up to it, are always there, with me. Hanging over me." He pushed himself forward from his seat and rested his elbows on his knees. His eyes were closed and his head lowered, running his fingers through his hair. "You were right, the first few months were my absolute worst, and I have moved on from those days. But I still feel like there's no real way to properly move on. I mean, how can I?" David lifted his head, his eyes landing on the closed door directly behind Allen before shifting to the bookshelves that dominated the entire wall on his right-hand side. "People say time heals everything," David said, now looking back at Allen. "But can time heal me?"

Allen finished scribbling into the notepad that he balanced on his crossed legs and removed his glasses. "Everyone's different,

David. Remember that," he said as he waved his glasses through the air. "Yes, a lot of people find that time does help heal their wounds. Maybe not over weeks or months. But years, sometimes decades. You don't need me to tell you that everyone processes their feelings differently. Even though it's been three years, that's not to say that you're suddenly expected to no longer carry this around with you. It's a heavy, heavy burden."

David slumped back in his seat, his hands tightly pressed together.

"What happened to you was extraordinarily traumatic, David. When the thoughts of what happened enter your head, it's okay to stop and reflect. Try not to bottle up what you're feeling, because you need to feel your emotions and experience them in order to move forward." Allen let out a sigh. "I think that's what's been tripping you up. Don't just rely on the fact that time can heal you. You also need to heal yourself."

David's forehead wrinkled. "I think about the good times every day. I think about it all before that moment." He shook his head.

"When those thoughts come to you, remember that it's okay. It's natural. As horrendous and as devastating as those memories are, stop pushing them away, because it'll only make it harder for you to overcome."

David didn't respond.

"I know that sounds like the worst possible advice, but it works. You know it does. It's facing the reality of the situation that will allow you to start properly healing."

"You'd think I'd know all this, and really I do. I loved my… what was it? Twelve, thirteen years in the industry."

Allen gave a smile. "You've always got the option to come back into it. You don't have to close that door. I know you've already sold your practice, but that doesn't mean you can't start again when the time is right."

David only gave half a smile as he shrugged. "I realised it was no longer for me."

Allen paused, glancing down at his notes before looking back at David. "Have you slept any better this week? I recall that being a major obstacle for you back when you were having these episodes."

David shook his head emphatically. "Still struggling. I don't know, it's like I'm destined to never have some deep sleep again. I just lie there for hours, waiting. Hoping to fall asleep. When that happens, my mind trails. I've found this time to be the worst for feeling low and having all of those emotions return."

"And you've still not spoken to your doctor about the possibility of medication?"

David repeated the shaking of his head.

"What about your dreams? When you do finally fall asleep, have you experienced the same recurring dream?"

David hesitated, his eyes unwavering. "The same one," he said before forcing an attempted smile, only for it to deflate as quickly as it had appeared. "Walking into the dark room and sitting down in front of the candle." He scratched his eyebrow and took a short, sharp breath. "Then the headlights just appear in the distance, but they're so bright and I can't see. They start coming towards me and all I can hear is the ringing."

"I can see how much that's affecting you."

David inflated his cheeks and blew out a mouthful of air. "I'm not like this all the time," he said as he patted the bags under his eyes. "Most days are better than others."

"This recurring dream that you're still experiencing is an indication of unresolved, persistent conflict. This comes back to what I was just saying to you about these thoughts that you have, and how it's important that you process them. We need to address this internal conflict you have before we can hope to see an improvement."

David shuffled in his seat, his eyes cast to the floor.

"Have you thought any more of going back to East Horsley? To your home?"

David's expression froze as if his lungs skipped an intake of air. His eyes moved around the room searchingly, unable to find anything of meaning to cling onto. He felt Allen's stare etching into him and so finally met his gaze. "Now and then."

"And how do you feel about it?"

David contrived another smile that lasted the briefest of moments. "Mad, I know. I still can't bring myself to go back to our old home. I can't bear to walk through that door again without them."

Allen propped his glasses back onto his nose and wrote into his notepad.

David watched him write. "Perhaps I'm not ready for that closure just yet."

"My only worry, David, is that this phase you've been in for the past three years may never resolve itself if you don't get this closure you so desperately need."

David glanced at Allen's notepad.

"How do you think you'd feel when you do return?"

He shrugged. "I don't know."

"Sadness? Anger, maybe?"

David's eyes glistened, his lips pressed shut.

"But perhaps that's not all you'd find. Perhaps you'd find a level of comfort in the possessions that are still there. Perhaps by the memories that exist in those rooms. By going through those rooms and those possessions, you'd be able to bring about that closure."

"The sadness and anger I can deal with. I have dealt with. It's the guilt and emptiness that gets me. It'd be too much. Too much for me to go back to right now."

"That's certainly something that you need to address, David. You can't let this guilt and emptiness, wherever it is inside of you, and no matter how much you suppress it, to eat away at you, bit by bit."

"I can't. Not now," David said in a hushed voice.

Allen slowly nodded. "Okay. We'll move on," he said, striking a loud line on the notepad with his pen. "Day-to-day, how are you? What's keeping you busy at the moment?"

David cleared his throat. "I'm a long way away from the days of being holed up in The Washington Mayfair Hotel with a pile of room service trays and a full-on beard, not doing anything with my time. I'm past that," he said as he straightened his back. "I've been keeping myself busy. Too busy, in fact, and I've not actually mentioned any of this to you yet."

"Oh? Have you taken up a new hobby? A new job?"

"For the past few months, I've been putting together a little project, and I've reached the point where I just need to make a few final touches."

"That's excellent, David. That's really, really good to hear. What kind of project is it?"

David let out the first genuine smile since the session began. "It's a project that's hopefully going to turn my grief into something meaningful. I've really struggled with what I've been through over the past three years and without your help I would've been in a much darker place, so I can't thank you enough." He scratched his head, his smile still evident. "I'm bringing together some very close friends of mine to try and make this project work. It's my dream to help people when their world is turned upside down just like mine was."

"That's very commendable, David. It sounds fantastic."

David's smile faded. "...but?"

Allen sighed. "You're a very intelligent, capable person, and whatever you set yourself upon, I know it'll be a tremendous success. I really commend you for wanting to help people, and the world needs more people like you."

"But?"

"But I'd recommend focusing on yourself for just a bit longer. You need the time and energy to concentrate on your own needs, not other people's."

David leant forward. "It's by focusing on other people's needs and improving the lives of others that I'll be able to heal myself."

CHAPTER 2

The car slowly rolled up to the small Victorian terrace, hidden amongst the capital's big-player buildings. Dated, yet full of character, Victorian terraces were the little gems of the city. Almost like a bird's nest in the bustling forest that is the great city of London.

From the driver's seat of his grey Audi, David peered at the house before him. The building itself was no stranger. Countless times had he walked through its doorway and countless times more had the homeowner left through the same doorway to meet with David. The quaint building was well matched with its current owner – its only owner for the last forty-six years. David glanced at his watch. 7:28 p.m. Punctual, as always.

Looking out through the windscreen, he soaked in an appealing view of London's skyline. Dark clouds ominously threatened overhead, adding to the picture perfectly. A mixture of dark shades from the buildings and surrounding atmosphere could make quite a lovely black and white watercolour painting – should a piece of artwork be ever so cruelly denied a lick of colour.

The cold wind that blew overhead crept into the car, tightening its grip on the suppressed temperature. He thanked himself for choosing his thick, brown coat and his dark grey scarf to shield him from the offensive chill.

Three sharp knocks on the passenger window released David from the absorbing view that had taken a hold of his attention. He quickly looked over at the window.

An elderly black woman stood before the car, hunched down so as to be at eye level with him. Her face told a thousand stories through her striking wrinkles. Plump cheeks and shy freckles, supplemented by her black, curly hair that propped up a large, colourful hat, resting evenly on her head. "Are ya gonna open the door and let me in, or am I walkin' on my own to the restaurant on my sixty-eighth birthday?" she said to David through the window, her eyes narrowed.

He quickly leaned over and unlocked the door, pushing it open. "I'm very sorry, Bev. How are you?"

She climbed into the passenger seat, accidentally flicking David in his face with her overly large hat. "Ooh, I'm much better now I'm inside away from the rain that's surely comin'!"

He rubbed his face.

"Ya cheeky sod. Not seen ya in nearly a whole year and yet ya lettin' me stand waitin' on ya car doorstep in this weather. I'm not ya cat askin' to be let in, y'know! My hair could have been ruined." Her Jamaican accent sounded even raspier when she was up close.

"My apologies," David replied with a grin. "I was in a world—"

"Let's go, Mr! I just can't wait for them spicy chicken wings again. And ya bet I'm askin' for double portions. *Girl* doesn't turn sixty-eight every day now, do I?"

Bev Walcott had no immediate family living in London, so David insisted he treat her on her birthday. Her daughter, who was in her early forties, had moved to New York when she graduated university. Bev's husband passed away in 2004 after a happy twenty-six-year marriage.

For almost fourteen years, Bev had been a very close friend to David and his family. Her kindness, honesty, and wisdom were refreshing traits which David regarded highly. The pair made certain to see each other as frequently as they could – as if a pair of lost souls had found comfort and support in one another.

With a smile on his face and his right foot poised on the gas pedal, David set off to the restaurant, buried deep inside the city.

David slid into the booth that encompassed a table in the corner of the restaurant. Bev approached slowly, her eyes fixed on the available spacing for her to also slide her way in. Shaking her head, she requested a chair so that she could sit on the open-end of the booth. She was too old to humour her chances of attempting to make her way in without budging the table all the way into the wall and suffocating David in the process. With her newly found spacious seat, it almost seemed as if David was at an interview without any plausible means of escape.

The pair each picked up their menu, opened it, and began sifting through the numerous options.

"Spicy chicken wings?" he asked.

"Need ya ask?"

He smirked.

A waitress appeared and took the pair's order. Two plates of spicy chicken wings for Bev's appetiser, followed up by a double cheeseburger with the side of peppered potato wedges. All washed down with a bottle of the house red wine. For David, he ordered a portion of the restaurant's signature dough balls with the melted cheese and garlic dip, quickly accompanied by a tomato and chili spaghetti arrabbiata. Since he was tonight's designated driver, a full-fat Pepsi would be his choice of drink. Living life on the edge.

"Thank ya for this, David. It's real special."

"There's no need to thank me, Bev. You've done so much for me over the years you don't even realise. Anyway, I know you're working too hard and too much these days. You should consider slowing down and cutting back on your hours."

"Slowin' down? Cuttin' back? *Noooo*. I enjoy my work, ya know that. It gets me outa the house and talkin' to people. Ya know me and ya know human psychology. We creatures are social and we like talkin' to people."

"You always have been a people person," he replied with a smile.

"Ya have no need to worry about me. It's me that's worried about ya, ya see."

"And why would that be?"

A drawn-out pause filled the booth, quickly setting up camp.

"Because," Bev started, "it's been three years, David."

The drawn-out pause had officially packed its bags, uprooted its camp and fled the scene.

"And?"

"And what has happened in that time? I'm worried about ya."

David stared down at his perfectly folded napkin on his perfectly clean plate.

"Before *everythin'* happened, ya had a beautiful home. A hugely successful business that was flourishin'. I don't understand what ya've done with it all." Her eyes were transfixed on his face, staring him down in an anxious manner – almost like parents do with their children when they say they've somehow managed to hurt themselves. "Thankfully ya have stayed in touch with me and have chosen to keep me in ya life for all of this time, but I don't see ya as much as I used to." Her words were now softer. "It's like ya've put me at arm's length and refuse to allow me any closer."

David's eyes shifted to meet Bev's gaze.

The waitress returned to the table, carrying three plates in a way that always fascinated David.

"Chicken wings?" the waitress asked.

"Spicy?" Bev questioned, looking at the waitress expectantly.

"Mhm."

"In that case, plant 'em down."

With the two portions of spicy chicken wings placed in front of a now-beaming Bev, and the warm dough balls in front of David, he once again met her eye. "Truth be told, Bev, I not only wanted to treat you tonight and catch up, but I also wanted to talk to you about exactly what I've been up to."

"Oh?"

"Enjoy your delicacies and we'll finish the rest of our meal, then I'll take you for a drink afterwards. We'll talk more about it then."

Without bothering with a response, Bev dug her hand into one of the plates, yanking out her first spicy chicken wing.

As the pair exited the restaurant, the moonlight above welcomed them to the abrupt coldness with a shimmering reflection from the wet concrete road. The night, with its dark and threatening clouds, had liberated itself by releasing its vast downfall of rain upon the city while David and Bev were enjoying their meal inside. With a clearer sky, but also with a much colder wind, the pair began the extensive journey to the Revolution bar – a whole fifty metres away. Bev made every effort to wrap herself up against the elements, tightly securing her coat around her body and propping her hat above her head; as if a colourful beacon against the backdrop of her dull surroundings. David simply slung his coat and scarf over his arm and set off.

As they walked, David caught Bev staring at him. "What is it?"

Bev smiled and shook her head. "No, it's nothin'."

He gave her a gentle nudge. "Come on."

"It's just," she giggled, "I appreciate how lucky I am to have such a kind and thoughtful friend."

"Oh, stop."

"And the fact that ya so easy on the eyes makes it even better."

"How much have you drunk?" David laughed.

David did still carry a somewhat youthful look; a glow that made him seem younger than his thirty-seven-year-old face really was. His layer of brown, prickly stubble shielded his face from the coldness of the weather and the warmth of a person's touch. His short, dark brown hair, one of his few regrets, showed subtle signs of thinning.

The bar was surprisingly quiet for 8:48 p.m. David had been a customer of this particular bar for many years and knew it well. With his group of friends while students at university, they would come into the city on Friday or Saturday evenings – sometimes both – for long drinking sessions of clubbing, partying and socialising. Over more recent years, however, the bar had regained itself from the grip of its student customers as they moved on to more designated student zones within the city. Locals and regulars alike seized the opportunity and reclaimed the bar.

David pointed out a small table at the side of the bar to Bev, who quickly sprinted towards it and threw down her hat on one of the chairs like an exhausted explorer would have thrown down a flag on unexplored territory during the Age of Discovery.

Handing over a £20 note to the bartender and receiving copper and two drinks in exchange, David glanced at the small TV on the wall behind the counter. A short news clip covered the story of Prince William and Kate, the Duke and Duchess of Cambridge, landing in Canada to crowds of Commonwealth fans. The news coverage then moved on to another story with the newsreader going into detail.

"It has emerged this afternoon that Eva Shields, the founding CEO of the major international media group Shields Corporation, has made a controversial statement towards people in poverty and the consequences of the state supporting them. In an interview released earlier today, the thirty-nine-year-old stated, *'I do think something needs to change with people on the poverty line in this country, we can't be funding them forever'*. These comments are the latest in a string of controversial missteps for Miss Shields whose reputation has suffered over recent months. The share price of Shields Corporation on the London Stock Exchange has closed one point six per cent down at two hundred and sixty-nine pence a share. Please join me again at eleven p.m. for another news bulletin."

David shook his head as he headed towards their table. He placed down a glass of *Blaxland Estate Shiraz* – red wine – in front of Bev, while he sat opposite her with another full-fat Pepsi.

"Ooh," she shrieked in excitement, studying the glass in front of her. "Why thank ya very much."

"You're welcome," David replied, sipping his drink as he glanced around the room.

Bev brought the wine up to her nose, smelling it before taking a larger-than-average mouthful. Her eyes opened widely. "This is fabulous."

David laughed. "Good."

A group of six women entered the bar, laughing and talking loudly. The group approached the bartender and were quickly diverted to a reserved table on the other side of the room.

"William and Kate have arrived in Canada," David said, looking back at Bev.

Bev smiled. "Let's not talk about the beautiful couple now. I'll catch up with their journey when I get home. But for now, I want ya to tell me what ya said ya would. What have ya been doing, David?"

David's lips parted. He readjusted his seating posture.

Bev kept her gaze firmly on him, narrowing her eyes.

David offered up a small smile. Bev was quite possibly his closest friend. No other person did he regard their opinion so high. "Well," he started, "I think you know that I'm no longer running my psychiatry practice."

"Anyone with an IQ over ten and access to the Internet can find that out, David."

"I sold it a while back. After what happened…" He looked for words across the table.

"In South Carolina."

"Yeah. After what happened, I lost my motivation. My passion. I couldn't cope with it anymore. It was just a huge money-making machine that I no longer loved. It…" he paused, searching for the words. "Turned me into something I didn't want to be."

Bev nodded.

"After I lost my girls, Stu took over and dealt with the business' day-to-day operations. Do you know Stu?"

Bev shook her head.

"I've worked with him for over a decade. It doesn't matter, but he ran the practice for me while I was coming to terms with everything. He also helped me with the sale when I finally decided what I wanted to do."

"And what is that?"

David gulped down a mouthful of Pepsi.

Bev's eyebrows tilted.

"I'm in need of a partner, Bev."

"A partner?"

"Yeah. Would you care to come and work with me?"

Confusion cast across Bev, settling in. "Work with you on what?"

"I was tired of my money-making machine of a business. I was tired of helping rich, narcissistic people who thought that because they were on TV and their bank account was full, they deserved everything. I was tired of doing nothing truly good in the world."

Bev nodded once.

"I'm launching a charity in seven days' time, and I'd love it if you helped me. Even if it's just temporary while I find my feet. I want you to help me start the next chapter of my life."

CHAPTER 3

Bev ran for the car as if a third portion of chicken wings were hidden inside. The rain thrashed down onto the pavement, bouncing back up at them as if the concrete was leaking. "Unlock it, unlock it," Bev said, cowering underneath her hat.

David fumbled his set of keys, finally clicking open the car with a beep. They dove inside, snapping shut their doors behind them. "Jesus," he started, "we didn't time that well."

Bev let out a boisterous laugh. "Ya said that right. There's not a dry patch on me."

Turning the heating onto the maximum setting, David started the car and slotted in his seatbelt. "Well apart from the damp ending, I think we've had a good night. Have you enjoyed it?"

Bev squeezed her hat, releasing droplets of water onto her lap. "I've had a wonderful evenin', David. I thank ya very much for it, ya've made it so special."

"My pleasure, Bev. I'm glad you've enjoyed it." He indicated to turn right and set off on Falcon Road. Even for a Friday evening, the streets were subdued; people hunkered in pubs and clubs rather than on the road.

Clearing her throat, Bev glanced around her surroundings. She looked back to David. "Ya never told me what happened when ya got back. When I didn't speak to ya for so long."

David quietly sighed. "You don't miss a trick," he said, braking at a set of red lights. "Well, the first thing I did was move into a hotel room in the city centre for close to three months." He rubbed his hands together in the warm air that blew toward him. "Sam offered I stay with her, but I refused. I had some sort of desire just to relinquish all form of responsibility; something staying with my sister could provide, but it wouldn't have been fair on little Ben. It wouldn't have been fair to have a depressed uncle take over his house."

"You stayed in a hotel for three months?"

The lights turned green and David set off once more. "The Washington Mayfair, yeah."

Bev looked out at the persistent rain. "That must have set ya back a fortune."

"It did, but the hotel had become something like a haven. Like a stronghold I could hide in whilst I just dealt with everything."

"I get ya, but ya should have come to me. Ya know I live alone and could have helped ya get through it."

"I know you would have, but I just needed to be on my own. Anyway, I discovered a prolonged residency at a hotel allowed you to see a lot. Business men and women stopping for the odd night. Couples spending a romantic weekend. Singletons, or committed-but-available people hooking up with one another."

Bev's eyes widened. "How unsavoury."

"Then I finally got the apartment on the twelfth floor where I'm at now."

"Ah yeah, it's quite a nice little place ya have now. Handy location, too. But what's happened to ya family home back in East Horsley?"

"I've still got it," David said, turning onto a one-way street backlogged with a queue of traffic. "Ah, this is where everyone's been hiding." He stuck the car in neutral. "I've had no reason to sell it or rent it out. I've just kept it the way it was the day we left."

"It might do ya good to move on, sell it. Ya know, might bring some closure."

David smirked and thought of Allen. He shook his head. "Another family's not going to make memories in place of my own. Nah, the place can stand empty until I'm ready to go back. I want everything just how it was."

"Fair enough," Bev said, watching the last water droplets fall from David's ear. "How do ya feel livin' in the city now? Do ya like it?"

"I dono, it's a weird one. When I moved into the apartment, I felt an overwhelming sense like I was being reborn. Living in a property without memories that would make my stomach churn the moment they faded in and out of my mind, you know? There's something about living on the twelfth floor of a building that I enjoy, too. That sounds a bit crazy. But it's like some childish emotion in me stirs when I look out of the living room window. The buzz and atmosphere of living slap-bang in the middle of the capital. Hearing sirens, and busy traffic at the dead of night, and a passer-by with their shouting and obnoxiously loud fits of laughter."

"Ya like that?" Bev asked, a single eyebrow raised.

David chuckled, said, "Surprisingly, yeah. But, I've got to be honest, I've also bought another place just out of the city."

The second eyebrow joined the first at the top of Bev's forehead. "How many houses do ya own?"

"I bought a third one in Wanstead. I know, I know," he said, turning away from Bev's expression. "I thought it'd be a nice retreat to go to when I've had a busy week in the city with the charity, you know. It's a two-bedroom country home right by Wanstead Park, just next to some woods and a beautiful lake. The guy selling it was from India and he was moving back there, so I got a good price."

"Check you out, Mr Monopoly."

David smirked, shaking his head as he rolled the car forward in a slow crawl. The queue of traffic gradually dispersed, with the pair able to continue their journey.

"It's a shame ya sold ya practice. Ya were so passionate about psychiatry once upon a time."

"Things change," David said. "People change."

Bev nodded. "I guess that's true."

"I mean I built it up from scratch just after university. It was a fifteen-year-old company and I managed to do everything I set out to achieve. It really was awesome."

"Take a left here," Bev said as she laid eyes on another queue of traffic ahead. "It'll lead ya straight onto the main road round the corner from my house."

David indicated and turned.

"Who did ya sell your practice to?"

"An American corporation that already owns a chain of practices in the U.S. and wanted to break into the British market. Whether they'll keep it as just a provider of psychiatry and psychotherapy, I don't know. They might branch out, or change it entirely, who knows."

"I remember comin' to the openin' of ya practice. Ya and Maria were so young." Bev smiled. "She'll be proud of ya, ya know. She'll be proud of ya opening this new charity and all the work ya're wantin' to do for people."

David brought the car to a stop outside of the terraced house. He kept his eyes on the grey scenery beyond the windscreen.

"I can see ya still carry a great sense of grief, David. I can see it behind ya glossy eyes and I can feel it in the words ya speak."

David mustered a short smile.

Bev placed her palm on his cheek. "I'm glad ya've moved on from the days of the hotel, and ya took me out this evenin'. If I can help at all with the charity, I will be there."

David wandered through the dense Wanstead woodland aimlessly having dropped Bev off at her home half an hour ago. He dipped below low-lying, over-stretching branches; an occurrence any six-foot man should be well aware of if deciding to stroll through the wilderness close to midnight. The fruit of the spring season was evident in the flourishing leaves, waving themselves proudly in the bitter wind. Young plants sprouted from the damp earth, fighting their neighbours for all-important space. The pathway on which many of the locals walked was neatly hidden in the undergrowth. Strangers to the land could easily miss it, crossing it entirely unaware. But David was no stranger to these parts anymore. The woods lay at the foot of his house and were the only element between him and a huge, concealed lake.

After walking for eight minutes, David reached the opening of the other side. The trees separated, giving way to his steaming breath in the cool air. The moonlight shone over across the brim of the calm lake.

For what seemed like miles, open land was all the eye could see. Nothing laid waste to the beauty that was this natural sanctuary. David had been visiting this site since he moved here, being informed by his estate agent of the close-by picturesque setting.

Tonight, no one else was in sight. David had only two birds circling overhead for company.

Perfect.

He walked towards a large, moss-covered rock that he usually sat on, but decided to sit in front of it on the grass, leaning back onto the stone. The cost of this, David soon realised, was an increasingly damp backside.

For fifteen minutes, David sat silently staring out towards the idyllic view, watching as birds dipped in and out of the water. Questions intruded into his mind, before being swiftly replaced by inspirations. Doubts dribbled in before being swept out by regrets. He dug into his right pocket, taking out his phone. Bringing it to life with a touch of the skin, they appeared A colourful picture of his three smiling faces staring back at him from one Christmas day many years prior. "This is all for you," he said.

An email notification from an unknown address popped up on his screen, blurring the three faces into the background.

David opened the notification with a tap.

From: 9h2k001yc@szxg.com
Subject: DAVID DALE

Welcome back to the real world, David. You've been hiding for so long, I thought I might never get a chance to speak with you.

I see you've been quietly busy these past few months and now you're back.

Back for good?

Let's see.

CHAPTER 4

"Including myself, there are now four trustees," David said into the phone. "Together we will be acting as the responsible persons that the Commission requires."

"An ideal number," a man replied. "May I take their details and roles within the charity, please?"

"Sure. Well, firstly, there's myself. I'll be acting as the Charity Director and Treasurer."

"Mhm."

"Then there's Bev Walcott who'll be a governor in the charity as well as my assistant. I'll also have Stu Jackson as The Chair, and the fourth person is Kristian Sinason who'll also act as a governor."

"*Sinason?* How is that spelt?"

David spelt the name out to the man.

"Thank you," he replied. "The relevant forms will be sent out and you should receive them in the next three to five working days. If you could complete and return them to us, that'd be great."

"Sounds good."

"Is there anything else you would like to discuss?"

"No, thank you though."

"Thanks for your call, Mr Dale. Provided the forms you return are satisfactory, there should be no reason for the Charity

Commission to not allow beneficial tax relief upon, or soon after, your launch."

"Brilliant, thank you for your time," David replied with a smile. The phone clicked off and he placed it down onto the table in front of him next to piles of documents and forms.

Bev emerged from the hallway, walking into the living room of David's central London flat. "Oooh, now in all my sixty-eight years, that is a lovely back scratcher ya have by ya bath. That baby works right into the tension, dunnit? Mhm-hmm," she said, emitting a slight shiver as if renewed by the experience.

David smirked. "I've just got off the phone with the Charity Commission. They've got everything they need."

"Brilliant," Bev replied, walking over to the sofa opposite David, popping herself down.

"I'll speak with Kristian and Stu when I get a chance and try and arrange a meeting in the next day or so. It'll be nice for you to meet them both, they're great. It'll also give us a chance to go over the details of the launch and a few final things I want to cover before we go live," David said before standing up and heading to the kitchen. "Would you like a drink?"

"A water'll be fine."

David plucked two glasses out of the cabinet, rinsing them under the tap. "Oh, there's a spare office key here on the counter for you, so you can let yourself in and lock up if necessary."

"Perfect," she said as she straightened her dress. "Tell me, how'd ya know this Stu and Kristian? Why them for the charity?"

David dried the outside of the glasses, putting them down onto the kitchen counter and filling them with bottled water from his fridge. He carried them over to the living room table and handed one to Bev while sipping from the other. "I've known Stu for years. We go back to the days of university. We never studied together; he was into his music and I was into my psychology. We just happened to get to know one another when we somehow ended up playing pool together in the student union bar on campus. We became good friends quite quickly. He moved to London after he graduated and has worked at several record labels since, as well as helping out with the practice."

"And Kristian? Where's he from?"

"Sweden."

"Sweden? How's he gonna help run the charity from Scandinavia?"

"He originates from Sweden, but he moved to the UK in his early twenties. He's a trained solicitor and will help with the legal side of the charity's operations. Don't worry, his English is impeccable."

"It's not his English I'm worried about," she said. "It's his gorgeous accent and, I presume, his blonde hair and blue eyes that might get me all fired up, y'know?"

David looked at Bev blankly, choosing to sip his water rather than reply.

Bev smiled to herself. She looked to the window and the world beyond it. "High up, aren't we? Quite scary."

"We're on the twelfth floor. Perfectly safe, of course."

Bev stood up and walked over to the window, peering outside.

"What is it?" David asked with a frown.

"I'm seeing if I can see Sweden from here, or at least hear their accents."

David started to clear away his and Bev's plates after their light lunch. Bev's visit was pleasant, her company always was. The opportunity to go over details of the upcoming charity also proved useful, igniting Bev's excitement.

Bev left for her own home ten minutes ago; her house just a short twenty-minute tube journey away, but Bev was no fan of public transport. The services, she said, were of a good standard and were vital in today's day and age, but the overcrowding of people and the fight for personal space was something Bev would not be willing to give a go. Nonetheless, she is a keen driver and still owned her own car. Adding up to an hour or so onto her journey time by driving in stop-start London traffic wasn't an issue for good ol' Bev.

David's mobile phone rang. He darted into the living room and checked the caller ID.

Unknown.

He picked up. "David Dale."

Silence.

"Hello?" David asked.

The line disconnected.

David stared at his phone, his forehead wrinkled. He placed it back down onto the counter and returned to the kitchen. Picking up a dripping wet plate and a cloth, he started to hand dry it.

The phone rang again.

Sighing, David placed the plate and cloth back onto the drying rack and approached the phone. This time, there was a caller ID. He answered, "Hello, hello. How are you?"

"Hey, I'm all good, thanks. And you?" a friendly female asked.

"Yeah, I'm well. What's up?"

"Just checking in. Do I need a reason these days for calling my big brother?"

David narrowed his eyes. "No, really. What's up?"

"Honestly, I can't believe you – okay, fine. I was wondering if you'd like to come and have dinner with us next week, if you're free."

"You want me to come all the way up to Lancashire for dinner? Is it Christmas already?" he replied, putting the glasses and cutlery into the sink.

"It'll be nice, don't you think?"

"Come on, hit me with the catch already."

"Well…"

"Well?"

"Just come and I'll tell you when I see you."

"Just tell me now so I can tell you if I can make it or not."

Silence.

"I've started seeing someone and I can't wait for you to meet him," she said.

Great.

CHAPTER 5

Slowly walking into complete darkness, David could just make out a square glass table and a single chair. On top of the table was a long, thin white candle, flicking its amber glow onto David's face as he moved closer. He pulled out the chair and sat down. The candle, now inches from him, instantly went out, leaving a perfectly vertical trail of smoke. He followed the smoke with his eyes, watching its trail disappear into the darkness above him. Two bright lights some hundred metres away switched on, and the sound of a car's engine roared through him as the two lights rapidly rushed forward. David's lips parted with a short intake of air as he looked back down at the table before him, the candle replaced by a ringing mobile phone.

David snapped open his eyes and immediately pushed his body up as he fought for a lungful of air. One deep breath after the other, he sat there, hands faced down by the pillow behind him, looking around his bedroom.

Sunlight had crept its way into the room with its full-frontal assault on the shielding window blinds. The new source of light provided the room with an alien warm glow, giving floating dust particles the platform to perform their acrobatic dances.

David felt the moist sheets covering his legs and wiped the sweat from his forehead and cheeks, glancing over to the alarm with his blurred, tired vision. He forced his eyes shut and held his head in his stuffy hands. He let his body drop back onto the bed and rested once again, looking up to the blank ceiling. He turned his head, looking to his right. Standing there, on his bedside drawer and behind his alarm, she was forever embedded into the picture frame as a constant source of comfort. Maria, holding out her first ever batch of home-baked bread rolls in their old family home. Her long chestnut hair tied back. A colourful apron hanging from her neck and wrapped around her body. Oven mitts on each hand, holding a cooling rack of nine bread rolls, each looking deliciously golden brown and perfectly round.

Kissing two fingers, David leaned over and placed them onto the picture before standing up and climbing out of bed.

Just as he stepped out of the shower, David heard the phone ringing. He wrapped the towel around his waist and walked quickly to his phone. "Hello?"

"Hi David, are you all right?"

"Ah, hi Stu," he returned, walking back to the bathroom to let the water drip onto the bath mat. "Yeah I'm fine, just outta the shower. Are you okay?"

"I'm grand. Listen, I've just gotten wind of a new casino opening tonight in the city centre. Well, I found out last night, but that's not the point. It's supposed to be a huge first night, heard everyone is going."

"You know I'm not a gambler, Stu. I'll pass."

"Our names are already on the guest list. I'll pick you up at eight."

The phone clicked off.

*

8:00 p.m. came around quickly. Another day of preparation evaporated into a gust of wind in what had become a tornado, sucking every second of time into it. A productive day, as usual. Tax forms, trustee forms and charity asset and office forms all filled in and ready to be returned. The website was finally ready, too, bringing David huge relief. A small company in Manchester was tasked with building the website, as well as its continual hosting needs. A tennis game of phone calls to and from the company finally paid off with the site looking professional, clean and easy to navigate. An enormous tick could be placed onto David's checklist of what was left to be accomplished before launch day which was rapidly approaching at breakneck speed.

David's phone sounded, vibrating on the arm of the sofa. Stu was outside of the apartment block waiting in his car. David finished his beer and placed the empty glass bottle on his kitchen counter next to other empty glass jars and bottles. With that, he put on his jacket, locked his door and hopped into the elevator.

David noticed Stu sitting in his car across from the apartment's entrance. Running over and jumping in, he asked, "Ever heard of peer pressure?"

"Give it a rest, you'll enjoy yourself. You need to enjoy yourself more often," Stu said, putting the car into first gear and setting off.

"You know I don't gamble though. Surely someone who does would be more fun to take?"

"Or I could just take my best bud whether he gambles or not," Stu replied, glancing at David.

David backed down.

"Anyway," Stu continued, "I don't wanna talk about the charity tonight. We've been planning and preparing for months, let's just take the night off and have a laugh, okay?"

David hesitantly nodded. "Okay."

The pair of them looked out of the windscreen, their gaze bouncing from car to building and back from building to car.

"Just one quick thing," David said.

Stu sighed, shaking his head. "One quick thing," he repeated.

"I've got Bev on board, bless her. I'd like you and Kristian to meet her in the next few days," David said, looking out of the window watching a car almost cause an incident after it quickly swerved into another lane.

"Sure thing. When were you thinking?"

"I'm heading to my sister's the day after next, and I won't be back until Wednesday, so then?"

"So late before the launch?"

"Why not?"

"No, it's nothing," Stu said. "Just seems a little late for us all to get together and have a meeting, is all."

"It'll be fine. I know you all so well that I can guarantee you'll get along fine."

Stu nodded slowly. He looked back to David. "Now no more charity related talk."

"Okay, okay."

"And lookie here. Something I picked up earlier today." Stu picked up a small object from the car's tray, hidden amongst a clutter of car park receipts and copper coins. He passed it to David. "All yours."

David looked at the object in his hand. A £50 casino chip. "What's this? How many times have I told you I don't bloody gamble?"

"Simmer down, golden boy. It's another night off for you. Be a rebel and humour me," Stu said with a smirk on his face.

"Mhm."

Stu leant forward, looking up at the clouds. "And I hope you brought an umbrella with you, because it's gonna absolutely piss it down."

The pair drove for a further twenty minutes before parking down a small, dead-end side road. The rain had managed to hold off, giving David and Stu the time they needed to reach the casino entrance. A small red carpet lay at its double doorway, guarded by two well-built security guards wearing black suits and earpieces. Stu stated their names and admission was granted. A wide flight of stairs immediately stood before them, which they ascended, climbing alongside reflective red walls with a golden shimmer. Stu and David reached the top of the staircase and entered the internal cavern that was the casino floor.

The doorway was on a high platform, overlooking the floor of activity. A mesh of sound blurred together and echoed off of the walls, hitting David like the music hits you when you enter an arena concert. The scurry of activity below them raised his eyebrows, the corners of his mouth daring to point upwards. David wasn't a gambling man, but the atmosphere was fascinatingly electrifying – and he had a £50 chip in his shirt pocket starting to burn a hole. Tables upon tables of games took up the majority of the floor. Blackjack, roulette, poker, craps. Up and down the side of the room lay small tables with stools and larger tables with chairs encircling them. An extensive bar, stretching wall-to-wall, was at the far side of the room. Hundreds of people were already here drinking, talking, laughing, and gambling. Waitresses – David couldn't see any waiters in sight – walked up and down the casino carrying trays of drinks.

David looked at Stu who was beaming, his smile stretched from one cheek to the other. Stu walked over to a booth to swap some cash into more casino chips, stashing them into his pocket. The pair then walked onwards, descending a short flight of stairs to participate in the heated, bustling crowd.

A lady immediately approached them with a tray of drinks. "Champagne?" she asked, holding out the tray.

Stu looked to David – still beaming – and took a glass.

David took his own, said, "Thank you."

"Isn't this great?" Stu asked, darting his vision in as many directions as he could.

"It's very nice. Very contemporary and decorative. Tasteful," David said.

"We're not here to survey the place," Stu said with a frown. "Come on, what shall we get started on first?"

"I couldn't even name you a single game, so you lead."

The pair drifted through the various groups of gamblers at different tables. As David followed in Stu's footsteps, weaving through the countless people, he caught a glimpse of a pair of eyes that rested squarely on him. From behind a packed roulette table, David saw a bald man in a black suit, staring. The man was tall, well built, and could have easily been in his mid-forties. The stare was constant and unapologetic.

Just before Stu and David reached a quiet blackjack table at the side of the room, David lost sight of the bald man in the midst of the activity.

"Blackjack. Do you know blackjack?" Stu asked.

"Er, is that the twenty-one game?"

"Yeah, yeah. Get twenty-one to win or beat the house with the highest hand. Go over twenty-one and you're out."

"Okay," David said with an uncertain tone.

Two players were already at the table, opposite the now-surrounded casino dealer. One of the players was middle-aged with round *Harry Potter* styled glasses. The other was older, sporting a long, frizzy beard that hid his mouth. David and Stu sat down to join, nodding politely to Potter and Frizzy.

"Be careful," Potter began, "this table's not got a great track record."

Stu smirked, said, "I'm feeling lucky."

"I'll watch a few rounds to see how it's done," David said.

Stu placed down a £50 chip and looked at his cards once the dealer had finished her dealing. Potter and Frizzy repeated the actions of: *look quickly and put on a straight face.* All three decided to keep their hand.

The dealer presented her cards, showing an eight of Spades and a Jack of Hearts. "Pay nineteen," she said.

Stu, Potter and Frizzy showed their hand. 19, 20 and 20. Win, win and win. Stu smirked again.

"You might've brought luck to the table, my friend," Frizzy said to Stu as the winning chips slid across to the three of them.

David smiled with a shrug.

"Are you playing this one?" Stu asked.

"Sure. Wish me luck," David said.

All four placed their bets and the dealer dealt their cards. Potter asked for another card before sighing and announcing he was bust on twenty-five. Frizzy asked for another card and then stuck with his hand. Stu also asked for another card, and then another, before sticking with his hand. David stuck with his two cards.

The dealer showed her hand. "Fifteen," she said. She drew another card. A seven. "Bust," she announced. She dished out the winning chips.

"Aha!" Stu said with a loud laugh. "See! We're doing so well already. You're up to one hundred pounds now."

"I know, that's crazy," David replied, joining in with the laughter. He glanced around the room at the other tables, looking across the crowds of happy and deflated faces mixed in together. As his eyes moved, he looked for the bald man. Out of the corner of his eye he noticed a white glow emitting from the entrance up on the platform where he and Stu had entered. He turned his body, looking up. A lady in a long, sleeveless and flowing white dress entered the casino. Her white-blonde hair tied up behind her head. Her face pale and youthful – from what David could see. A long, silver and gold necklace draped from her neck with several unique bangles around her arms and wrist.

Where have I seen that face before?

A thin Asian man wearing colourful clothes was by her side. Three men in black suits with stern expressions were on her tail, scanning the crowd. David noticed that people from other tables had also clocked the lady's entrance and were looking in her direction.

"David? David?" Stu said with a forceful nudge in the arm.

David looked back around at the table. "Sorry," he said, placing a £25 chip down and taking a quick look at his dealt cards. Two tens.

Potter stuck, and both Frizzy and Stu asked for another card each and lost. David stuck.

The dealer showed her hand. 21. "Unfortunate," she said before collecting the chips and cards.

"Ouch," Stu said. "I'll be right back, gonna find the loo."

Potter and Frizzy also ditched the table, leaving David alone. He smiled awkwardly to the dealer before swivelling on his stool a full 180 degrees. Then, there she was. Right in front of him. The lady in the long, flowing white dress staring into David's eyes. The gentle touch of makeup highlighted her complexion, along with her deep blue ocean-like eyes. The dress screamed elegance, reminding David of a Greek goddess he learnt about as a kid in a distant memory. The woman's expression didn't change as she moved to the side of David and approached the table. Her colourfully dressed male friend was by her side and the three men in suits were still on her heel.

"Could you fetch me a Martini, darling?" she said to the man in the thousand-coloured jacket. Her hauntingly soft-yet-firm voice, wrapped up in a traditional, southern English accent, sounded enticingly provoking.

"Right on it," he returned.

"Get one for yourself and Rocco, if he's still joining us."

"No, he's not. He called me before we set off; he's goddamn working, isn't he?"

"He chose to take an extra shift instead of joining you to the opening night?" she sniggered. "Ah well, more Martinis for the two of us."

The man let out a louder-than-necessary laugh before heading off into the direction of the bar. The lady looked at David and then to the casino dealer behind the table.

"Ah, Blackjack," she said.

David put down the remainder of his chips. £75 worth. "I'm in."

The lady in white glanced at his bet. She dug into a tiny bag that she propped onto the table and withdrew a single chip and placed it onto the table. "Put me in for a thousand," she said.

David raised his eyebrows, his eyes fixed on the chip.

The dealer dished out her cards.

David shook his head to the dealer when offered another card.

The lady looked at her hand and hesitated for a moment, contemplating. "Give me another," she said. She was handed another card. "Stick."

The dealer presented her hand. "Nineteen. Pay twenty."

David showed his hand, a ten of Clubs and an Ace of Diamonds. "Twenty-one."

The woman smiled at the sight of the dealer's hand and flicked her cards in the dealer's direction. "Congratulations, Mr…?"

The dealer collected the £1,000 chip and passed David his winning £75 chips.

"David Dale," he replied, offering a smile and his hand.

She returned the smile and took his hand, shaking it softly. "Shields," she said. "Eva Shields."

The light bulb flicked on. That's where he had seen her face before.

The pair stepped away from the table and started walking together, without meaning to, through the crowds of players. Heads turned and eyes glared in Eva and David's direction. Tongues quietly wagged.

"What is it you do, Mr Dale?" she asked.

David heard somebody gasp as Eva walked past. "I used to run a private psychiatry practice here in London, but that was a while ago now. I'm actually preparing to launch my own charity. In four days, in fact."

"How selfless of you. Very commendable."

Another waitress carrying a tray of drinks approached them. Eva took one for herself, David declined.

"So, Mr Dale. How much of a gambling man are you?"

"I'm not one at all, as it happens. I'm here with a friend who is," he said, starting to look around for Stu.

"A shred of your DNA is obviously geared towards taking risks. You wouldn't be gambling or at a major casino opening night if you weren't."

"Would you say only risk takers make it past the poverty line?" David asked, giving Eva a knowing look.

Eva instantly gave a wide smile, showing her immaculate white teeth. She restrained a laugh. "My comments were majorly misconstrued. I was being questioned on the UK's welfare system, the reporter knew exactly what she was doing. She knew comments like those coming from someone like me would stir up controversy. I don't know why I played into it, really."

They continued walking, sifting through people laughing in the midst of the glory of winning whilst others showed their losses by their pale faces, drained of all colour.

"I don't expect you to believe me," she said.

David looked for words in the crowd.

"I'm all for helping people where I can," she said before taking another sip from her glass. "It's just over the years I've obviously not made the best of friends with some people in this country, and I think the attitude of people toward me represents that quite well. It's rather sad, really."

David glanced behind him at the three men in suits that were closely following. "May I ask who," he motioned, "they are?"

"You can't be somebody in this city without a guarantee, Mr Dale. Too many people would love to see my head on a silver plate. On any plate for that matter."

"Do you really feel that way?"

"Of course I do."

"But how do you cope with that? How do you get through each day thinking that some people don't like you, and maybe don't like you enough to want to hurt you?"

The pair reached the stairs leading up to the exit as David noticed the thin male in his colourful jacket with an irritated expression standing at the top, holding two Martinis.

Eva stepped in front of David and the three men ushered from behind him to be by her side. She passed her empty glass to one of the men before turning to David. "To live in fear is to not live at all. And besides, Mr Dale, I choose to live by my motto: Don't cry over spilt milk, because it may have been poisoned."

CHAPTER 6

David didn't know a great deal about Eva Shields, only what he had seen in the media. Despite being only thirty-nine years of age, Eva had incredible influence over the country's media – and this privilege did not come with a *Get out of the public eye free* card. Owning one of the largest corporations in the country, which also spanned its wings across a further eight countries, Eva Shields was a hot topic in the world of gossip and current affairs. Her competitors, both public and private, wanted her viewers, her readers and her listeners. In current affairs, Eva didn't hold back when it came to politics and business; she ruthlessly lobbied government ministers and politicians for anything she deemed against her, her corporation, or her beliefs. At a time of heavy BBC cuts and other competitors dwindling in the aftermath of the 2008 financial crisis, Eva managed to make the Shields Corporation flourish.

Eva was only twenty-nine when she launched the company using her inheritance from her late father's estate. Shields Corporation quickly went from strength to strength, with Eva deciding to sell 49% ownership on the London Stock Exchange. After a much-anticipated first day of selling the Shields Corp. stock, disappointment set in. Lack of demand sent the price plummeting. Three days later, Shields Corporation announced the purchasing of five businesses, absorbing them into its operations to strengthen its infrastructure and boost its supply chain. It also released its latest magazine, centred on the corporation's main competitor's unruly management techniques, naming and shaming several senior managers who had been caught in scandalous late-night romps in the office. The Shield Corporation's online blog then centred on Eva Shields herself, featuring a twenty-four-paged interview and countless modelling shots in a variety of revealing clothing. She was already a major celebrity – why not write and release one's own exclusive?

Eva's efforts doubled the company's stock within months. But as quickly as her reputation soared, it started to sour. A spate of negative headlines covering her controversial comments and accusations of corporate negligence started to dog the corporation and raise questions of Eva's character.

David slammed the car door behind him, holding his brown leather bag up over his head as he darted across the road as quickly as the traffic would allow him. The clouds had split open, releasing their entire savings of water upon the drenched city. This batch of rain was persistent. Continuously, no-end-in-sight persistent.

David leapt over a puddle at the foot of the kerb, landing mid-sprint aimed at the main entrance. The charity's offices were being rented on a floor of a relatively modest tower, located a few streets from his city apartment. Its central location demanded a big monthly cheque but offered David and his team an easily accessible and resourceful home for everything charity related.

Rushing into the building, he lowered the bag from over his head – his hair still saturated despite his best efforts. David returned the nod from the security guard. The guard slowly, it seemed, beginning to recognise him as a frequent visitor. When David first secured the floor of offices, the guard constantly referred to him as Darren, stopping him in his tracks every morning to ask for ID and security clearance.

David took the elevator up to the third floor. The doors slid open, welcoming him back with a cheerful *ding*. The office space was quite possibly a bit too much room than he or the rest of the team really needed, but it was nice to have for potential future expansion. Breathing room.

The walls were whitewashed with a light blue tint, mimicking a clear summer sky in contrast to the drab weather outside. The carpet was short and dull, in need of a replacement. Office furniture, however, was contemporary and professional. Rather lawyer-like, he said to the young estate agent that showed him round on the day he decided to take it. A row of comfortable-looking seats for waiting visitors lay against a wall leading into the main, large room. A mix of shelves with documents and books accompanied the seats, preventing their loneliness. Desks were cast across the room, installed with desktop computers.

David had only taken three steps into the office before Bev descended on him. "Good mornin', I've had two calls," she began, now walking alongside David. "A man from the Charity Commission wantin' to discuss a section in our Governin' document, and a man from a local newspaper wantin' some details on who we are, what we're intendin' on doin' and who's behind it. I must say, this is the first journalist to actually get in touch for facts."

David agreed, murmuring in response as he opened the door to his private, walled office. A tall, leafy bird-of-paradise occupied a corner of the room. A large window displayed the dullness of the dark clouds outside and a semi-distant River Thames, close enough to make out its murky water.

A vintage wall clock, a watercolour painting of a couple walking their dog in a valley, and David's master's degree in a platinum frame decorated the walls. His desk was bulky and dark brown, with a far-reaching slim computer monitor mounted on top of it. A telephone and a heap of paperwork were scattered across the remainder of the desk.

David walked in and immediately gave rest to his feet by diving onto his chair, shaking the leftover rain from his hair. "Do you have their numbers?" he asked.

Bev leaned over the edge of the desk, handing him a post-it note.

He glanced at the numbers and names scribbled impeccably neatly onto it. "Thank you very much," he said as he stuck it onto the top of the heap of papers.

"I met Stu this mornin', by the way."

David raised his chin, looking to her. "Ah, great. Did he introduce himself?"

"Yeah, he came into the office almost as early as I did. Almost got a fright," she laughed. "He told me a few stories about ya two when ya were younger in ya uni days. Sounds like a lotta fun. He seemed a lovely man, I'm glad he's on board."

David smiled. "Good, I'm also glad. Thanks for your help, Bev."

She returned the smile, turning around and heading for the door. "Oh," she said, looking back to him. "He also mentioned about last night, the two of ya goin' to the new casino? He said he saw ya all up close and personal with that lady off the TV and in those magazines. Y'know who I mean."

"Eva Shields," David said, blinking slowly with a slight nod in a way to say, *it's true.*

"Aye, that's the one! Heard lots about her. Very sexy, rich lady. Ya behave yourself now, won't ya!" She laughed her loud, contagious laugh.

David dismissed Bev's comments with the shaking of his head and a subtle smirk.

Bev exited his office, closing the door behind her with a giggle.

Oh, Bev.

David glanced over the heap of paperwork, familiarising himself with the organised mess. He shook the computer mouse, bringing the monitor to life and checked his email. A dozen spam mails and a couple of genuine messages. For some reason, his mind was crammed full of thoughts about Eva. The visual of her arriving last night in the long white dress repeated, flicking through his mind like a broken light. The way she glided through the crowd of gamblers in the midst of the casino action, as if she owned the place. For all David knew, she quite possibly did.

He opened up Google Chrome and searched her name. The results flowed in instantly.

About 9,800,000 results (0.19 seconds) – Google returned.

David glanced through the various articles and web pages on the first page. A *Wikipedia* page, an official website of her own, the Shields Corporation official website, links to the company's stock details. Even several fan bases sprung up, detailing their enthusiasm to be *a Shield* – another one of those nicknames that celebrities give to their fans.

He opened four different news articles written about her. An *Independent* article entitled EVA SHIELDS' EMOTIONAL PLEA FOR EQUAL RIGHTS. A website article from *Digital Spy* with its title of EVA SHIELDS AND THE SHIELDS CORPORATION: TOO MUCH POWER? A *BBC* article entitled SHIELDS CORP. INVESTIGATED OVER £45M BLACK HOLE. David started reading the four-month-old *BBC* article.

SHIELDS CORP. INVESTIGATED
OVER £45M BLACK HOLE

Published: 08:02 GMT, 10 October 2025

Scotland Yard have this morning announced their intention to conduct a 'full and thorough investigation' into internationally renowned Shields Corporation. The news follows a tough week for the corporation as some shareholders have lost confidence in the company's founder after a huge £45m was found to be unaccounted for in its annual financial reports. The corporation's purported mass business dealings with both international and UK companies have also plagued the company in recent weeks.

The massive financial black hole, discovered on Thursday from leaked financial—

David closed the webpage and opened a second article.

EVA SHIELDS' EMOTIONAL
PLEA FOR EQUAL RIGHTS

Published: 16:43 GMT, 9 April 2025

Eva Shields has released a video, directed at the government, pleading for equal rights for women.

In the 4-minute clip posted on her own website, Miss Shields called for transparency in senior job roles in large companies and equal pay for equal work, saying, "not enough is done to give women big jobs in the city".

Miss Shields grows more emotional as the video continues. "I know of women in large companies here in London that get paid half of what their male colleagues earn," she said. "I know of women struggling to make ends meet as they're underpaid for their worth. It isn't right and the government needs to fix this problem now."

You can watch the full video here.

As well as building a successful company with a vast audience reach, Miss Shields has concentrated on a plethora of other projects including modelling, writing and publishing. To date, she has appeared on elven separate magazine

44

There was a knock on the office door. "Yeah?" David said.

The door popped open and Bev stuck her head in. "David, one more thin', are ya in the middle of somethin'?"

"No, come in."

She swung the door open and slid through the giant gap. "I just wanted to run through the invitation list with ya."

He frowned. "The invitation list?"

"For the charity launch event."

"Oh," he said, blinking hard. "Of course, sorry. What were you thinking?"

"Well," she began, "we obviously want to invite people who will be able to both support the charity and propel it into their own circles of influence," she said with a grin, as if behind an elaborate master plan. "I've already sent out invitations to four news stations, six newspapers and eight magazines. Stu has emailed me a list of celebrities and people in the public eye who he thinks could attend and help put the word out there, as well as possibly make a donation. They include TV presenters, film stars, authors, radio presenters, and business figures. I've forwarded ya the email."

"Sounds brilliant, sounds like you've got a good handle on this."

"Well have a read through and get back to me, and if ya can think of anyone else who ya would like to attend then let me know."

"Thanks, Bev. I'm quite excited."

"Me too!" She turned and headed for the door.

David leaned back in his chair. "Oh, Bev."

She turned back to face him.

"Just in case you were thinking to, there's no need to send Sam an invite, I'm visiting her for dinner tomorrow. I'll invite her then."

"Alrighty."

"And," he paused, "could you please send an invite to Eva Shields for me?"

CHAPTER 7

David's train journey from London Euston to Wigan North Western was uneventful. The train was swamped upon arrival by eager passengers wanting a good seat with a table, for reasons unbeknown to him. The four-to-a-table seating arrangement was the most frequent victim of littering by people with a sheer disregard for their fellow passengers. Read newspapers – now considered trash – coupled with used tissues, empty packets of crisps and coffee cups left to keep the lonely tables company. Passengers needing to excuse themselves so that they can get up and leave the train when their station rolls in, attempting to not step on any toes. Yes, David wasn't a fan of sitting at tables on trains. A little, out of the way seat by a window was all he needed.

The one-hour and fifty-five-minute journey gave David the time he needed to work on his speech for the charity launch event. With now well over sixty celebrities invited, and a further thirty journalists from the media, it needed to be on point and informative. His first moment in the world of philanthropy needed to make an impact that would resonate brightly both now and into the organisation's future. And to do this, David didn't need a table.

An email came through to his computer, letting off a high-pitched ping that turned heads around the carriage.

David tapped down his laptop's volume and opened the email, another from the same unknown email address that messaged him back at the lake. The email was blank but contained a single attachment. He glanced around at the people sat near him.

No one was looking in his direction.

He clicked on the attachment, opening it.

A screenshot of an American news article from three years ago flicked open. The huge bold letters took up half the screen, screaming at David with deafening silence.

TRAGEDY IN SOUTH CAROLINA: 3 DEAD, 2 HOSPITALIZED.

David instantly closed the image and slapped shut his laptop.

As David wandered along the dirt track beside the overgrown bushes that lined the edge of a farmer's field close to Sam's house, he thought of nothing but his sister.

Sam's life was, in ways, constantly in a suitcase. At the age of nineteen she went backpacking through France, Belgium and Germany with her best friend. When Sam returned a year later, she found her home uninteresting and dull; a boring life in one constant place with no change, diversity or mix of culture. At the age of twenty-eight she fell pregnant and decided to relocate to Euxton for a simpler, cheaper and less polluted lifestyle. She rented a tiny cottage on a quiet country lane, which the postman far-too-frequently forgot existed. Ben, her son, appeared soon after and the numerous holidays and constant travelling flew out of the window. Since Ben's birth, Sam had enjoyed only three fleeting romances, the last being almost twelve months ago.

David pushed open the fragile rusted gate with a gentle nudge before stepping into the tiny, overgrown garden. He closed the gate behind him and knocked twice on the painted wooden door, its colour difficult to see in the evening darkness. After a scurry of audible activity, the door opened, allowing the internal light to shine on David's face and reveal the door's turquoise colour. Sam stood in the doorway with a smile as bright as the glow behind her. Wearing a baggy cream jumper, oversized grey joggers and fluffy brown slippers, she plunged forward and hugged David, letting off a high-pitched screech.

"Just in time!" she shouted, her grip tight. She slowly released him from her clutches.

"Just in time for what?" David replied, following her inside.

"Dinner. I did invite you here for a meal, you know."

The house was warm and consoling compared to the dark, frosty weather outside. The cottage was modest, but in a comfortable and homely way. Old-fashioned features were prominent throughout, from the original brick walls to the low ceiling with thick wooden support beams. A welcoming smell of home-cooked food filled the air.

"You look well," David said.

"Thanks. You look a bit tired. Are you all right?"

David shrugged, said, "I'm fine."

A dog, a cross between a Golden Retriever and a Labrador, sprinted towards David from behind Sam. It jumped up and down, off and on to David.

David leant down, being careful not to be head-butted in the face by the dog's rock-solid head and gave him a hug. "Long time, no see, Shadow."

Shadow's tail wagged relentlessly with force.

"Evenin'," a deep, male voice said.

David looked up at the doorway to the lounge where Sam had disappeared into and where Shadow had just emerged. The owner of the voice stood, leaning against the doorframe, one foot casually crossed over the other.

David straightened his back. "Hi. Richard, is it?" he asked, offering his hand.

Richard's sleek hair was brushed entirely to one side. His longer-than-average nose propped up his circular black glasses. He accepted the hand, shaking it with a squeeze. "David, nice to meet you."

Sam could be heard from behind, "Off there now, Ben, and get ready for your dinner. And say hello to your uncle, please." She then raised her voice, "How was the train, David?"

David glanced over Richard's shoulder.

Ben threw down a PlayStation remote controller onto the sofa and strolled towards David with a grin, said, "Hi Uncle David."

Richard swept himself to the side of the doorway as David made his way past. Ben leapt into David's arms, being swirled around the living room like a fighter pilot.

"Ahhhhh!" Ben shouted.

David plonked him back on the ground, feeling the strain of Ben's weight in his arms. Kids don't stay kids for long.

Sam rushed in to switch off the TV. "Shadow, drop that, please," she said as she pushed him away from a plastic Pikachu figurine.

"Don't worry, he'll go through his teeth before he goes through that solid thing," Richard said.

Sam swayed her hand in the air as to say, *Whatever.* "Your timing is perfect, David. A few more minutes and we would be eating cremated Yorkshires. Let's eat," she said, heading into the adjacent, teeny dining room. "I've got you a San Miguel, is that all right?"

"That's fine, thank you," David said as he sat next to Ben on one side of the table, opposite Sam and Richard. The table held an array of dishes, bowls and plates. Four empty plates waiting for food and eight full ones waiting to be emptied. Carrots, mashed potato, roast potatoes, peas, Yorkshire puddings, sweet potato. A single plate overflowed with Quorn meat-free sausages, and a large celebration nut roast lay in the centre of the table – the main attraction.

Sam was a devoted vegetarian, had been for close to twenty years. Something she picked up while travelling and would soon phase out, or so her parents had thought. Weeks passed, followed by months, before rolling into years and Sam's passion for meat-free food, both for health reasons and for the concern of animal welfare, held intact. Her parents weren't exactly thrilled to have to cook two separate meals on a daily basis, but for some nights, to Sam's delight, the only meal prepared was purely vegetarian.

"The nut roast has an awesome apple and cranberry sauce over it, by the way. Gotta give it a whirl," Sam said. "Okay, come on already, dig in!"

The four started exchanging plates, passing around the veg.

"How's school then, been busy?" David asked, passing the peas to Richard.

"It's okay. Been doing geography. I know where Spain is now," Ben said.

"Good lad, that's good goin'."

"Yeah, and I can sometimes remember where India is, but I usually forget and have to check."

"Soon you'll know where every country is, and you'll be able to tell your mum where you want to go for your holiday," David said with a smirk.

"We went over some maths yesterday, too, didn't we?" Richard said.

Ben nodded, chewing on half a roast potato.

David looked to Richard as he sipped his beer. "So where abouts do you live, Richard? In Euxton?"

Richard swallowed a mouthful of mash. "Preston currently. Just by the marina."

"Ah. I'm not familiar with Preston, not been in years."

"I bounce around a lot for work, but Preston's not that bad."

David plucked two Yorkshire puddings from the plate. "What do you do?"

"I'm a business researcher. At the minute, I'm based on an assignment in the North West. It's decent if you like travelling the country."

Sam hurriedly chewed a slice of the nut roast. "See how we've clicked? He loves to travel!"

"I guess so. What have you been doing? How's work and life?"

Sam cut up a sausage, sliding some mashed potato onto it. "Very well, thanks. We've a meeting next week with a potential big-time supplier from the Netherlands, so busy prepping for that. Other than that, I can't complain much," she said before chomping on the forkful.

"Does Russ still work there?" David asked.

She nodded, mumbling with a full mouth.

"Is he ever going to retire?" he laughed. "Bless him, he's a good egg."

Sam swallowed. "How's the charity goin'? Are you all ready for the big day?"

"Couldn't be better, cheers. I think we're ready. It's mad that the launch is only two days away, it's come round so quick."

"We can't wait for it," Sam said.

"Launching a charity sounds pretty stressful," Richard said before taking a sip from his glass.

"Thanks," David replied. "Oh, and I even managed to land Bev Walcott. She's joined."

"Ah, I love her," Sam returned, grabbing the bowl of carrots.

"She's one ace lady."

"Is that the same Bev you were telling me was a good friend of Maria's?" Richard asked.

David stared at Richard.

"I'm sorry," Richard said. "It's not my place to bring Maria up. Sam only told me about her yesterday, I'm sorry."

David took a deep, prolonged breath. "No, it's fine. Yeah, it's how I met Bev, through my wife. About twelve years ago, or something like that."

Ben's cogs finished turning as he gulped down a chunk of roast potato, said, "And I know where France is, too!"

Sam carried the last of the plates to the kitchen as Richard and David both offered to do the washing up. She declined, leaving them alone in the dining room.

"How long is it you and Sam have been seeing each other then?" David asked before polishing off his beer.

"Er, it'll be four weeks tomorrow."

David nodded. "Very early days then. She's an amazing, loving woman."

"I know, she's something."

"Do you have any kids of your own?"

Richard shook his head. "No, no. Not of my own."

David subtly picked a bit of nut roast out from his teeth as he nodded. "What got you into business research then? It sounds hard work if you're moving about all the time."

"Nah, it's all right. I have a really good employer who makes it worthwhile."

"What exactly do you research? It's not like lab coats and experimental research, I take it."

Richard laughed. "Heck no. I usually have to locate and dig out the weeds, if you will."

"Sounds intriguing," David said, tapping his fingers on the table. "Well if you make Sam happy then I'm more than happy."

Sam emerged from the kitchen and hugged David from behind, wrapping her arms around his neck and kissing his cheek. "Thank you."

He patted her arm.

"Mum!" Ben shouted from the living room.

"What?" she shouted back.

David shook his head, his ear deafened.

"Come look!"

Sam let go of David and wandered into the living room, closely followed by David and Richard who had each cracked open another bottle of beer. She gasped as she saw the violent mess on the floor. Bits of Pikachu were spread across the carpet, leading up to Shadow who lay in front of the TV, still gnawing his way through the plastic toy.

"Well, Pikachu really has peaked and been chewed," Richard said.

CHAPTER 8

David had stayed the night on Sam's sofa after excavating the furniture for console controllers, toy cars and bundles of dog hair. Sam's dinner was just what David needed, as was the company of family. Richard's introduction was pleasant, making David hopeful of a future. A normal, stable future for his sister and his nephew, filled with the love and comforts that everyone deserves.

The train journey from Wigan North Western to London Euston was eventful to say the least. The train was an unfortunate forty-eight minutes late, purportedly due to a broken-down train further down the tracks. Once it had finally arrived, the platoon of impatient people surged forward, storming the doors and fighting for every inch of space. There was no luxury of turning down a table seat today. When the train hit Warrington Bank Quay, a first aider had to be summoned from the depths of the station to assist an elderly passenger two carriages down; a further delay of close to half an hour.

The one-hour and twelve-minute delay to David's journey also carried its benefits; extra time to sift through emails and finish final preparation for tomorrow's big launch.

Looking at his watch, he sighed.

Late for the meeting.

There is something about returning to one's home city after being away, David thought as the taxi strolled deeper into the concrete jungle, finally arriving at the charity offices a little more than two hours late. The security guard smiled to David as he ran hurriedly for the elevator; David's returned expression of his lips spread open and his teeth clenched.

The elevator doors opened on the third floor.

"And just as we're finishing up, he arrives," Stu said, eyeing David step out behind the doors. Stu sat around a large, circular table with Bev and Kristian. Mounds of paperwork and scribbled-on notepads surrounded them.

"I'm sorry, I'm sorry," David said, rushing into the office and putting down his bag by a vacant seat. He threw his coat over the back of the chair. "I forgot to charge my phone at Sam's so I couldn't call."

"Your laptop has email ya know," Stu smirked.

David shook off the comment. "Stuff's been on my mind. Sorry."

"Travel problems?" Bev asked, clicking her pen.

"Train was severely delayed. But I'm here now. Bev, I see you've met Kristian. Kristian, Bev," he said, gesturing from one to the other.

"We have met now, thank you," Kristian said in his slight Swedish, slight London-adopted accent.

David could almost see the glow in Bev's eyes as Kristian spoke. "Please, summarise the points before we all head off. Where are we up to?"

"Well," Bev started, "we were discussing the invited guests, as well as the schedule for tomorrow. Stu has only just mentioned that he would also like to say something alongside ya, but it'll be impossible to fit into the schedule at this late point. I'm sorry, Stu."

Stu shrugged in a childlike sulk.

David leant back in his chair, said, "Hit me with the schedule."

"Guests are arrivin' at the ballroom at six thirty. Security, red carpet and drinks on arrival have been organised," Bev said, flicking through her notepad. She found what she was searching for. "We'll then leave the guests to mingle and talk to one another. We will also be in the midst, makin' sure everyone is well and introducin' ourselves. We expect everyone to have arrived by seven thirty, where we will let David loose on the stage to formally introduce the charity. His words will be spoken and a short four-minute video prepared by Stu will be played to support your speech." Bev looked at David. "Have ya finished ya speech, David?"

"Yes, it's all sorted."

"Excellent. Around eight o'clock we will initiate our first fundraisin' campaign and try and sign up some of the celebrity guests to help. The buffet will be on from eight forty-five and interviews will be enabled from nine o'clock. Is everyone alright with this?"

The three men nodded.

"Good, cos I'm not changin' it now!" Bev said, laughing to herself.

"How do you think it'll turn out?" Kristian asked. "I mean, I'm surprised by how many people have said they'll come, to say we're an unknown group of people launching an unknown charity. Think there'll be no-shows?"

"Of course there'll be no-shows," Stu said in response. "But haven't you been reading online? There's no official word out yet in national papers or on the radio, but people are already aware of David."

David leant forward. "What do you mean, *already aware of me?*"

Bev's forehead wrinkled and her eyebrows dipped, her eyes flittering between Stu and David.

"David, I'm sorry to bring this up, but what happened to you three years ago was a big story over here, you know that," Stu said. "People are clicking on to the fact that the David who is launching this charity is the David that was involved in what happened three years ago. People can see what you had, what you've lost and given up with your psychiatry practice, to now turn it all into something good. How many people would do that?"

Kristian nodded.

"David, you are more of a driver for this project than I think you realise," Stu continued. "People are behind you as a person, and that is going to rub off on the charity. I think all of this might end up better than any of us expect. Just wait and see."

Right now, all David wanted to do was sit by the lake and clear his head, not *wait and see.*

"See ya later," Kristian said as he left the office alongside Stu.

Bev and David waved them off as they also prepared for their departure. Bev made her way around the office, checking all the computer monitors were switched off. David sifted through the paperwork on his desk, checking if there was anything worth taking home with him. He picked up a few unopened envelopes with his name on and tucked them into his bag.

"How was Sam and Ben?" Bev asked, approaching David as she placed her handbag strap up onto her shoulder. "Still adorable as ever?"

David smirked. "They were actually really good, thanks. It's crazy how quickly kids grow though, Ben's getting quite tall."

"They sneak up on you," Bev said. "I know with mine, one day I was always helpin' her around the house as she could never reach anythin', and then the next day it's me askin' her for help getting somethin' down from the top of the bookcase. The legs of a model, my girl."

David stared at his bag.

"I'm sorry, I should have thought before I started talkin'—"

"No, honestly, Bev. It's fine." He snapped shut his bag. "You know, Cassie would have been eleven this year. Eleven."

Bev's lips parted. "Here, sit down," she said, gesturing to the chair.

The pair sat down, looking at one another.

Bev continued, "Y'know, I wish I could have been a part of this charity back when I was younger and when I had more energy. Back then I was just workin' in meaningless jobs, assistin' senior high-flyers. And truth be told, I would have loved my Bill to have seen me doin' this kinda work. Bill was so big into community givin' and doin' things that were right." Bev glanced away from David and smiled to the wall. "I don't wanna have any regrets with this." She looked back to David. "But I still know, in my heart, that Bill will be proud of me. So ya need to take comfort in knowin' that ya Maria, and ya Cassie and Sophie, wherever they may be, they will be proud of ya, David."

He nodded slowly, absorbing the words.

"Ya're an incredibly strong man, and what ya're doin' with this charity is so inspirin'. It will be for a lot of people who come to see us launch it tomorrow. Take comfort in knowin' that, my dear."

David rubbed his dry eyes, taking in several deep breaths in the process. "Thanks, Bev. That means a lot."

Bev blew out a mouthful of air as she climbed to her feet. "Whoa, things got pretty emotional then, didn't they?" She laughed. "What are we like, eh?"

"We're definitely quite the pair," David said before putting on his coat.

"Now come on, home time. It's a big day tomorrow. I might actually stop off for some spicy chicken wings for supper on the way. That'd be nice, wouldn't it?"

CHAPTER 9

In contrast to the cold weather that Britain had been forever enduring, the night of the charity launch brought with it a warm breeze and a clear sky; something the entire population were vying for. Although the sun still set early and dark descended on the city, the stars came out to support the event, dazzling in solidarity. The warm air allowed the arriving guests to leave their jackets, coats, scarves and gloves at home. Women strode down the elaborate red carpet leading into the venue in long, short and sleeveless dresses. Some men arrived in suits, particularly those representing businesses. Others wore casual, open shirts with their favourite, recently polished black or brown shoes.

Stu had been right about the online comments. Media had slowly gravitated to the launch event. A line of journalists set up along the red carpet to document exactly who was turning up to support the unknown charity, led by the *heartbroken widower and psychiatry-practice-entrepreneur-turned-charity-founder.* Those journalists lucky enough to have been invited set up inside the venue with their notepads and interchangeable lens cameras.

David adjusted his grey tie and pressed down his jacket, looking at his reflection in the mirror. For David, tonight was most definitely a suit night. His emotions were strung across a far-reaching spectrum, from excitement and nervousness, causing his feet to tap at their own will and his fingers to fidget. His stomach performed unappreciated somersaults; all the while he could not bring himself to stop smiling. Countless months in the making had led up to this very night. The night he is to declare this charity open and operational, here to serve the general public wherever it can.

The door to the small makeshift dressing room opened and Sam popped her head in. "You okay?" she asked. She slid through the gap, bringing Ben with her.

"Hey, guys," David said.

"You look handsome," Sam said, smiling. "You really do scrub up well for things like these, don't ya?"

He smirked, looking down to Ben. "You all right, bud?"

Ben, dressed in a checked red shirt that was tucked into his trousers, nodded a confident nod.

"Richard wished he could come, but he's meeting people tonight for work. He's sorry and wished you plenty of luck," Sam said.

"Not a problem. That's nice of him though." David led the way into the main venue hall, which was beginning to fill up nicely.

The large room with its high ceiling was gorgeously decorated. Typically used for business functions, university graduation parties and banquets; the room had a history of entertainment as it used to host international dancing competitions. The ceiling and walls adorned gold-coloured patterns and symbols encrusted into them. Balloons ran up and down the walls of the room, lining it with bright, in-your-face colour. Large tables with white-cloth surfaces and oak chairs littered the floor. The tables hosted bouquets of flowers, encircled by tiny fairy light candles. David could already see guests observing the room and questioning the charity's actions by hosting such an upstate event. One journalist was even scribbling into his notepad, glancing around at the room.

Ben asked for a drink and so Sam scurried off to the bar with him for an orange juice.

Stu crept up on David. "Lookin' good, Mr Charity Launcher."

David turned to Stu, noticing the well-groomed man in a burgundy suit. "Not bad yourself, Mr Charity Accomplice."

Stu laughed. "Cheers, bud. What did I say about the turnout? You're going to quickly become a hot topic, David. I just need to be standing next to you when they come for those pictures that'll end up in the morning's papers. That'll get me some much-needed female attention."

David cast an unimpressed frown at Stu.

"What?" Stu nudged David, "I need to settle down."

The flow of people into the venue kept up its pace. Mixtures of black, blue, grey and brown suits took over the bar, presumably men from businesses scattered around London. Elegant and well-dressed women flooded the room, mingling in between the crowd. David recognised only a few people in his first glance. A well-known daytime radio presenter who had a name for supporting new charities, several authors, and a handful of well-known TV presenters. Even a few recent *Love Island* rejects accompanied by a handful of Z-list reality stars.

"Oh, by the way," Stu said, lowering his voice and glancing around the room. "Kristian has brought a big group of Swedes over from Sweden. Some are his family who are here to support him, and others are his friends and associates that are interested in the charity."

"Uh huh."

"Well," Stu said, now pointing out the large group of people dominated largely by blonde hair, "guess who's lapping up the Swedish accent?"

David eyed the group, taking note of the number of heads with thick, blonde hair. Then, amongst the group, he saw Bev. Her eyes wide, her ears tipped up as if listening to a masterpiece of a song for the very first time.

"Well, I best get introducing myself, shouldn't I?" Stu said before patting David on the back and heading into the sea of people.

David headed for the bar and asked for a bottled beer. He looked to the men in suits, on the other side of the bar, who were partaking in what looked like a very tight-knit discussion. The bartender returned with the beer.

"Ah, David," said a voice behind him.

David turned, holding his bottle, and noticed him.

"For a second there I thought I got the wrong person," Allen said with a soft laugh.

David beamed a smile, instantly offering his open hand. "I can't believe you've come."

"Wouldn't miss it for anything," Allen said. "How are you feeling? Nervous?"

"We're not in one of our sessions now," David laughed. "No, but really, I'm feeling okay. Yeah, a bit nervous, I mean, the turnout is pretty incredible."

"Yeah, you've done well here, David. I'm so pleased for you. I hear you're also giving a speech, I'm very much looking forward to that."

Over Allen's shoulder, David saw another white light emitting from the entrance doorway where guests were still pouring in. Another white light that radiated, grabbing David's attention.

There she was. She had been invited and she had shown up. She wore a short, white, strapless dress, which draped down at her sides. The dress was ruffled in the glowing material, overflowing with intricate detail that would send fashion-lovers into a frenzy. From across the room, David couldn't fully appreciate Eva's exact specifications this evening, but he already knew she would be glamorous and graciously elegant. She spotted David and held his stare. People crossed their path of vision before she wandered off into the crowd with an entourage of four men. David thought he could hear people gasping by their surprise of her arrival. Some even headed in Eva's direction; the possibility of networking and socialising with such a magnate of a businesswoman would do legendary tales for one's social circles or career.

"Your speech?" Allen prompted.

"I'm so sorry, Allen," David said as he gave his head a slight shake. "Yeah, I should be doing my speech any time now, really."

"Ah, excellent. Well, I wish you the—"

"David!" Bev said hurriedly from the midst of the crowd. "It's seven twenty-eight! Ya need to get ya self together and head for the stage, please. And abandon the beer!"

David took his last mouthful from the bottle before placing it onto the bar. "Ah, here we go. We'll catch up later, Allen. Thanks again, so much, for coming."

Allen nodded. "Good luck." He spotted Bev through a gap in the crowd and waved.

Bev waved back with an animated smile.

Heads turned towards David as he made his way through the crowd and to the stage at the end of the room. Long, creamy-yellow curtains draped from each end of the platform, with a dark blue curtain covering the very back wall. David tucked into his inner jacket pocket and removed some handwritten notes before stepping up onto the stage. The room's lights dimmed and the platform lit up, signalling David's presence to the audience.

Everyone's eyes were now set on him as he stood behind a dark mahogany podium. Mouths were closed and ears were alert.

Journalists poised their pens against their notepads and ensured their cameras were in focus.

The room was overcome with silence.

David clicked the microphone on and cleared his throat. "Good evening and thank you to each of you for coming tonight to this launch event. Your being here tonight shows just how strong a community can be when we all come together, from hugely different walks of life, and work together to support one common goal. My name is David Dale, and tonight I'm presenting to you a project that I have poured my heart and soul into. I've been wholly supported in this endeavour by the other founding members Bev Walcott, Stu Jackson and Kristian Sinason; of whom all are here tonight." He looked out to them with a confident nod. "This evening, we are launching a non-profit charity organisation centred here in London, focusing on everyday people who are facing hardship and adverse circumstances of which we aim to help make a significant difference with."

The audience provided a small round of applause and journalists began to take the first round of photographs.

David narrowed his eyes, trying to lock out the beaming flashing lights. "It is with great pleasure, honour and pride that I present to you, Down Dream."

The dark blue curtain behind him dropped, revealing a huge digital poster of the charity logo and slogan: *Down Dream. Lifting Lives, Building Dreams.*

The audience applauded louder.

"Thank you. I understand the name Down Dream could be misunderstood, but I want to tell you how it came about. When I was a young boy and frequently had nightmares after watching grown up horror movies and listening to kids at school talk about Freddy Krueger and Jason Voorhees…"

The audience chuckled.

"I would be petrified of going to sleep and having another nightmare. After a while, my dad tucked me into bed and told me that nightmares are just another form of the normal dream that we experience. It's just that the nightmare is a *down* dream, a dream that needs to be uplifted and cheered up."

David made eye contact with Stu and Kristian as they stood side by side. Stu nodded once, Kristian smiled.

"From then on, I always referred to my nightmares as down dreams. This name symbolises the way in which something that seems so haunting and sinister, so dark and disastrous, can be viewed in another light. If someone is having a nightmare of a reality, a way can be found to uplift that situation and make it better, just like my nightmares as a child. I want to portray the message that things can be changed, things can be uplifted and real dreams, as a result, can happen."

Another round of applause.

David swallowed, his mouth and throat suddenly dry. "Three years ago," he said, clearing his throat, "I experienced the worst day of my life when I lost my wife and two daughters." His eyes hid from the audience and fixated on the notes that lay on the podium as the corners of his mouth instinctively pointed downward. "It was the darkest time of my life, and the pain I experienced on that day will always stay with me until the day I die." He pulled his head upward and looked out to the audience. "Since that day, I've battled with my own down dreams and wondered why I'm still here. What is my purpose?" He wavered, darting his eyes to Bev for reassurance.

She gave a tender smile, her eyes glistening from the stage's light.

"It took me a long time, but I've realised my purpose now is to spend my life doing what I can to help those who are in need. Working with other charities and local government, we will be targeting a whole host of locations where people feel vulnerable and could benefit immensely with some added help. The homeless, the unemployed, those navigating grief, those struggling with everyday hardships."

Sam's beaming face shone through the crowd, drawing David's eyes to her.

"Domestic physical and mental abuse, for example, is a bigger issue than people know. Not everybody in this country has access to the help that they need or know where to find it. Not everybody in this country has family members they can rely on or talk to. We want to face all of these issues and offer friendly and supportive assistance wherever we can."

The flashing cameras continued.

"I am so pleased to announce that for our first point of action, Down Dream will be opening our very first homeless shelter tomorrow evening, with a capacity of almost eighty beds."

A long applause rung out.

"Now I'd like to play you this short four-minute video that will—"

David stopped talking as he noticed the shift in attention from the crowd. The audience were all looking at the other end of the stage, no longer holding their gaze on him. He shifted, looking in their line of sight. There she was again, right in front of him, walking up the stage towards him. Eva Shields climbed the five steps, each foot causing a loud tap that echoed out across the room. A few subdued inhales of air could be heard from the audience. David caught Bev's eyes, her mouth hanging open in astonishment. Cameras were flashing and clicking at an exponential rate.

Eva's neck was bare, a statement in itself, with her long blonde locks again modelled into a sophisticated style on her head. The draped parts of her dress swayed by her sides in an uncontrolled dance. "A beautiful speech, David," Eva began, addressing both David and the audience, as she reached the podium, now stood next to him. "A truly inspirational cause. I personally thank you for creating such goodness in our dark world. I hope everyone in this room supports David and Down Dream unconditionally like I will. You are quickly becoming a beacon that everybody can look up to."

Click, click, click.

David forced a smile.

"I'm sorry for delaying your video, but it's because of your amazing cause and inspirational story that I would like to kick-off the fundraising for Down Dream right now." She lifted her chin and let her eyes look down across the faces that were looking back up at her. "There are a lot of wealthy, high-profile people in this room. Please get out your fat wallets and overweight purses, people." She smiled a devilish, gorgeous smile. "Because the highest bidder gets a twenty-four-hour date with me."

The room stirred into commotion with loud gasps and whispering.

"Not only that," she continued, "but I will also personally endorse whatever it is you come from. If you're a business owner, I'll endorse your business. If you're a singer, I'll endorse your record. If you're a presenter – you catch my drift."

The room loudened with chatter. David looked into the audience, spotting Stu and Kristian who both shrugged. Journalists shouted out to Eva, wanting answers. Lights flashed continuously, cameras clicking uncontrollably.

Eva's possession of the stage was now unrivalled. David didn't even want to try and persuade her to get off the stage and tell her to stop interrupting Down Dream's official launch schedule – to Bev's dismay – partly because who could possibly guess how much Eva could raise for the charity, both in the value of a donation and the value of vital press exposure.

Eva placed a hand on her hip. "Not only that, but I will triple whatever is raised."

David couldn't help but join Bev in hanging open his mouth. His glance to Eva provided him nothing, so he looked back to the crowd for answers.

"Get yourselves on a twenty-four-hour date with me and who knows what'll happen. Things could get steamy and we could get hitched, or you can interrogate me and launch your own career with an exclusive no one else has access to." She laughed. "Who'll start the bidding at ten thousand pounds?" She looked out to the audience, her eyebrows raised.

"Ten grand!" a man shouted from the back of the room.

"Thank you. Anyone else?" Eva asked.

"Fifteen!" shouted another man.

"Ooh, I do recognise that voice," she said, looking to the left of the room where it had come from. "Ah, Taylor, it is you! How's things?"

"Twenty-five grand!" the man at the back of the room shouted once more.

"Forty thousand!" shouted a lady.

Eva allowed a subtle smile.

"Forty-five!"

"Fifty-five!"

"Sixty thousand big ones!"

"Sixty-six thousand pounds!" a lady shouted.

Eva crossed her arms. David stood still, remaining uncertain of what the hell to do.

"Eighty-five thousand pounds!" a newcomer male bidder shouted.

The room buzzed, springing Eva into action.

"I've got eighty-five thousand pounds. Do I hear any better for a twenty-four-hour date with me? Oh, and that endorsement thingy for whatever it is you do."

Some audience members were shaking their heads in disbelief.

"Going once. Going twice. Any better on eighty-five? Surely I'm worth much, much more than that?" Eva paused. "Gone!" She pointed out the male bidder who seemed awfully happy with himself. "Thank you, sir, for your bid and for supporting Down Dream. Phil, please go and speak to that gentleman about settling his payment."

Phil, apparently one of her security, weaved his way from the steps of the stage over to the man.

"And, now my end of the bargain," Eva said, holding out her palm, accepting a long chequebook from one of the members of her entourage. "I just knew I would need this tonight." She scribbled down onto a cheque and tore it from the book. She stood next to David and handed it to him in a symbolic gesture.

Click, click, click.

Eva leaned into David as he accepted the cheque. "It is with great honour that on behalf of the Shields Corporation, I donate one hundred and seventy thousand pounds to Down Dream. We'll have the winning bidder's payment of eighty-five thousand pounds collected shortly."

Click, click, click.

She turned to David with a smile and whispered, "There you go, Mr Dale. Two hundred and fifty-five thousand pounds to give Down Dream the best possible start. Try not to spill the milk."

"Don't forget that you're not going through this alone," Allen said, slumped behind the desk in his home office. "There are more people out there with similar issues, and I would highly encourage you to seek out those support groups local to you." He nodded as the voice whispered through the phone. "Alright, take care of yourself and I'll speak to you on Tuesday. Goodnight." He hung up the mobile phone, placed it down onto his laptop, and removed his glasses, allowing him to rub his eyes as if a deep itch needed urgent attention. He had arrived home from the Down Dream launch event thirty minutes ago with one of his long-term clients needing another late-night check-in call. He switched off his laptop and placed his glasses in their black leather case.

A long-haired black cat jumped up onto the desk, but as its front feet made contact with the summit, its hind legs failed to reach the same height, bringing the cat crashing back down to the floor with a thud. It quickly scurried out of the room.

"That was pathetic, Jasper," Allen said with a shake of his head as he rose to his feet. "We're becoming a right pair of old gits." He turned on his heel, switched off the light, and stepped onto the landing. As he approached his bedroom door, he caught the sound of another thud from downstairs. He stepped toward the staircase banister that overlooked the hallway, already covered in darkness with no lights on. He listened.

Silence.

"Bloody cat." He approached his bedroom once again and entered it, leaving the door ajar as he always did in case Jasper wanted to join him through the night. He brushed his teeth in the en suite bathroom and threw his crumpled shirt and trousers onto the armchair in the corner of the room. His mobile phone beeped as he connected it to its charger on the bedside table. He climbed into bed and flicked off the lamp, turned over, and dug his head into the pillow.

What could have been several seconds passed. Then the staircase creaked.

Allen patted the bed softly. "Come on then."

Silence.

He splayed out the duvet, creating a small flat area with no lumps or bumps next to him. He patted the bed again.

The sound of Jasper clawing the cat scratching post in the living room directly below the bedroom rung through Allen like an alarm.

The bedroom door slowly nudged forward, scraping along the carpet.

Allen tentatively rotated his head, his hands gripping onto the bed sheets. The bedroom door was now wide open. Allen stared into the empty pitch-black doorframe, desperate for his eyes to adjust to the darkness. Then, without warning, a figure of a man sprung from the shadows.

CHAPTER 10

The launch of Down Dream and the commotion that surrounded Eva's fundraising antics became the definition of an overnight media whirlwind. The following morning brought the relentless ringing of phones and the constant stream of emails. Journalists from newspapers, magazines and news stations around the country tried any conceivable way of contacting David for a statement. News was already spreading, jumping the English Channel and reaching international lands. A new founding of a charity is one thing, but for it to be founded by a man with such a tragic background and who had reached millions of sympathising people, is another thing. Mix in the headline-grabbing involvement of controversial and trend-setting Eva Shields who went as far as renting out an entire day and night with whomever bid the highest price was out of this world. For this one, the media found itself swivelling on its unprepared toes.

Bev didn't know what had hit them. "Two hundred and fifty-five thousand pounds. My lord, we hadn't even officially opened by cuttin' the ribbon yet, and she already landed us a quarter of a million pounds," she said from the back of the car, her eyes fixated on the other side of the window.

David nodded. "We owe her big. It's why I agreed to do this. It's not something I'd normally do."

"No, I know. It's the least we can do."

"Do you reckon, though, that Eva might have only done this for us in order to try and improve her image?"

Bev shifted her sight, resting a frown firmly on David. "What do ya mean?"

David shrugged. "She's been in the press recently about some negative comments she's made about poor people. I'm just thinking perhaps her actions last night were a publicity stunt to improve her image."

Bev immediately shook her head after realising David was serious. "Give over, David. Ya far too pessimistic. If she wanted to improve her image she could have done that in any old fashion. Ya happened to bump into her the other night at the casino launch, which obviously spurred her into helpin' us last night. Let's just be thankful for her assistance and not question it."

The car came to a stop on the busy road in the centre of London. David and Bev thanked the driver before stepping out of the car, leaving behind a copy of the first newspaper they could find that morning; its front page plastered with David and Eva's face.

Now stood in the morning's faint sunlight that only just managed to breach the clouds, Bev looked up at the building. "Is this it?"

David nodded. "Shields Tower. Eva's Head Office."

Silently, they both looked at the enormous, shiny building, as if it had just been cleaned for their arrival. A wall of scaffolding encompassed what looked like an entire side of the building, with men in bright orange and yellow high vis jackets walking up and down the suspended platforms, hard hats propped up on their heads. Bev and David exchanged a quick glance before heading into the entrance.

At the time of Eva's purchasing of the tower in 2011, formally owned by a billionaire Brazilian banker, it was widely reported on in the national news. *What will happen to the iconic London skyscraper?* Despite the controversy surrounding the building's sale, everybody's expectations were exceeded for the tower was soon to become a major landmark in British business and broadcasting. Across its forty-six floors, six separate arms of the Shields Corporation operate. *Shields TV*, *Shields News*, *Shields Radio*, *Shields* (magazine), *Shields Weekly* (blog), and *Shields Publishing*.

The lobby was extensive. Modern glass walls shone a reflective representation of shiny, contemporary business. Escalators linked the ground level to a second, open floor that overlooked the lobby. Men and women dressed in shirt and tie or formal blouses and dresses sprawled the cavern, speedily darting in various directions with bags and phones in hand. A huge Shields Corporation logo confronted all who entered, hung high against the far wall. A desk of women with their hair tied back, wearing striped, black jackets lined a circular desk, accessorised by slim monitors. David and Bev approached one of the women.

"Good morning, may I help you?" the lady asked, her hair tied back and her teeth as sparkly as the glass walls.

"Good morning. We're from Down Dream, we are—"

"David Dale?"

"Yes, that's me. And this is Bev Walcott," he motioned to Bev.

"Very well." The lady tapped onto her keyboard, staring at the monitor without a blink. "Here are your cards." She placed two white plastic cards on the desk before them. "Carry them with you. They'll grant you access to where you need to go. Do not deviate from where you are required. The building is undertaking some renovations on our east side, so there is some construction works on some floors, but there's plenty of signs so you can't make a wrong turn."

"And where is it we need to go?" Bev asked.

"Follow that man who is waiting for you," she said, pointing to a man at the top of one of the escalators. "He will take you to Shields Radio where you are due to go live shortly."

"Thank you for your help," David said, taking the two cards and passing one to Bev.

The pair made their way to the escalator and stepped on.

"Ya've certainly made yourself a powerful friend, David," Bev said, looking around the gigantic room.

At the escalator's summit, the man introduced himself and led the pair to a lift where they headed for the eighth floor. Once there, the man headed back into the lift and disappeared. David and Bev were quickly seen to by a young lady who, after introducing herself, detailed the exact plan. Bev was asked to remain outside in the waiting area, but she would be able to see and hear David talking to the radio presenter through a small window in the middle of the wall.

Before David knew it, he was being pushed inside the soundproof room and was shaking hands with Sarah Collings, a forty-something-year-old with short brown hair who had been presenting on Shields Radio for the past five years. He had heard of her before but had never personally tuned into her show. She pointed David to the vacant seat, opposite herself, and motioned to put on the headphones. She clicked a button. "And that was Ed Sheeran with *Camera*. Now, as promised, Shields Radio has a treat in store this morning. Everyone is already talking about Eva Shields' actions last night at the launch of the brand-new charity, Down Dream. Mr David Dale, the charity's founder, has been catapulted into the public's eye with his new non-profit organisation." Sarah smirked at David. "Well, we have David here for you now to tell us more about himself, the charity's goals, and what he thought of last night's events. Plus, you'll get your chance to call in and speak to him one-on-one." She allowed a small pause, her eyes still on David. "David Dale, good morning and welcome to the show."

"Sarah, good morning. Thank you so much for having me on."

"Thank you for agreeing to join us. Can we get you anything, or are you all right?"

"I'm fine, thank you," David said. "I had a coffee on the drive over here and I don't want to be testing my bladder's limits while on air."

"Alrighty then," she laughed. "So, David. Last night you launched Down Dream, a brand-new charity."

"Yeah, we did. The event went a lot better than I anticipated. We put a lot of time and resource into the launch."

"From what I've heard, I understand Down Dream is aimed at helping people in any burdened circumstance, is that right?"

"Yes, that's right. If you're unemployed and struggling with your bills, speak to us. If you're homeless and are sleeping rough on the streets, speak to us. There are so many underlying issues out there, which a lot of people don't think about because it doesn't affect them. But there are thousands of people who need help and charities up and down the country, as well as government bodies, are struggling with the demand. Down Dream is here to help and do what we can to assist people in all sorts of circumstances."

"I see. I understand you have your own background of running a psychiatry practice, which you left a few years ago. Is that correct?"

"Yeah. Shortly after leaving university where I studied Counselling and Psychotherapy, I setup my own practice that massively snowballed. The practice really grew over a matter of years and became a brand that still helps thousands of people with their personal issues. I'm actually hoping to bring a form of this service into Down Dream at some point down the line, but that's for the future."

"You sound well qualified to run your own charity then. Do you personally still offer psychiatry on the side? Like freelance or anything like that?"

"No, I don't."

Sarah nodded. "And are you single, David?"

David hesitated, his eyebrows tilted inwards. "I am."

"Ooh, I wonder how long that'll last with all the ladies that'll be swooning for you now." She laughed. "On a serious note, though. I understand you once were married, and had two daughters?"

David swallowed, feeling almost frozen in place. His history, his background; it was all going to be brought up. His life was now in the public domain. "That's correct," he said with a splintered voice.

"I remember the tragic story airing on this show, what, was it three, four years ago now?"

"Three years," David said, his jaw locked and his tone dull.

"That must have been a huge, life-shattering loss. I'm terribly sorry for that." She looked down to her desk, as if reading some notes. "Do you think what has happened in the past has led you to where you are today? Launching your own charity?"

David held his gaze on Sarah, his expression blank. "Completely, yes."

She nodded several times. "Okay, a quick song now and we'll return with David Dale, the founder of new charity Down Dream. Call in now to have your chance at speaking with him," Sarah said before clicking a luminous green button. "Are you okay, David? Don't worry, we're off the air while the next song's on."

"I'm fine," David returned, offering a contrived smile.

"I'm sorry, it was insensitive of me to bring up the past."

David shook his head with a raised palm. "Honestly, it's fine." He glanced over at Bev through the glass window. "This phone-in thing, what can I expect?" he asked, looking to Sarah again.

"Truth be told, I have no idea. It changes every time we have someone new on the show. Some phone-ins can be very sweet and complementing, others can be quite to the point and direct. Don't worry, I'll be here. You're in safe hands," she said.

David caught Bev's eyes as she pressed her lips together in a sympathetic expression.

The few minutes passed quickly as Sarah started speaking once more to the nation. "I'm still here with David Dale, the founding leader of the new London-based charity, Down Dream. If you've seen the papers this morning or if you've read the online news articles and blogs alike, you'll already know all about him and what happened at the charity launch event last night involving Eva Shields. David, could you fill in any listeners who've been hiding under a rock?"

David tried a laugh, but it came out like a mumble. "Of course I can," he said. "Well, in the middle of my speech, which was opening the charity to a room full of guests, Eva boldly entered the proceedings and walked onto the stage. She ended up auctioning herself in a twenty-four-hour date that the lucky highest bidder could enjoy. I don't know who the winner was, but a person ended up paying eighty-five thousand pounds for that opportunity, and Eva made an extra donation, tripling the amount."

"Wow," Sarah said. "Your first night of fundraising was pretty successful then."

"It really was. We're very grateful to Eva and what she's been able to do."

"If you would like to donate to Down Dream and assist in their charitable operations, you can visit their website, or ours, for details on how to do it. Right, let's get some people on the line." Sarah pressed several more buttons. "Tom on line one, good morning."

"Good morning, Sarah," said the voice through the headphones.

"What would you like to say or ask David?"

"Well, I want to ask David how he's funded opening a charity and laying on a grand launch event, when his only bit of fundraising so far was last night? Oh, and I also wanted to say I think he's doing an awesome job and more people should pay attention to organisations like this because, like you say, a lot of people don't give a lot of issues much thought."

"Hi Tom," David started. "Thanks for your question. Down Dream, so far, has been exclusively self-funded by myself. I've poured a lot of money into this project because I want it to be a success and I think it'll have the potential to aid thousands of people and change lives for the better. Moving forward, we aim to launch a lot of fundraising initiatives to cover the costs of our work which we'll be posting about online. Thanks for that nice comment, too."

"Good answer," Sarah said. "Okay, James on line two. What would you like to say or ask David Dale?"

"Hi Sarah, great show. I wanted to speak to David personally because he really interests me."

"Hi James," David said.

"Hi," James said. "David, how exactly were your family killed?"

David's eyes widened. His body stiffened. The words rang through the headphones and refused to leave his ears.

"You're a filthy scumbag seeking attention and fame," James said.

Sarah tried to butt in. "Excuse me—"

"Watch your back, Mr Dale, because we've got our eyes on ya, you mother—"

Sarah terminated the call.

CHAPTER 11

It had been twenty-three minutes since the interview hastily concluded, with Sarah and the team from Shields Radio profusely apologising for the unprecedented phone call. Never had they ever, they swore, received a phone call with such expletive and direct language to a guest of the show. And it was true. The Internet was ablaze with comments on what had happened, with the topic becoming the second most trending subject matter at its peak; trailing behind the hype of a newly released trailer for yet another Marvel superhero movie.

"David, are ya comin'?" Bev asked from inside the back of the taxi.

David didn't respond; too transfixed to the phone in his hand buzzing with relentless notifications. He was frozen in place beside the open taxi door.

"David," Bev repeated, this time louder and with a snappy sense of urgency.

He looked up from the screen, his forehead crinkled. "No, no," he quietly said, glancing up and down the busy London road. "Go straight to the office. Stu and Kristian will be there." He looked back to his phone. "I'll meet you there in an hour or so."

"An hour? David, where are ya goin'? We need to talk about what just happened."

David shook his head before clicking off his phone. "I'm sorry, I just need to meet someone first. I'll see you at the office," he said as he started walking away.

Bev watched him walk away with a faint muttering of upset.

"Are you ready?" the taxi driver asked.

Bev outstretched her arm and pulled the door closed with a firm tug. She told the driver the address of the charity offices and dug into her handbag for her phone. As she pulled it out, she found it already ringing. "Hello," she answered.

"Bev, where are you? I've tried calling David but he's not answering," Stu said.

"We've only just left the studio. David said he needed to go somewhere, I dono."

"What happened in the interview? Kristian and I heard the whole thing. Who was that guy?"

Bev released a built-up sigh, which earned her a glance from the driver through the rear-view mirror. "Ya guess is as good as mine. I really don't know the answer to that one."

"Did the people at the radio not say anything? Did they not take his details before they let him on air? Surely they do some sort of checks before they let people on."

"Yeah, I guess so. They just said there weren't any signs he'd act the way he did. For me, the real question is why."

"A prank, maybe." Stu exhaled loudly down the line, with the faint sound of Kristian talking in the background. "What's the plan then? Are you coming here?"

Bev rubbed her eyes. "I'm on my way now. I won't be long."

"Okay. I hope David's all right. Must have shaken him up a bit."

"He seemed really distracted. It looked like it got to him. He said he'd meet us at the office in about an hour, so we'll see how he is then."

"All right, Bev. I'll see you shortly."

"See ya soon," she said before hanging up. She dropped her phone back into her bag and pushed her legs up against the chair in front of her.

The taxi driver's eyes caught Bev's in the rear-view mirror for a second time. He laughed. "You heard that bloke on Shields Radio earlier? Boy, now that was a moment, weren't it?"

David allowed the door to slam shut behind him, causing a loud bang to reverberate around the small waiting room. A man who appeared to be in his early thirties looked up from his hunched seating position on the pale green sofa, sitting in the same right-hand corner seat that was typically always vacant when David arrived at his usual hour.

The receptionist had already changed her focus from her computer screen to David as he entered. "Jesus, David. The other day you saturated me with your bloody umbrella, now you're scaring me with loud bangs." She laughed, "What do you have in store for me next?"

David lacked any notion of a smile.

"Are you okay?" she continued. "I didn't think you were booked in to see Allen until tomorrow evening."

David placed both of his palms against the counter, as if pausing for a breath. "I'm sorry, Kate, I need to see him now. I need to swap my appointment."

She frowned. "Is everything okay?"

"I'm just not feeling great and I need to speak to him. I tried calling him."

"David, I'm very sorry, but I don't think that'll be possible."

"Look, I don't mind paying extra to squeeze me in."

"It's not that." Kate glanced back and forth to the waiting gentleman on the sofa. "Allen missed his nine o'clock appointment, and now he's almost fifteen minutes late for his ten thirty appointment."

David hadn't realised, but his lips parted in genuine shock. Never had he heard of Allen being late for an appointment, let alone miss one.

"It's not that we can't squeeze you in," Kate started, "it's just I don't really know if he's coming in or not. I've tried texting, I've tried calling, but I'm not hearing anything back."

David shook his head slowly. "Right."

"Apart from that, I don't really know what else to say. I'm sorry."

David looked toward Allen's office door, and then to the waiting gentleman on the sofa. He returned his eyes to Kate. "Okay, I'll just come back for my appointment tomorrow. Please let me know when you hear from him." Without giving her a chance to respond, he turned his back and left, once again leaving the door to slam shut behind him.

"What the hell was that all about?" Kristian asked as soon as he clocked David step foot in the office.

"I honestly have no idea." David replied, solemnly walking toward the group.

"Sounded like someone wasn't happy with Down Dream," Bev said, her shoulders slouched.

"Why though? What have we done? What has David done? We're running a goddamn charity, for god's sake," Stu said, kicking his feet underneath the shared table.

David took a seat at the same table in the centre of the charity's office, looking at the three downcast expressions that perfectly reflected his own.

Bev let out a sigh before taking a short, sharp breath. "We've gotta stay strong and move past this. We're new to the scene. Some people may not like that. Some people, whether a prank or not, might think of us as a target. That's fine – well, it's not, but ya know what I mean." She took another short breath, her eyes looking up and down David's face. "We just have to stick together and stay strong. We're bound to face hurdles. We just have to make sure we jump over them."

Kristian nodded hesitantly.

Stu flicked from Kristian and David, waiting for their reaction.

"It was obviously directed towards me and not the charity. It was a silly man with silly, empty words. Nothing more," David said, offering a timid smile.

Silence.

Bev cleared her throat. "Right, let's move on. We have a few hours before we need to be at the homeless shelter. The press are still goin' crazy about the launch last night and are dyin' to get their hands on ya, David. It'll also be a great opportunity for the rest of us to raise our profile as governors of the charity and project Down Dream's goals. This launch of the homeless shelter is our first major step and we need to gather as much interest and support as possible. We really need to network strongly, people."

The four of them slowly stood from the table after a murmur of agreement. Bev wandered off with Kristian, beginning to detail advice on his outfit for the event.

David lingered at the table and Stu noticed. He leaned forward, gaining David's attention. "It's not right, David," he said in a hushed voice.

"What's not right?"

"This situation. Nobody goes to the effort to say the things they did without a reason. No, nobody goes to the effort to *threaten* somebody without a reason."

"Honestly, we need to move on like Bev said. As bad as it was, we can't let it get to us. It was one silly man. Please, let's get ready and go out."

"David, the man said *we've got our eyes on ya*. There's more than one silly man."

CHAPTER 12

The car stopped in front of the entrance to the homeless shelter on the fringes of Mayfair. The building, formally a hotel, had been purchased and renovated extensively. The vast majority of it had been completely stripped back to the plaster and refurbished. Now, with a new lick of paint and nearly eighty brand new beds, the building could play temporary host to some of London's homeless. From the pavement, the building was aesthetically pleasing with traditional, city-like architecture giving it a sense of character that comfortably stood out from its neighbouring buildings.

David stepped out of the back of the car, suited and booted in a black suit and tie, accompanied by Stu, Bev and Kristian.

An uproar of noise from the awaiting journalists, paparazzi and a dozen gathered pedestrians ensued.

"David! David! Over here!" one reporter shouted.

"David! Look here for a quick picture!"

"David!"

"David! Can you describe your relationship with Eva Shields? David!"

The four made their way towards the building's entrance, stopping at random to speak to members of the crowd. David was asked about what was said to him on Shields Radio earlier in the morning. Stu was asked about his role in the charity. Bev was asked about her relationship with David. Kristian was asked how he had met David.

After answering countless questions and having many photographs taken, the group entered the homeless shelter, passing the initial reception area and heading straight to the large communal room that was now buzzing with more journalists, representatives from other non-profit organisations from up and down the country, and prominent members from the local city council. The room was alive with bustling discussions and the clinking of glasses. Large and colourful banners were scattered around the room with various facts on homelessness, poverty and the rising use of food banks.

As more and more people noticed the group's arrival, faces turned their way. One person started clapping, leading to a cluster of people clapping. After a few moments, the entire room had erupted into a unanimous round of applause. In return, the four smiled and raised their hands as a thank you.

"Ooh, how lovely," Bev said, raising an open palm in a royal-like wave. "Now remember, mingle and project the charity's goals. We're here to raise critical support."

David, Kristian and Stu nodded in unison behind Bev's line of sight.

"Now disperse my charitable firecrackers!" Bev exclaimed, heading towards a group of journalists holding notepads, cameras and microphones.

A well-dressed middle-aged lady approached David, sporting a blue blouse and a matching long skirt. Her bulky gold necklace jangled as she approached. "Mr Dale. Lovely to meet you," she said, holding out her hand. "My name's Rochelle Parkins, Director of R.P.A Trust."

David accepted her hand, shaking it gently. "R.P.A Trust? Whoa, thank you for coming, Miss Parkins. I've followed your charity for a long time. You do some incredible work." Her shake was much firmer than David had anticipated.

"Thank you very much, that means a lot."

"Honestly, your work last year in Blackpool was inspiring. The number of people in education that you've helped is amazing."

"We do try our best in reaching as many as we can. Spreading the assistance is all we can do."

"I'm honoured you've attended our opening event of this homeless shelter," David said.

"My pleasure. I'd actually be quite interested in working closely with Down Dream in the future. Who knows."

"That would be great. We're focusing on this homeless shelter right now, but we'll be launching some new initiatives in the coming weeks, so I can get in touch to discuss."

"Excellent," Rochelle said as she took out a small business card. "Here's my details."

David took the card, glancing at it. "Thank you, Rochelle."

She nodded once, smiling. "I'll let you greet your guests."

He watched her walk away.

"Mr Dale," an unfamiliar voice said.

David glanced to his side, noticing a tall, well-built man approaching. The man was wearing a white suit of seemingly exceptional quality. His dark hair was of medium length and brushed neatly backwards in a wet-gelled form. A thin layer of defined facial hair encompassed his tanned face. A woman was attached to his left arm, her arm interlinked with his. At least two men, also dressed in suits, stood closely behind them.

"Good evening," David said.

"I don't believe we have yet met. Quentin." He moved his right hand forward, offering David a handshake as the lady detached from his arm.

"Pleasure to meet you, Quentin," David said.

"This is my wife, Rose Zicela," he said, overemphasising every one of his words. He turned to look at her.

David moved his focus to the woman before him.

Her brown eyes moved from the floor to confront his. Their never-ending depth consumed his focus, as if luring him inside. Her amber-brown, wavy hair left loose and hung down her back with some strands coyly dangling beside her cheeks. Her neck was bare, but her strapless red dress that flowed to her heels demanded appreciation.

Before David could bring himself to say something to her, Quentin interjected, "You've had a busy few days, haven't you? Congratulations on the charity launch. Down Dream, isn't it?"

David reluctantly shifted his focus from Rose back to Quentin. "Er, yes, thank you very much. Thank you for coming and supporting us, too."

"No, not a problem. It's our pleasure to support organisations like these, isn't it, sweetheart?" he said, glancing at Rose.

She remained silent, her eyes flittering up to meet with Quentin's.

"How long have you been working on the charity?" Quentin asked.

David said, "Er, far too long to remember now. It feels like a lifetime. But I'm so glad the ball is rolling. We've had such a successful launch. The only way is up now."

"I'm pleased for you. Must be quite a stressful thing to do, I imagine?"

"Yeah, it's been one hell of a journey. Worth it in the end though," David said, glancing around the room for any sight of Bev,

Kristian or Stu. All that greeted him was a crowd of unfamiliar faces. The two men that were standing closely behind Quentin were staring in David's direction. One of the men was obviously older than the other; his skin tired and his head completely bald, with a prominent scar splitting his right eyebrow in two. As David took a second to process the face, he remembered where he had seen the man before and instantly dropped his lower lip.

Quentin smirked. "I saw a clip from your launch last night. You really reminded me of my brother. He used to be so selfless."

David wanted to frown but instead forced a silent smile.

"I would love to work with you, Mr Dale. In a type of partnership, if you will."

"A partnership? Of what sort?"

Quentin smiled a wide smile with narrowed eyes. He looked at Rose, said, "Could you tell Harold that we'll be leaving shortly and to bring the car to the front? That's my girl."

Rose instantly looked to the floor before taking another look into David's eyes. She turned her back and walked towards the scarred, bald man, said a few words, and then the pair made their way towards the exit.

Quentin and David watched her walk away.

"Such a beautiful specimen, isn't she?" Quentin said. He turned back to face David, a smile plastered across his face. "Now, Mr Dale. This partnership of ours," he said, stopping himself in what sounded like mid-flow. "It's going to be hugely beneficial to the both of us, you see. I'll be able to provide certain assurances and guarantees that no other person or organisation can provide Down Dream."

David frowned. "I don't understand what you're saying, Quentin. What did you say your last name was again?"

"I didn't." He cleared his throat, glanced around the room, and then placed a tight grip onto David's shoulder, still with the smile on his face.

David moved uneasily on the spot.

"Mr Dale. You pay for my services. This fundraising for Down Dream, just throw a little my way every month. Then, happy days."

"You're asking me to give you some of the charity's donations?"

"I'm telling you that for our partnership to work smoothly, you'll need to pay for my services, yes. Don't worry, these assurances I can give you are invaluable."

"I don't know who you are or what you're playing at, but you must be insane if you think I'll be freely handing out the charity's donations to anybody."

Quentin tightened his grip, digging his bony fingertips deep into David's shoulder blade.

David grimaced, reaching for his shoulder but finding his hand only pulling at Quentin's.

Quentin moved a step closer with stern eyes and whispered, "Think about it, Mr Dale. You've been back on the scene for five minutes. I'd personally like to see you around a little bit longer than that." Quentin leaned back, sharing another prolonged smile. "Think about it, Mr Dale," Quentin repeated. He released his grip on David's shoulder, patted his arm with a strong slap and turned to walk out of the building.

David stood, speechless, putting every effort into stopping his hands from shaking.

CHAPTER 13

David could feel his hands tremble. The few moments he had just shared with Quentin had left them physically shaking, but then he realised his arms, too, were wobbling, and his feet jittered against the floor.

Stu approached. "David? Who was that guy? I was watching from the other side of the room."

David's focus shifted from the exit to Stu, then back to the exit where he had just left. "His name was Quentin."

"He looked pretty serious. What was he saying to you? Do you know him?"

David looked at Stu, said, "I think he is—"

"You guys," Kristian said, bursting into the conversation with an energetic mood. "I've just been talking to a lady from Southwark Council here in London. She's so excited about our charity and has already started some discussions internally about our operations. I think she'll be able to open up some channels of communications across a lot of regional councils, which will be an awesome benefit." Kristian took a moment to register both Stu and David's expressions. "Is everything okay?"

David kept his eye contact with Stu. "I think he's connected to that man, from the radio."

"He? He, who?" Kristian asked.

Stu's eyebrows dived. "You think this guy, Quentin, is somehow involved with the radio guy from this morning? James, or something? How? Why?"

"I don't know why," David started, "but my gut just tells me. It's too coincidental and too similar."

Kristian shook his head. "What do you mean, David? What's happening?"

"I don't quite know yet, but I've got a really bad feeling."

"I've never seen you like this before. He's really rattled you," Stu said.

David flexed his fingers, then shook his hands to try and stabilise them. He took a deep breath before he spotted a representative from the Charity Commission that he recognised walking towards him. David tilted his head and gave Stu and Kristian a stare with slightly raised eyebrows.

"Ah, Mr Dale," the representative said, now stood next to Kristian with a confident rolling of his shoulders. "Your homeless shelter is magnificent, you must be really proud."

David's eyes looked out to the crowd.

"David?" the man enquired.

"I'm sorry, sir, but could you please excuse us for a moment?" Kristian asked. Without waiting for an answer, Kristian placed a hand under David's elbow and led him away.

"Where's Bev?" David asked, walking through the loud room filled with chatter, both Kristian and Stu by his side.

Stu walked on the tips of his feet, raising his head up above the crowd and scanning the room. He dipped his head back down. "Last I heard, she was speaking to someone from Shelter over by the stairs about five minutes ago."

"We need to get together and talk about what just happened. I don't feel comfortable at all," David said, forcing a smile at a guest he had locked eyes with.

Several journalists and guests approached David but were waved off as the group cut through the raft of people to get to the staircase, walking at an urgent pace.

Bev stepped out of the ladies' toilets, taking a moment to look up and down the room for any faces she hadn't yet spoken to. As she picked out a person to mingle with next, the phone in her jacket pocket vibrated. She pulled herself against a wall, out of reach from the majority of the noise, and removed her phone, checking the caller ID.

Unknown.

She tapped the screen. "Hello, this is Bev Walcott speakin'."

"Good evening. Are you the person that handles all insurance policies for the charity Down Dream?"

"I oversee the policies, yes. Whom am I speakin' to?"

"My apologies, Miss Walcott. Where are my manners? My name is Peter James from S and F Insurance. I'm calling to see if you currently hold insurance policies for your premises in central London?"

"For which property? The homeless shelter, or our offices?"

"*Both.*"

"Yes, we do. We finalised an agreement with our provider last week for both buildings."

"Ah, what a shame. I was hoping to offer you a very generous policy, Miss Walcott."

"Well thank ya anyway."

"No, thank you," the man replied before clicking the phone off.

Bev hesitated for a moment, tentatively bringing the phone down from her ear. She blinked several times and then straightened her expression, pocketing her phone and looking up once again to the lively crowd of people. However this time, she was scanning the densely populated room for a face she did recognise.

Stu reached Bev's side, giving her a minor startle. "Found you. Bloody hell."

Kristian and David were close behind, walking in towards the circle they were forming.

"Are ya all right?" Bev asked, noticing the strained looks on the faces in front of her.

David spoke first. "I think we're being targeted."

"What do ya mean, ya *think we're being targeted?*" she repeated, putting on a display with her hands as she quoted his statement.

David sighed, glanced around the room and then motioned for them to follow him. "Let's speak in private."

Bev followed David as he led his friends-come-colleagues out of the hectic main room and down a corridor to the side of the property. Stepping through a door and closing it behind them, they huddled close together in a small, quiet room, decked out with low wooden tables, a handful of sofas, and scattered chairs.

"Come on, tell us what the hell you're all worried about," Kristian said.

All three pairs of eyes were directed at David.

He gulped, caught his breath, and said, "Truth be told, I don't know, but from what I do know, I don't like the sound of it one bit." David's eyes flicked from person to person. "This morning, the call in on the radio."

"That isn't anythin' to worry about. It was a deranged loner with nothin' better to do," Bev said.

"My gut tells me it's more serious than that. He said *we've got our eyes on you,*" David said in a stressed tone. "*We.*"

Bev shrugged. "Right, so there's a handful of deranged loners out there. So what?"

"I don't quite think they're deranged loners," David said.

Stu and Kristian remained silent.

"Why not? Because they were able to correctly dial the right number for the radio show?" Bev asked. As soon as the last syllable left her mouth, her eyes widened. Her upbeat spirit spiralled downwards in free-fall as her eyes met the floor.

David shook his head. "No," he started, "I think one of them was here tonight. A different man, because he sounded nothing like the guy from the radio. A well-dressed guy, well groomed, who you wouldn't take for some deranged loner. He came up to me. He looked well off. He was with a timid-looking woman. But he seemed intelligent, intellectual. He threatened me, out of everyone else's range for overhearing. He grabbed hold of my shoulder and crushed it." David paused, catching his breath. "He was delivering a message. He wants a cut of the charity's donations, and he seemed pretty determined to get it."

"Bastard! Who does he think he is?" Kristian snapped.

David raised a finger to his lips. "Shh. Don't let this get out."

"Did you get his name at least?" Kristian asked.

"Er," David paused, "yeah. He said his name was Quentin." He paused again, but for longer, his eyes frozen still. "I've also got a horrible feeling that one of the men that was with him was watching me," he said, turning to Stu, "at the casino the other night when we went, Stu."

Stu frowned. "You saw one of them at the casino?"

"Well, I can't be sure, but I think so. I'm sure it was him."

"Right, let me get this straight," Stu said, his hands held out as if demanding the stage. "So a guy calls you this morning over the radio and insults you, then some rich bloke with a quiet woman comes to our homeless shelter launch event and threatens and assaults you? And you reckon one of the guys who was with this Quentin guy was watching you at the casino?"

David's shoulders fell as he exhaled loudly. "Sounds crazy, but yeah, that's about right."

"Then we need to contact the police," Stu said, his voice slightly raised.

"I think things may already have gotten worse," Bev said before David had a chance to reply.

All eyes set on Bev.

"What do you mean?" David asked.

"He called me, just before you found me outside the loo just then."

Stu's eyes narrowed. "Who called you?"

"The man from the radio. It's only just hit me. I recognise his voice completely now."

Silence cast itself across the room for the briefest of moments.

"You mean he has your number?" Kristian asked.

"It's publicly listed for Down Dream administration," Bev said. "He called and said he was from some insurance company, S and F Insurance, or somethin' like that. He was askin' if we had insurance policies for the shelter and our offices."

Stu's lips quickly parted, his eyes no longer narrowed.

Kristian looked blankly at Bev. "Why would some nutcase call at this time in the evening and ask something like that?"

David took a step back. "We need to go to the offices. Now."

CHAPTER 14

David and Stu left Bev and Kristian behind, leaving them to try to salvage the opening night. Confused faces watched the pair rush to leave the building, with some unanswered questions thrown their way. Bev, David thought, would be able to come up with an excuse decent enough to explain their urgent departure.

From the passenger seat of the car, Stu looked at David who was driving just a tad over the national speed limit. "Do you really think they'll have done something?"

"I think it's likely, but we don't know these people. We only know what they've said, not what they're actually capable of."

Stu glanced around the city's streets, lit up from the countless lampposts that hung overhead. A faint trickle of rain showered the windscreen, appearing from out of the darkness of the sky. "If they have," Stu said. "I mean, if they have..." He exhaled loudly with a shaking of his head.

"Then we have reason to be worried," David said, making eye contact with Stu.

They drove for a further eleven minutes, bulldozing through an amber traffic light and narrowly missing the wing mirror of a parked Honda. As they pulled up outside of the charity office building, the area seemed quiet and peaceful, as if nothing more than the usual dribble of light traffic had passed by. The building looked normal; nothing set on fire and nothing in a heap of rubble.

They left the car and hurriedly made their way into the entrance of the building. The entrance hall was dark without a single light lit.

"Where's security?" David asked, the quickening pace of his breathing catching him off guard.

Stu looked around. "He should be here. The door was open."

David glanced outside and noticed the streetlights he had just passed were on. "There's not a power cut in the area, so I don't know why the lights are off."

They both slowly wandered the hall, approaching the security desk opposite the entrance; typically where twenty-four-hour security personnel would sit. The desk and its contents of a computer and keyboard remained undisturbed, but the chair behind it was empty.

"Do you know where the light switch is down here?" Stu asked.

"No idea. Let's just head up to the office."

Keeping close to one another, they went straight for the stairs and slowly climbed their way to the third floor. As they stepped through the first doorway that led them out of the stairwell and into the third-floor landing, they could already see that things weren't right. Shattered glass covered the floor, and a strong gush of cold air forced its way through a broken window. They exchanged a glance to one another, both of their faces effortlessly reflecting the same concerned expression.

"Oh my god," David said, walking over glass and pushing open the main door to Down Dream's offices. The pair tentatively stepped inside where only darkness and cool air met them, causing a chilling tingle to roar up David's spine.

Stu tentatively followed the wall to the lightswitch, where he flicked it on.

David's mouth dropped open as the lights displayed the full office. "No," he said, his eyes taking in as much as he could see.

Stu couldn't help but gasp.

Tables lay overturned, their computers smashed and scattered across the floor. Chairs split into several pieces. Beautiful pictures and paintings that once hung on the clean, white walls were now ripped and torn, overthrown by the splashes of red paint that had been carelessly lashed across the entire room. Windows were broken and a handful of ceiling lights destroyed, having created a floor of glass shards. What seemed like imprints of baseball bats were embedded into corners of the walls, tables, chairs and doors.

David and Stu slowly looked around the havoc that was once their tidy office.

"Jesus Christ," Stu said before digging out his phone from his pocket and dialling 999.

David lowered his head, feeling as if the splinters of wood from the tables and chairs were cutting into every part of his body. He looked around the room from his stationary spot before making his way to his own office, the door ajar and the lights off. With darkness inside David's office, but bright lights overhead in the main room, the window that looked into David's office reflected his tentative approach as he stepped closer. In the background, he could hear Stu speaking to an operator and requesting the police, the worry that lined his voice so evident to hear.

David gently pushed his office door, peering inside. Still stood in the doorway, he reached in and felt along the wall for the light switch before touching something cold and wet. He flicked on the light and immediately noticed the blood-red paint on his fingers. He took a step forward and looked up at huge, capitalised letters that dominated his office wall.

KILLER.

David stared directly at the word, his eyes transfixed and his feet seemingly unable to take him elsewhere.

A groaning sounded from behind him, startling David enough for him to instantly turn around as if prepared to face the intruder. There, hunched on the floor in front of his wooden desk, lay the security guard, tied, gagged and semi-unconscious.

The police and an ambulance had arrived within twelve minutes, with the former beginning to question Stu and David, take photographs of the wreckage and dust for fingerprints. The paramedics treated the woozy security guard and ushered him to hospital as a precaution for concussion.

David and Stu perched on a small stone wall alongside the pavement, their backs to an array of shrubs and flowers. The earlier rain had subsided with the clouds overhead separating, leaving an eerily quiet and clear night.

David had just gotten off of the phone with Bev, informing her of the latest developments. His emotions ran high when she began to sob down the phone, questioning the motive of such thugs. David held himself together; now was not the time to falter.

A man in a long, grey overcoat approached David and Stu; his age in the mid-forties, his hair dark brown and his face an uncanny resemblance to a Hollywood actor, or so David thought.

"Good evening, gents. My name is Detective Thomas McField. I'm sorry about your office, but I'm here to ask you a couple of questions, if you don't mind?"

"Sure," David started as he pushed himself to his feet, "but you could start by going to question Quentin, the guy who turned up at our event this evening and threatened me as he crushed my shoulder."

McField looked confused, said, "Hold up, hold up. One step at a time, right?" His eyes rolled over the building, landing back on the pair. "Right, so you're David Dale and you're Stu Jackson, is that correct?"

They nodded in agreement.

McField pulled a small notepad from his pocket, clicked a stainless steel pen, and started scribbling. "And the offices on the third floor, the ones broken into and trashed, they're the premises of your charity? Down…" He stopped to think.

"Down Dream, yeah," David replied.

"And you think someone called Quentin is involved?"

"He *is* involved. Our charity was launching our homeless shelter tonight and he turned up with a woman. Rose, I think her name was. He came just to threaten me. That's what this is about tonight, he's sending a message."

McField noted down the names. "And what kind of message is that?"

"He's obviously showing us what he's capable of. He's after the charity's money."

"Can you give me a description of this guy, and the woman?"

David gave the detective descriptions of what he remembered.

McField pondered on the spot. "No offence to Down Dream, but small start-up charities don't typically have a lot of money, do they? They rely on charity shops and volunteer fundraising for donations."

"You're right, but," David hesitated, "we raised a quarter of a million pounds yesterday, in one night."

"And you think he's after this money now?"

"Yes, why else would he be doing this?"

"I'm not sure," McField started, "but if he's capable of doing what he's supposedly done tonight; overpowering a security guard, wrecking a secure office space and getting himself onto the guest list to your event, do you not think he'd have bigger fish to fry? So to speak."

"We didn't have a guest list for this event. We sent out invitations to people we wanted to come, but really anyone could walk in."

McField raised his eyebrows.

Stu looked up at David. "What if he knows your background? What if he knows you're worth the trouble?"

"What do you mean by that?" McField asked.

David paused. "I have some money," he said. "It's what's launched this charity. The media have already reported on it though. It isn't hard to find out on the Internet."

McField nodded. "Okay."

Stu pushed himself from the wall and stood straight.

McField looked up to the third floor windows of the building. "Oh, in your offices," he said, now looking back at Stu and David. "There was a word painted onto one of the walls."

David slowly blinked.

"*Killer*," McField said matter-of-factly. "Do you have any idea why someone would write that?"

Stu shrugged, his head gently shaking. "Because they're bastards playing with us?"

McField's eyes remained on David.

David wrapped his arms around his chest. A deep frown cast across his face.

"What about you?" McField prodded.

"I, er…" David started, looking around the floor for the words. He forced his head up to look at the detective. "I lost my wife and two daughters three years ago in an accident. An accident that was my fault."

"And these sick bastards must be using that to get to him," Stu said.

"Right," McField said, glancing back and forth between Stu and David. "It's late so I'll let you two get off home." He pulled two cards out from his inner jacket pocket. "Please take one of my cards. If you think of anything else, or you'd like to talk, give me a ring on that number." He turned his back and began walking to his awaiting car. "Oh," he said, stopping and turning back around. "One last thing. What were you both doing at the office so late?"

"At the shelter launch – the event we were talking about – Bev, our colleague, received a call from someone who was asking about our insurance policies for the offices and for the shelter," Stu said. "Bev realised that she recognised the man's voice from another threat that David got earlier this morning, on a phone-in on Shields Radio. We put that together with what Quentin said and did to David and decided we'd better make sure the office was all right."

David nodded. "And Bev mentioned that the caller said they were from S and F Insurance, if that helps?"

"I'll check it out. Thanks for that," McField said. "Our team will need continuous access to your office over the next couple of hours at least, but if we need anything further, we'll reach out."

David nodded. "Sure."

"Take it easy. I'll be in touch," McField said before turning around and walking towards his car.

Stu headed home. David, at first, headed to his city apartment before instinctively changing direction and instead drove to his house outside of the city, by Wanstead Park. After arriving and immediately walking into the woods, he soon re-emerged on the side of the lake in the dead of night. The sky was fine and the lake picture-still. He sat by his familiar stone and reflected in his own private sanctuary.

As he stared out across the shaded lake, his mind faded to nothingness, as if the non-stop events of the day had completely subdued him.

His phone vibrated in his pocket, bringing him back to reality. He checked the caller ID but didn't recognise the number. He debated for a moment before his curiosity overcame his cautiousness. "Hello?"

"Is this David Dale?" asked a man with a soft squeak to his voice.

"Who is this?"

"My name is Alex Haynes. I'm an investigative journalist and I—"

"Whoa, news travels fast. No, I don't want to sell any stories, thank you."

"No, no, I'm not wanting to interview you or scoop your story."

"Then why are you calling at," he checked his phone, "half twelve at night?"

"I know what's happened to you today. I know about Quentin."

Hearing the name so unexpectedly forced David's lips apart.

"I've been investigating him for years and I know somewhat about his operations," Alex said. "I'm writing a report that I want to use to expose him for what he is, but to do that I need more information. Meet with me tomorrow and I'll tell you exactly who you're dealing with."

CHAPTER 15

The morning papers, which everyone at Down Dream hoped would be reporting the successful homeless shelter launch, instead focused on the extent of the damage to the charity's offices. Information had already seeped its way into the media's hands overnight, and the country was waking up to read all about it. Questions were rife and the sympathy poured in. Morning TV showed reporters outside of the offices, recounting police statements and archive photos of the offices before Down Dream's subsequent residence.

David ordered the group to withhold any comment to the media. Adding fuel to the fire could easily exacerbate the situation, he thought. As he drove through London with the phone on hands free, David shook his head.

"Honestly, I'm coming with you," Stu said through the line.

"You're not. And it's too late now, I'm already on my way," David said.

"Then tell me where you're meeting him and I'll meet you there."

"No, I need you to concentrate on the homeless shelter. It's open now and we have to start taking people in. People are going be relying on us. I need you to start working with the various agencies I forwarded to you this morning. We also need those posters out and around London, only half have been distributed so far."

"Bev can handle that."

"Bev is already too busy trying to manage the mess at the office to get the place up and running again."

"What about Kristian, what's he doing?"

"He's up in Edinburgh for today and tomorrow, attending that Equal Opportunities conference. Didn't you see the memo?"

"No," Stu said with an annoyed tone.

"Thank you for offering to come with me, but I know I'll be all right. I've looked this guy up and he's who he says he is. I'll call you when I'm on the way back."

"Okay."

"Don't worry about it, Stu. Honestly."

Stu blew out some air that translated into a loud muffled noise in the car.

"I'm gonna have to go as I'm not far away now."

"No worries, David. Call if you need me. I'll speak to you soon."

"All right, speak soon." With that, David clicked off his hands free and turned the car's radio back on – until he heard a news bulletin detailing the ransacking of Down Dream's offices, to which he turned it back off.

David arrived at the location, parking in a vacant bay opposite the building. He stepped out of the car, realising just how nice the weather was with the strong sun radiating down from the centre of a clear, blue sky. A gentle wind blew away the majority of the sun's heat, so the day could have been a little warmer, but David didn't mind. Dressed in his short-sleeve white shirt, tucked into a pair of old jeans, he crossed St James's square. For all of the years he had lived and worked around London, he had never visited The London Library. He approached the building, taking a moment to appreciate the traditional English architecture. The building's stone looked almost marble, and the iron railings outside the front door accentuated its overall character.

Upon stepping through the entrance, David scanned the unfamiliar area. The dark wooden walls glistened with polish after having recently been cleaned. The air was heavy with the smell of oak and paper. A young lady behind a short counter looked at him blankly.

"Hi, I'm meeting somebody here. Alex Haynes?" he said.

She frowned, opened her mouth to speak, but was then cut off by a soft, high-pitched voice coming from the corner of the room.

"Mr Dale?" a man said, coming from David's right-hand side.

David turned to look at the man before him. Stood in the doorway, he looked back at David with a wider smile than David was expecting. He was slightly shorter than David and possessed messy red hair that looked overdue a wash. His stubble was unkempt and out of control, like a wildfire in the driest of forests. Thin, wire glasses sat firmly on his nose, his dark eyes piercing through the glass.

"Yes," David responded. "Alex Haynes?"

"Indeed. Thanks for agreeing to meet me at such short notice." He turned to the young lady. "Thank you, Julie," he said, before gesturing for David to follow him. "Please, if you will."

David glanced in the direction of which Alex was now heading and slowly drifted along after him.

The pair entered a large open room, the walls lined with books upon shelves and more books upon more shelves. A metal walkway wrapped itself around the room, suspended above them; a second floor in which visitors could access the highest of shelves.

"Been here before, Mr Dale?" Alex asked, weaving in between desks, tables and chairs.

"Sadly not, it's a beautiful place. And, please, call me David."

"Ah, yes, okay, David. This library was founded in eighteen forty-one, you know, by Thomas Carlyle. A teacher, philosopher, and a writer, amongst many other things. He was respected in quite a few circles."

David nodded out of view.

"It's a real shame you haven't been before, it's a gem of a place," he said, looking over his shoulder with another wide smile.

The pair meandered through several corridors before appearing in a small, square room. A pattern of pale and dark grey tiles panned the floor. Three of the walls were lined with oak panelling, with large, rectangular paintings hung upon them. The fourth wall was overwhelmed by stacks of shelves, filled to the brim with red leather-bound books. In the centre of the room lay two small tables, each with two chairs on either side. A vintage-looking lamp with an orange glow sat in the middle of both tables.

"Please, do take a seat," Alex said.

David obliged, pulling out a chair and sitting down.

Alex joined him at the same table. "Now you're probably wondering why I've asked you to meet me here, at The London Library of all places."

"The thought's crossed my mind."

Alex removed his glasses and started to clean them with a cloth from his trouser pocket. "Well, it's a public place so you feel a little more comfortable, at the same time having a little bit of privacy so we can have a chat." He slid his glasses back on, pocketed the cloth, and let out a smile. "Don't worry, I'm no friend of Quentin."

David contrived a smile. "You said you have information?"

"And I have."

"Then who is he? Do you know why he seems to be targeting Down Dream?"

"Ah," he said, holding an open palm in the air for a second. "In exchange for all of my information on Quentin, I want to be involved in everything between him and yourself."

"What do you mean, between him and me?"

Alex cleared his throat. "Unfortunately, David, he isn't targeting Down Dream. He's targeting you."

David repeatedly blinked as if unsure what he had just heard.

"In exchange for the information I have on him, I need you to guarantee you'll let me be a part of everything that's going to happen. The report I'm writing is extensive and its main purpose is to crack his world apart, but I have vital information missing. If you can help me, I could finish this."

David swallowed as he stared at Alex. After a few moments, he said, "Tell me what you know."

"I've gotta ask that you keep all sensitive information that I tell you to yourself. I'm going to be describing a lot of the information I'm sitting on, and I can't afford to let this get out. Not yet."

"You have my word."

Alex leaned in, placing both of his elbows onto the table. "Okay. I first came across Quentin in two thousand and nine when I was given the task at my local paper to write an article about a huge brawl that occurred in the car park of a pub one night. I know, not how you'd expect the story to start," he said with a quick smirk. "During the brawl, one man was stabbed and unfortunately paramedics couldn't save him. The suspect, a guy named Lee who could be clearly seen on CCTV as the person who did the stabbing, was detained and arrested. The story seemed like any other knife crime incident involving men linked to gangs. That was until Lee's trial. He admitted to the stabbing and killing of his victim, but argued persistently that he was paid to carry out the attack and that his alleged employer was a Londoner named Quentin."

David joined Alex in leaning on the table.

"Lee's confession of the murder was enough to send him down and the police, as well as the judge and jury, ignored all mention of Quentin, the man who supposedly orchestrated it. Six weeks later, prison guards found Lee in the shower room. His wrists had been slashed that many times that his hands were hanging off."

David grimaced. "So Quentin's some gangster with contacts in prison?"

"Oh, no. This was sixteen years ago. Like I said, that was only the start of the story. After I found out about Lee's death, I gained an interest in this Quentin fellow. Did he exist? Was he so pissed off with Lee for disclosing his name to the police that he had him killed? And so my hobby for keeping track of this Quentin was sparked. Since then, I've come across his name from people's accounts of criminal activity, witnesses, and connections to crimes within the city on a few dozen occasions. He's reclusive and has grown rapidly in power since his days of pub brawls." Alex shifted uncomfortably in his chair. "I'm afraid to say, David, that I believe from two thousand and sixteen or seventeen, Quentin took over as the leader of a far-reaching underground criminal organisation."

David motionlessly sat, his eyes fixed on Alex, but only able to picture Quentin's assertive expression from the homeless shelter launch. David reached for his shoulder.

"I'm sitting on a story that's going to tear open Quentin's underground world of crime. Once this gets out, the media are going to have an absolute field day."

"You said that you think he's targeting me personally, rather than Down Dream. Why?"

Alex coughed. "Excuse me," he said, wiping his mouth. "Yes, David, I'm sorry to say it, but it's true. With people like Quentin, especially Quentin, it all boils down to one thing."

"Money," David said.

"Exactly that," Alex said with a firm nod. "It's no secret that you sold your psychiatry practice recently for millions. The American takeover was well reported on, as was your profile from what happened to you with your family."

David winced at the mention, his eyes downcast.

"I'm sorry, David, but Quentin's coming after the source, and you've funded Down Dream, you've got the ball rolling. If Down Dream continues to do well, he'll probably want a cut of that as well as whatever you've got."

"Tell me what Quentin does nowadays. What is this organisation? What do they do?"

"There's no official name for them, unfortunately I haven't had the pleasure to ask. They're based here in London, and from the information I've gathered, they always have been. They do operate internationally though, with several links to Europe, mostly eastern. Operationally, Quentin nowadays focuses his trade on money laundering and extortion, where it is that you come in. I know their previous bread and butter, if you will, was sex trafficking and people smuggling; taking advantage of migrants coming into Europe from the Middle East and Africa."

David shook his head. "Jesus Christ."

"I've only heard the faintest of rumours of a previous extortion he's made recently, which was with a foreign investment firm that setup a branch just outside of Canary Wharf."

"What happened?"

"If the rumours are true, the firm lost a helluva lot of money and staff members who couldn't hack it. The firm never went public with it for some reason. Probably PR."

"You've withheld this story all this time?"

"No, no. I've slowly built up my knowledge of what's going on over the years. It's only in the past eight months that I've dug up a lot about Quentin and his operations."

"Then what's stopping you? Why haven't you published it already?"

"There's one missing piece of the puzzle. A link that needs to be there, but just isn't. Without it, the credibility is questionable, even with the information I've already got."

"What kind of link are you missing?"

"A strong one, and it's here in the UK. Quentin's money laundering has died down over recent years due to the UK and other European governments and agencies picking up on his actions. Something's helping him, effectively boosting his cash flow."

"And I assume you have suspects?"

"So far, there's a huge list, but I'm working on it."

"Who are they?"

"I can't tell you their names just yet, but there's a politician and a senior figure in the police force in that list."

"My god, what the hell is going on?"

"Troubling, ain't it?" Alex said, leaning back in his chair.

"It's unbelievable. What kind of world do we actually live in?"

Alex shrugged. "A brutal, insane world. David, this information I've told you is sensitive. I can't have you repeat any of this outside to anyone. If word gets out, Quentin would come looking for me. I've been so careful up to now. Please."

David nodded. "You have my word." He scratched his head and looked down at the table for an answer. He shifted in his seat, his eyes darting across the room. They rested back on Alex. "After all these years, why haven't the police touched him? No offence to you, but you can't be the only one who's got this information on him and his group."

"You're right. I believe the NCA has been watching him for a long time now, but haven't acted. Your guess is as good as mine as to why."

"The NCA? The National…"

"The National Crime Agency, yeah."

David's eyes narrowed as he processed the unravelling details. "And what about the woman who's with him? He brought a lady to our shelter event where I met him."

"You must be talking about Rose."

"Yeah, Rose. She didn't come across as the wife of a ringleader."

"Rose has been on the scene since early two thousand and nineteen, or so I can tell. None of my sources or the information I've gathered can suggest how they met, apart from the fact that she's of Italian descent. The first I saw of her, they were married, so I dono."

"Why's her being Italian important?"

"Remember I said Quentin used to focus heavily in sex trafficking?"

David shook his head in disbelief.

"This all came from his contacts in Italy beforehand. I've spoken to people who've dealt with Quentin's direct associates, purchasing women for evenings, or for trips abroad."

"So because Rose is Italian, you automatically assume Quentin has kidnapped her? Forced her to be his wife?"

"I'm assuming, yeah. For so many years Quentin's been a single man with women coming and going. Then one day, bam, he's married to a woman I've not seen or heard of before."

David leaned back in his chair, letting out a long, drawn-out sigh.

"David, a word of warning. Quentin is a vastly powerful man with contacts everywhere. I couldn't even possibly begin to think who or where all of them could be, only those careless enough to have been identified over the years by my various sources."

David nodded slowly, the picture of Quentin still at the forefront of his mind.

"Do you want my advice?"

"Yes," he said.

For the first time in their conversation, Alex lowered his voice. "Do what you can to avoid all contact with him and his associates. If you have to, do what you can to keep them happy. Angering them can only lead to devastation. If you have to, play along with whatever he says. I'm still working on this missing link, and hopefully I might get it if he keeps in close contact with you now, but once I've got it, this story will be in every paper across the country. Don't you worry, David. We'll get him. We'll get him."

David's mobile phone began to ring, vibrating loudly from his pocket. He pulled it out and glanced at the caller ID. "I'm sorry, I'll be one second," he said before standing up, taking a few steps towards the exit of the room, and answering. "Hello?"

"Mr Dale," the woman said before clearing her throat. "It's Kate from Doctor Allen Henderson's office."

"Oh, hi. My appointment's not until later this afternoon, isn't it?"

Soft sobs sounded down the line.

David moved his eyes around the library. "Is everything okay?"

"No. It's Allen," she said, her voice breaking. "He's dead."

<h1 style="text-align:center">CHAPTER 16</h1>

Bev's efforts to refurbish the ruined office were slow and tedious. In the six hours that she had so far given to the task, having had to wait for the police to confirm their work was complete, she had almost finished the required fixes. Painters and decorators were sourced within the city to quickly re-paint the entire office space, ridding it of the devilish red paint. Broken ceiling lights were replaced and a local locksmith was drafted in to exchange the office locks. A mechanical keypad at the side of the front door was also installed, requiring a code to now unlock. Bev had also organised the speedy delivery of a whole set of new computers, desks, and ergonomic office chairs.

The office was slowly beginning to resemble its former self, as if nothing had happened. Bev's mind, however, couldn't be fixed quite as easily and kept returning to the thoughts of those responsible. Returning to the red word hidden behind the fresh, wet paint.

John Fairburn hadn't showered for five days. His beard was out of control, and his overgrown hair was reaching the point of becoming matted. He wore his usual clothes – the only ones he owned. His sand-coloured waterproof jacket had seen better days, but waterproof clothing was hard to come by. His khaki, baggy pants were getting worn and frayed. Tears, scratches and stains of dirt plagued the unwashed fabric. His shoes, thankfully the correct size to fit his feet, were the only objects he owned that were of a moderate condition; he had a skip from the East End of London to thank for that.

Sad to say, John had grown accustomed to his way of life and now accepted the fact he was a homeless, middle-aged man with no quality of life. Nothing to do. Nothing to look forward to.

Most days were overwhelming and, at times, too much to handle. The constant need to be aware of one's surroundings and the massive energy drain that was the never-ending fight to survive.

However today, something felt different. On his mid-morning stroll, a generous passer-by with a northern accent approached him, offering a bottle of water and a sandwich. Come early afternoon, he had a pleasant chat with one of the few people he would deem a friend. Fellow homeless acquaintance, Lacey, mentioned the opening of a brand-new homeless shelter, opened by a brand-new charity. She told him of Down Dream and the man who was behind it. Doctor David Dale, psychologist-turned-entrepreneur-turned-philanthropist.

"I'm good as I've got myself in at Hector's, but you should get hold of this Dale guy," Lacey had told him, "and he might be good enough to sort you out. Worth a shot, ain't it?" Before she left him, she gave him the poster she had torn down in Walworth.

John hadn't used one of the red phone boxes dotted around the city for years but felt today was the day. With the poster in his hands, he inserted three dirty 20p coins that he had been carrying around for two days into the machine and dialled the number carefully.

Three rings later, the other side picked up.

"Good afternoon, this is Down Dream, how can I help?" Bev asked.

"Er, hi. I saw this number on a poster and I'm, er, hoping to speak to David. David Dale?"

"I'm afraid he's not in the office at the moment, can I help?"

John didn't know how to answer, all of a sudden fixing his eyes on his shoes as they pattered up and down on the dirty floor. "Er," he started, "I'm looking for a place to stay."

"I see. Can I take ya name, chuck?"

"Yeah, it's John Fairburn."

"Okay, John, my name is Bev and I work with David. Where is it ya callin' from? I could give ya directions to our homeless shelter; David should be callin' in there sometime soon."

"Er." He pushed open the phone box door. "I'm right in front of Victoria Station." He looked around, said, "The building across the road is Stockley House."

"Ya're quite far away actually, ya at least a good few miles."

John sighed, turning his back on a group of young lads as they walked past the telephone box.

"Not to worry, chuck," Bev said. "Cross the road to Stockley House, I'll call a taxi for ya now."

"A taxi? But I don't have money for one."

"No need to worry about that, I'll call for one now and settle it over the phone."

John raised his eyebrows. "Wow, thank you. Thank you so much." It was at this moment that John Fairburn truly felt that for the first time in a long while, luck was on his side.

Later that afternoon, David arrived at the homeless shelter to oversee its first day of operation. Despite strong demand from people in need at the start of the day, interest seemed to wane by midday. The flashy opening event the night before, with a heavy presence of cameras and journalists may have contributed to some keeping their distance, or so a handful of volunteers and staff members theorised. A steady trickle of people in search for temporary respite arrived sporadically.

"An accident?" Bev asked from the other end of the line.

David drooped his head with a heavy sigh. "That's what they're ruling. Apparently, he slipped in the bathroom, hit his head in the bath, and drowned."

"How incredibly tragic. Ya knew him well, didn't ya."

"I've been seeing him for years. I was supposed to see him this afternoon. He even came to Down Dream's launch event."

"I'm so sorry, David."

David pushed back in his seat. "I've known him for well over a decade and he's been my therapist for the past three years." He forced his eyes shut and clenched his free fist. "I can't believe this has happened. I really can't."

"Look, the offices are almost back in shape. Come over once ya done at the shelter and we'll talk more. Ya know I'm here for ya."

David exhaled loudly. "Cheers, Bev. I'll see you soon." He clicked off the mobile and placed it onto the low table in front of him. Sat in the small tea and coffee room in his charity's homeless shelter, he could see a few guests were helping themselves to the provided refreshments. They noticed him looking, and so he attempted a smile.

The door to the room opened and Stu popped his head through the door, said, "Afternoon. Are you busy?"

"No, I'm not."

"Good, there's someone wanting to speak to you."

David nodded. "Sure, pass the phone," he said, holding out his hand.

Stu smirked and in response pushed the door open fully and let John Fairburn into the room.

David attempted a second smile, looking up to the man before him.

"John, this is David. David, this is John, he's just arrived to stay with us tonight," Stu said.

David rose from his seat and offered a hand whilst Stu left the room and closed the door behind him. "Hello. David Dale."

John accepted David's hand and shook it. "Hi, nice to meet you."

"Nice to meet you, too. Please, please sit down. Would you like a tea? Or a coffee?"

John shook his head as he claimed a seat. "No, thank you. I'm quite all right at the minute."

David sat back down, noting John's old jacket and dirty khaki pants. "How can I help?" he asked, regretting the obvious question instantly.

"Are there any free beds going? For tonight?"

"Of course there are. You're very welcome here."

John nodded several times then glanced over at the other guests.

"How are you? How are you keeping?" David asked.

John cleared his throat. "I'm not too bad. Had a nasty cough a few days ago, but it's faded now."

"Is there anything else I can get for you? If you need any meds for your cough..."

"No, I'm fine. Your hospitality is very kind."

A moment of silence filled the air. John spoke first. "Heard this place just opened. It's nice. Well, nicer than a few others I've stayed in."

"Thanks. We opened last night. We're a new charity and this is our first shelter. We're hoping to open a few more up and down the country in the coming year or two."

"That's fantastic."

David looked at the man's beard and neglected head of hair. "While you're here, if there is anything in particular that you require, just let me know. There are quite a few floors to this place; each floor has two bathrooms so help yourself to a bath, or a shower. Once I get you checked in I'll show you to your room and we hand out some basic toiletries, too. Toothbrush, toothpaste, shampoo, that kinda stuff."

John restrained a smile, quickly looking to the floor with flush cheeks. "Thank you."

"It's what we're here for."

John looked back at David. "You know, I used to be a client of yours."

David looked blankly at John. "A client? Oh, of my psychiatry practice?"

"Yeah, I think it was seven, maybe eight years ago now. I used to meet with Claire every Tuesday evening."

"Bloody hell, it's a small world."

"Back when I had the disposable income to see a therapist," John said with a slight laughter underlining his comment. "I used to speak to her about my drinking. She was a bloody good listener, and gave me some great advice, though I frequently ignored it."

"I remember Claire. She was a brilliant psychiatrist."

"She definitely identified a fair few syndromes I was facing. You know, I convinced myself I was on the path to a fully blown recovery? I think I even convinced Claire. She was so enthusiastic about my progress, both with my drink and with my relationships with my family." John shook his head.

David slowly leant forward, placing his elbows on his knees and melding his hands together. "Is that how you lost your home?"

John's eyes darted around the table before settling on David. "That's how I lost my job. Losing a job to alcoholism doesn't score highly with potential new employers. Not having a job and fighting the urge to drink myself to sleep every night cost me my marriage. The divorce sealed my fate and here I am. Years down the line with bankruptcy on my shoulders and someone's discarded shoes on my feet."

"I'm really sorry to hear that, John. Do you keep contact with your ex-wife at all?"

John swallowed, hesitating, his eyes wandering.

David held his gaze, searching John's face for answers.

John's eyes found their way back to David. "I have a seven-year-old son. My ex got full custody. I've not seen him for eight months."

"What, why?"

"She doesn't want him seeing me like this. Would rather tell him I'm working away." John frowned, as if bracing for a wave of pain. "It kills me more than anything. Sleeping rough I can take. Coming across dodgy characters who want to steal from me, hurt me, I can take. But not having contact with my boy..." John lost his voice as he wiped his face.

David nodded knowingly, swallowing hard. "I'm incredibly sorry to hear that, John. I lost my wife and two daughters. It was the single most painful experience of my life. I still carry that weight with me every day." He let out a subtle cough, clearing his throat. "But someone once told me that we may be products of our past, but we don't have to be prisoners of it. I applied that by picking myself up from depression and persistent suicidal thoughts and launched this charity. I turned heartbreak into hope."

John's focus was transfixed on David, hanging onto every word.

"You don't have to be trapped in your past. It doesn't define you. You can improve things. You can rebuild and reconnect with your son. You will do."

"You're right," John said. "I need to get myself straight, then get back into my son's life. I can do it."

Detective Constable Thomas McField released an exhausted sigh as he rested his feet on the bin underneath his desk. He stared at the Bonsai tree that sat next to his computer monitor; a gift from his girlfriend for his birthday four months ago. Why was it, he thought, that his colleagues received expensive watches and city breaks away to foreign capitals from their partners, whereas he received a glorified miniature tree? A hidden message, perhaps? Other than the thought that his better half was testing his nurturing skills for a future addition to the family, he couldn't think of anything. He shivered.

"Detective, I've got the results back," a female officer said, standing over his desk with a brown folder in her hand.

McField took his eyes off the Bonsai and looked up at her. "Shoot."

She opened the folder and leafed through the contents. "Well, S and F Insurance sure doesn't exist. Not in the UK anyway."

"Are you sure?"

"Positive. There's other variants of the name, but nothing close enough to warrant investigation."

"Mhm," Thomas mumbled. "And what about the forensics?"

"Forensics gathered at the offices are non-existent. No fingerprints, no foreign DNA traces of any kind. Not even a muddy footprint."

"Well shit a brick. And technically?"

"Our investigations into the phone used to ring Miss Walcott led to a brand-new pay-as-you-go SIM that was purchased earlier the same day. A burner. Lastly, and I'm sorry to be the bearer of such crappy news, but we all agree with you in that the CCTV cameras in and around the building caught nothing we believe we can work with. We saw three hooded, masked figures, all average height. They could be anyone."

McField kicked the desk. "Come on, Natalie. No leads whatsoever? Not even a glimpse of a face, or a slight trip up somewhere on the footage?"

Natalie shook her head. "Sorry." She dropped the folder down onto his desk. "What about the security guard from the building? What did he have to say when you spoke to him this morning?"

"He was still a little woozy, but he couldn't remember anything of value. He practically mimicked your conclusion: masked men, average height. He just said one minute he was looking at his computer monitor, the next minute he looks up and sees three men running at him. He must have been hit over the head with something at that point as he next remembers waking up in an office, looking up at David Dale."

"Talk about nothing to go on," Natalie said with an exaggerated shrug.

"Then I guess the only piece of tangible evidence we do hold is the name David and Stu gave us."

"Provided the man that David and Stu spoke of gave them his real name."

McField looked back to his Bonsai tree, counting the number of branches for the fourth time that day. "Quentin is quite the unique false name to give."

"Thank you so much for all your help," John said, accepting the freshly folded towels from David.

"Don't mention it," David replied. "The bathroom is down the corridor, second on your right. If you need anything else, just let me or anyone downstairs know. Food's from six thirty."

John nodded, looking around the large bedroom. Two beds lay against each opposing blue wall. A large bay window consumed the far-reaching wall, allowing the loud, orange sunset to be noticed. He looked back at David with a genuine smile. "Thank you, David."

"Like I said, don't mention it," he said before turning and walking towards the flight of stairs at the end of the corridor. His mobile buzzed in his pocket as he descended the stairs. He answered. "Hello?"

"Ah, Mr Dale. How are you?"

He recognised the voice immediately. "Eva, hi," he said, taken aback by her calling. He stood still in the middle of the staircase.

"I'll take it that you're well then."

"Yeah, sorry. I'm, er, I'm okay, thanks. How are you?"

"As well as one can be, you know."

"Good, I'm glad." He looked around, taking one step down.

"I have a very important question that I need to ask."

"Oh?"

"Yes," Eva said. "Very, very important indeed." She hesitated, leaving a moment's pause. "Are you ready for the question?"

"Fire away."

"What are your dinner plans this evening? I have a reservation for two at the Chiltern Firehouse and I just cannot go alone."

CHAPTER 17

Stepping into the office, Detective McField felt an electric rush of nervousness that spread from his inner core. It wasn't every day that he was called into his superintendent's office. In fact, McField had only been in the office on three separate occasions. The first, when the superintendent congratulated McField on his promotion to Detective Constable. The second, to be briefed on a highly sensitive case involving a member of the royal family. And the third, to be given a formal warning in regard to his addressing of the said royal family member by an accidental, expletive slip of the tongue.

Being called into Detective Superintendent Christopher Forrest's office was something of an event, although this time, for McField's fourth visit, its specialness was heightened by the fact he was summoned late into the evening when most others had gone home.

"McField, take a seat," Christopher said, momentarily glancing up from a document he was reading on his desk. The desk was bulky and expensive, with a thick, wide frame that shone a golden varnish. A small green lamp stood in one of the desk's corners, whilst a thin computer monitor took up the other.

Two uncomfortable-looking, red leather chairs with large copper-coloured buttons sat opposite the desk where McField took a seat. For a minute, the room was silent. Christopher bided his time meticulously reading every line of the document whilst McField sat awkwardly still, counting the picture frames that hung on the room's walls.

Christopher Forrest had been Detective Superintendent for nearly six years. In his late fifties, Christopher had an old-fashioned moustache, perfectly curled and pointy at its tips, which he meticulously checked every so often. His eyes dark blue, which stood out in the faint light like sapphires amongst the rubble. He spoke with a slanted mouth, one half carrying the words whilst the other took a permanent break and barely moved. "I wanted to speak with you, regarding your current case," he finally said.

McField nodded, unwilling to divert his eyes away from the superintendent's mouth. "Down Dream and David Dale?"

"Yes. I read in your preliminary report that the charity's office had been broken into and damaged, and that Mr Dale had received multiple threats of violence, one involving a face-to-face encounter with a man called Quentin."

"That's correct," McField said. "I've since done a little bit of digging into this Quentin and I've found all sorts of cases where his name has appeared in the past. Up and down the country, his name crops up and for whatever reason, he's never been brought in to be questioned or spoken to by a member of the force, or so I can tell."

Christopher sighed as he signed the document with a rushed stroke of the pen and placed it on the top of a pile of papers next to his monitor. "Yes," he said, setting his sapphire eyes firmly on McField. "Quentin is an unfortunate character that I tend to try and not dwell on."

McField tilted his head and raised an eyebrow. "I'm sorry, Sir, I don't know what you mean."

The superintendent ran his fingers across his moustache. "The matter of fact is, that as you are assigned to this case, you are on a strict need-to-know basis. And the truth is…"

Leaving his inner-city apartment, David locked the door behind him, took the elevator down to the ground floor, and climbed into the awaiting taxi. Wearing an open, white cotton shirt under a semi-formal brown jacket, he felt adequately dressed to dine in the 'celebrity hangout' of London restaurants, or so he gleaned from a quick Google of Chiltern Firehouse.

David stated his destination and the taxi driver headed off. The journey would only take twenty minutes or so, enough time to check some emails on his phone. Bev had emailed with an update of the offices, giving the go ahead to re-open tomorrow. Stu sent a memo to everyone with the details of the latest volunteers at the shelter, along with the details of a few new colleagues who have joined to handle admin, the website, and assist with event scheduling.

Only ten minutes into the journey and the taxi driver piped up, looking at David in the rear-view mirror. "You've got yourself a little friend," he said.

David looked at the driver as he gestured behind them. A black Mercedes Benz two cars behind and turning in every direction in which the taxi went. "Are you sure?"

"Been taxi drivin' for eighteen years, I know when someone's followin'."

"Well it's no friend of mine."

The taxi driver looked at David through the rear-view mirror again, this time with a twinkle in his eye. "Want me to lose him? I could do, easily."

David looked out of his side window. "No, not yet."

The taxi turned left and the car directly behind didn't. The Mercedes followed, now only yards apart. As they came to a stop at a red traffic light, David quickly snapped a photo of the registration plate on his phone using the front-facing camera as if he were taking a selfie. He wrote a text message and sent it along with the photo to Alex Haynes. If anyone could confirm whether or not the car was related to Quentin, it was the journalist.

The taxi soon pulled up outside of the Chiltern Firehouse restaurant. David sat for a moment and watched the Mercedes continue driving, passing him by without a fuss.

"Seems to be all clear," the driver said.

David leaned forward from the back of the car and paid the driver. "Thanks for that," he said before stepping out to a roar of noise and light. Photographers camped outside the building flashed their cameras, snapping the moment David was caught off guard. He instinctively shielded his eyes. The taxi drove off and he was left to face the crowd alone. He started walking towards the large double-door entrance when all of the attention suddenly left him. No more flashing lights blinding his eyes, and no more shouts of his name. David looked over his shoulder towards the limousine that came to a slow stop and was now attracting all of the attention.

The rear door automatically opened, as if on cue, and outstepped the dinkiest of feet in a pair of red stilettos. The legs followed. Long, long legs of smooth, flawless skin. The red dress, cut just below the knees, hugged the woman's body in its entirety. The woman looked up and out of the vehicle. Flowing blonde hair spilled out from behind her shoulders to also cover the side of her face. She saw David and beamed a Hollywood smile.

"Eva! Eva! A picture here!" shouted one photographer.

"Miss Shields! You look stunning! Who are you wearing?"

"Eva!"

Two security men appeared from the other side of the limousine and clambered to form a barrier between the photographers. She stepped up toward David. "Good evening, David."

He finally closed his mouth to form a sentence. "You look amazing."

She gave a little grin. "Thanks."

A doorman wearing a traditional top hat appeared from inside the restaurant and opened the two doors, though his eyes were firmly set on Eva. "Miss Shields, welcome back to the Chiltern Firehouse."

"Thank you," she said, stepping inside and immediately scanning the room as if it were under inspection. The hustle and bustle of intimate chats lined the restaurant. The open kitchen at the far end of the room shone with blazing amber flames over steaming pans.

A gentleman in a tailored white suit approached, his smile impossible to hide. "Eva, my dear. Welcome back," he said in a French accent before kissing her hand.

"André, so lovely to see you again."

"Please, please, let me show you to your table. We've reserved you the exclusive seating, of course."

"Of course," Eva said.

André looked at David and then raised an eyebrow. "And you must be David Dale, the hot news of the moment."

David couldn't think of anything to say.

"It's a pleasure to meet a noble charity leader," he said before looking back at Eva. "Come, come," he said, flicking around and walking into the restaurant. They left the initial entranceway, passed several tables, and stepped out into a small garden courtyard, boasting large exotic-looking plants and vines that ran up the stone walls. They continued, passing through a small room with high ceilings and hanging light fittings before climbing a few steps to a secluded, exclusive area. They sat down at the table for two that overlooked the rest of the restaurant. Eyes looked up at their presence as whispers made the rounds.

André cracked open the bottle of champagne with a pop, poured two glasses half full, then placed it in a standing ice bucket at the side of the table. He disappeared briefly and then re-emerged with two menus, handing them to Eva and David. He disappeared once more.

Eva leafed through the first few pages. "Been here before?"

"I haven't, no. I hadn't even heard of it until you invited me, which was very nice of you, by the way. Thank you."

Eva continued looking up and down the menu. "The food is mediocre and the champagne is sewage, but they do have some very attractive model-type waiters." She looked up, as if trying to spot one.

David couldn't stop his eyebrows from jumping.

"What are you looking at me like that for?"

"Why do you come here if you don't like the food?"

She rolled her eyes, said, "I didn't say I don't *like* the food. It's edible." She laughed. "I'm being cruel. I only really show up to the place every now and then to keep my status of being a regular guest. Image is everything."

"Oh," David said, turning his eyes back to the menu and trying to decipher the names of the dishes. His focus couldn't help but shift to the large numbers next to each option.

"How are you, David? You seem a little... off."

David lowered the menu, noticing Eva's eyes staring squarely at him. "Yeah, I'm, er." He quietly laughed. "Well, I'm not great, to be truthful."

"Oh?"

He pursed his lips together, his forehead wrinkled. "Earlier today I found out that a very good friend of mine passed away."

Eva's hand reached to cover her open mouth. "Oh my goodness. I am so sorry."

Shaking his head, David raised his menu once more. "It's fine, I, er. It's not something I really want to dwell on right now. It's incredibly raw."

Eva nodded. "No, I understand. You poor thing."

It wasn't long until one of the model-type waiters approached the table and took their order. The young man, dressed in a perfectly ironed white shirt and spotless black pants, nodded eagerly to each of their requests. He then collected their menus with a friendly smile and hurried off.

"So, Eva. Why is it you invited me to dinner tonight?"

"Must I have a reason to invite a friend to dinner?"

"A friend? Wow, we didn't even know each other a week or so ago, and now you've massively helped my charity and you're taking me out for dinner."

Eva giggled. "If it's meant to be, it's meant to be." She sipped her drink. "What are your thoughts on the sewage?"

"Oh, you mean this champagne that tastes ludicrously expensive?"

She nodded, her tongue poised at the edge of her mouth as if waiting to react to his answer.

"I think I'm going to ask for a pint when the waiter comes back."

She pushed back in her chair and laughed. "That bad?"

"I wouldn't use the word *bad*. I'm sure it's the taste for loads of people, but I'm just not a champagne drinker."

"Ah, I see. The bubbles don't float your boat, as it were."

David shook his head, scrunching his face in distaste.

"What does float your boat?"

"Are we still talking about drinks here?"

"We can talk about anything you like," Eva said, leaning her elbows on the table.

David laughed.

Eva waited patiently.

"How's the competition with the BBC going?" David finally asked.

"It's going. The BBC is on its last legs and is slowly eroding. Their fragrant political bias is dizzying. It's quite a shame for the country, to have such a gem of a national institute wither and die over a long period of time. Though we all know public corporations can't last long when set against huge private firms." She smirked. "Look at us, it's our tenth birthday in five days' time and Shields Corporation has never been more successful." She tapped her fingers against her arm. "Now, stop avoiding the question."

David smiled, looking down to his lap to hide his face. "I'm a simple man with simple tastes."

"I don't think you are a simple man."

"And what makes you say that?"

"I'm good at picking these things up from people."

"Well put it back down, it's not yours to pick up," David said.

After a few silent moments of eye contact, Eva burst into laughter.

The handsome waiter reappeared, carrying several plates. He placed the dishes down in front of the judges-to-be as they scrutinised the immaculate presentation of their food.

"Wow," David said, his eyes bouncing from each plate. "And could I also get a pint of Stella, please?"

The waiter nodded and then proceeded to the bar.

Eva delicately picked up her cutlery and started picking through the contents of her plate. "So, David, how is Down Dream operating so far since its inception? How has my contribution helped?"

"Enormously, actually. We still can't quite thank you enough for giving us such a pedestal. I think you've really kick-started everything for us."

"My absolute pleasure."

David bit into a small slice of chicken. "We were hoping to use that money, your contributions in particular, towards the cost of targeting areas in and around London on an awareness campaign. Getting our name out on the streets, you know?"

"*Were* hoping?"

"Yeah. Unfortunately, when our offices got broken into and practically demolished—"

Eva interrupted, her hand placed across her full mouth. "Oh, god. I'm so sorry, I forgot all about that."

"It's okay. We've just had to assign some of our funds to refurbishing the offices. It's cost us a fair bit, but it's nothing we can't handle."

"Oh, David, that's awful. I shouldn't have forgotten. How serious was the damage?"

A golden pint was ushered to the table, followed by David's thanks. "The usual you might expect from a pack of thugs. Nothing absolutely disastrous."

Eva nodded. "Good. That's good to hear." She sipped her champagne. "Have the police found those responsible?"

"No, not yet. I'm expecting to have an update from the detective who's looking into it. Hopefully he'll have some leads."

"Do you have any enemies who'd want to do something like that?"

David shook his head, swallowing a mouthful of food. "I'm not the typical bloke who has enemies. Since launching Down Dream though…" He looked blankly at his plate. "Nah, it doesn't matter."

"What is it?"

"It sounds a bit crazy, but, since I launched Down Dream, things have started happening. I mean, meeting you for one is just crazy. But," David gulped, "I think the charity's being targeted. Maybe even I am."

"Who would target a charity?"

David outlined the events of the past few days, describing the moment he met Quentin.

Eva maintained solid eye contact throughout the explanation. Finally, as David finished, she sat back in her chair digesting the food in her stomach and the descriptions in her head. With the taste of champagne renewed on her lips, she gently leant forward and whispered, "Whatever's going on, David, I'm here for you. Remember that."

CHAPTER 18

"Well, they've signed on the dotted line!" Stu said with a childlike grin.

David and Bev almost leapt from their seats in the newly refurbished office of Down Dream. Clutching on to each other, the pair bounced in their chairs.

Stu put down his mobile phone. "They've gone and bloody done it! They've agreed to a twelve-month sponsorship and they're sending through the final details now."

"My god, that's amazing," David said, unable to contain his smile. "Well done, everybody!"

"A twelve-month contract with one of the biggest drink makers in the country. This could easily turn into a lifelong sponsorship, David," Bev said. She placed her hands on his cheeks. "Maria would be so proud of ya, y'know that?" she said before hugging him tightly.

"Think of the exposure on this. Down Dream printed onto millions of juice and pop bottles up and down the country. This could really put us onto the fast lane."

A loud noise rang from the office's entrance, making the group look over. Kristian rushed through the door, dumping his several large bags of luggage onto the floor.

"Kristian, welcome back," Bev said.

Stu wandered over to him. "You look shattered, pal."

"I am," Kristian said in a dull drone. "The train last night was cancelled so I slept in the station overnight and got the six o'clock train this morning."

"Bloody hell, you should have gotten a hotel instead of sleeping rough," David said.

"It's all right. I was busy working anyway. I've been tapping away on my laptop all night," Kristian paused with a smirk, and then said, "I've managed to bag us a speaking spot at the Equal Opportunities event next month."

"A speakin' spot?" Bev asked, bringing a hand to her chest, her eyes wide in shock.

Kristian nodded with a satisfied smile, his eyes closed.

Bev and David cheered in unison. "That's better than we were hoping for," David said. "That's quite the platform."

"Wow," Stu said. "We'll have to get working on some material for that right away. I'll start thinking about it later."

"What an amazin' day for progress," Bev said. "We should stock cheeky bottles of somethin' fizzy here for milestones like these. Even a Buck's Fizz would be just nifty."

"Oh, has something else happened?" Kristian asked.

Stu nodded. "APM Drinks has agreed to sponsor us for at least a year."

"APM Drinks? The company that makes those strawberry and banana smoothies?"

Bev exaggerated the nodding of her head.

"I love those," Kristian said.

"They are good. We've done well to land them," Stu said.

"Indeed," David said, pushing the chair he was once sat on under the table. "Thank you everyone for your efforts so far. I'm so, so excited for our future."

"Anyway, I best head off," Kristian said. "I've not been home yet and I'm dying for a shower. I'll catch up with you all later." He picked up his luggage and left the office with a wave.

"Right, we best crack on then," David said.

"Hopefully APM will send over those documents sharpish," Stu said, leaning down to his computer to check his email.

Sitting down at his desk in his office, David took a moment to himself. He looked up at the wall that once had the word KILLER written across it in red paint. He pushed away the troubling thoughts of Quentin and attempted to replace them with the positivity of what Down Dream was achieving. He shook his head and brought his computer to life with the rattling of the mouse. Opening Google Chrome, the MSN home page that initially confronted David caught his attention. A news headline featured a name he was becoming so familiar with. Then he noticed something else in the title that made his body stiffen. He clicked on it.

EVA SHIELDS AND DOWN DREAM'S DAVID DALE SHARE ROMANTIC DATE DAYS BEFORE VALENTINES

Published: 10:36 GMT, 11 February 2026

It seems heartthrob philanthropist David Dale is repaying the gorgeous Eva Shields for her fundraising contributions to his newly opened charity, Down Dream. The pair were pictured together last night as they visited the exclusive Chiltern Firehouse restaurant in downtown London practically hand-in-hand.

A source from inside the restaurant witnessed the two dine together. "They seemed very close, especially since they've not long known each other. They're both incredibly good-looking and would make an exceptional couple."

David's phone vibrated on his desk, his ringtone filling the office. He looked at the caller ID and picked up. "Hello, Sam. How are you?"

"Eva Shields?" she asked down the phone, her loud voice lined with excitement.

"Huh?"

"It's all everyone's talking about at work. People can't believe that you're my brother and you're dating Eva Shields. I mean, Eva bloody Shields!"

"Look, I'm not even dating her. She invited me out for one meal and that's all it was."

"That's not what the magazines and news sites are saying."

"Come on, Sam, you have more brain cells than that. Your brother's telling you I'm not dating the woman. Who are you gonna believe?"

A moment of silence.

"So you're not dating the multimillionaire?"

"No."

"The one with the media empire? And the lovely Chanel and Gucci handbags?"

David rolled his eyes with a heavy sigh. "No, I'm not."

"Goddamn."

"Jeez, Sam, I didn't know you'd be this disappointed about me still being single."

"Well you're gonna end up with somebody eventually. Just it would be really awesome if she had a big mansion and expensive clothes that I could borrow."

"Sorry to let you down then."

"Nah, it's all right. But hey, how amazing is Down Dream doin'? There's articles about it everywhere. You know, Stacey and Fearne at work fancy you. When I told them you were my older brother, they couldn't believe it. I had to bloody show them photos to prove it."

David laughed as he shifted in his chair. "Oh god."

"They're now asking to meet you, but I told them you don't venture up north much, especially now you've got your charity."

"I was there just the other day."

"Yeah, but you know what I mean. It's not exactly a whole lot that me and Ben get to see you."

David picked up a pen and started fidgeting with it. "How is Ben? Still doing well with school?"

"Yeah, he's fine. Still learning his geography, bless him. He enjoyed seeing you the other day. We all did, Shadow and Richard included."

"Things still going okay with Richard?"

"Yeah, we're doin' good. Barely seen him this week, actually. He's been working a lot of nights, so don't actually spend a great deal of time with him, but it's okay."

"Well fingers crossed his night shifts die down a bit and he can spend a bit more time with you and Ben."

"And Shadow."

"And Shadow, of course," David said, clicking his pen with a smirk. "Listen, it was awesome chatting, but I best get back to some work."

"Yeah, no worries. It was lovely to chat. We should do it more often, especially now you're making friends with A-listers."

"Oh shush. Thanks for calling, I'll speak to you soon."

"Speak to you soon. Bye."

David hung up and took a moment to smile as he stared at the phone's screen, watching it fade to black.

Kristian eventually made his way inside his flat after having to apologise to the taxi driver that he was 40p short of his fare and had locked his debit card by incorrectly entering his PIN three times earlier at the train station. He threw down his luggage bags onto the floor of his hallway and dumped his coat on the sofa as he headed straight for the bathroom. He switched the shower on, letting the strong gush of water warm up as he removed his phone from his trouser pocket and placed it onto the side of the sink. He undressed, tossing his clothes straight into the wash basket in the corner of the room. The shower steamed the glass and he dived in carefully.

His phone rang.

Thinking it could be related to work, he dipped back out, leaned over, and read the caller ID.

His mother.

"You can wait a couple of minutes," he said to himself, charging back into the shower.

The phone stopped ringing, but then started up again almost instantly.

Kristian groaned loudly in frustration. Debating for a moment, he reluctantly turned the shower off, stepped out, and hastily answered the phone without checking the caller ID. "Ja, Mor, hej," he said, his Swedish accent thick.

"An angry Swede, what a liberty," the male voice on the other end of the line said.

"Who is this?"

"My name is Quentin and I'm a good friend of Davi—"

Kristian hung up and put the phone back onto the side of the sink.

It immediately started calling again. Number withheld.

Kristian stood still, watching the ringing phone. A floorboard in the corridor just outside of the bathroom creaked, pulling his attention to the door that stood ajar. He felt his chest tighten, his breathing short and deep.

The door started to move, gently opening until it couldn't open any further, nudging against the opposing wall. As he stood naked, almost shivering from the combination of cold and fear, Kristian looked into the eyes of the tall man in the doorway. Instinctively, he took a step back.

The bald man was dressed in a suit with black leather gloves on both hands. A scar split his right eyebrow in two. He motioned to the ringing phone with a single flick of his eyes.

Kristian timidly edged forward, picking up the phone along with a scrunched-up towel from underneath the sink. He brought the phone up to his ear with one hand, holding the towel against his chest with the other. He answered.

"Hang up the fucking phone once more, Kristian, and I'll have Harold show you some fucking respect!"

Kristian kept his eyes on the man in front of him. His legs felt unsteady and weak as they trembled.

Quentin took a deep breath and blew down the phone. "Now, let's start again, shall we? Hello, Kristian. My name is Quentin."

Kristian's lower lip shivered, unable to respond.

"No need to be scared, my little Swede friend. I don't mean to be the big, bad wolf. People just turn me into it when they don't listen. Do you understand?"

Kristian finally spoke with a crack in his voice. "Yes."

"Excellent. I love being on the same page. Now, I have a little favour to ask of you. Nothing major, just a nice little task for you to complete for me, okay?"

Kristian remained silent.

"I'll assume that's okay then. So, I would like you to have a little word with our mutual friend, David. The man is turning me into this big, bad wolf, you see? I'd like you to pass him a message, from me to him."

"Why me?" Kristian managed.

"Because, my little turnip – I mean Swede – I think you'll have a little more impact after our conversation than I would if I were to deliver the message myself."

Kristian pressed the towel firmly against his chest.

"The message is simply that David needs to start cooperating with his good friend Quentin, because Quentin doesn't like being the big, bad wolf. Not anymore, oh no. I'm getting tired, very tired, and everything would be so much easier if he just listened to me. Tell him that because of the messing around so far, I want twenty-five thousand pounds a month. Could you tell him that for me, Kristian?"

Yes," he whispered.

"Excellent stuff. It's people like you that help get things done. Thank you for this, Kristian. Oh, and one more thing to mention to him, if you could. I know about his flat in London and his old family home in East Horsley, so there's no hiding, especially from the big, bad wolf." Quentin let out a little chuckle. "Now I won't keep you any longer, I know you've just got back from a busy business trip and you want to unwind. I look forward to hearing of David receiving my message. I'll be in touch with you again if I find out he hasn't. Thanks, Kristian. You've been grand. Now if you could just say *Quentin's the boss* for me, Harold will get out of your hair."

"Quentin's the boss," Kristian said.

The line went dead and the man left the bathroom doorway and walked down the apartment's corridor.

Kristian heard his front door open and close. He rushed to the bathroom sink, gripping on to its sides for support. As he caught a glimpse of himself in the mirror, he now realised his whole body was uncontrollably shaking.

CHAPTER 19

Driving in inner-city London at 5 p.m. is unwise. David, however, didn't think of this before he jumped into a taxi at Down Dream's offices and asked the driver to take him back to his city apartment. The entire way there they hit every traffic light going, as well as participated in a minor-to-London but major-to-everywhere-outside-of-London traffic jam. David thought of the very same thing he always thought in these instances: maybe the tube isn't such a bad idea.

Alanis Morissette's *Ironic* started on the radio.

The elderly man of a taxi driver with a bald crown on the back of his head shuffled in his seat. "What a tune."

"It's a good song," David agreed, his eyes cast outwards to the sea of red brake lights. To his surprise, the taxi driver began to sing.

"*An old man turned ninety-eight, he won the lottery and died the next day.*" The driver looked at David in the rear-view mirror. "Do you know this next line about the death row pardon two minutes too late?"

David looked at him, gave a slight, uninterested nod.

He laughed hysterically, said, "I used to think she sang 'a death row *hard-on* two minutes too late'. Now that would have been tragic!"

Not soon enough, the taxi pulled up outside of David's apartment building. After paying the driver and telling him to keep the change, David slammed the building's entrance door shut behind him and proceeded inside.

Similar to Down Dream's offices, when going up to his floor in the apartment building, David always preferred the elevator. A *ding* sounded and the doors rolled open on the twelfth floor. Stepping out and turning the corner in the corridor that led up to his front door, he stopped with a sudden pound in his heart. The automatic lights on the floor had not yet detected his movement and remained off, but he could make out a figure that was resting against the windowsill in the dark corridor, right next to his door. Outside light shone on the figure, creating a shadow against the wall.

Someone was waiting for him.

David could make out a somewhat slender figure, possibly wearing a long overcoat. A large hat, or at least what looked like one, rested on their head.

As neither him nor the figure had yet moved, he gulped in anticipation. Then, he saw it shift. The person seemed to look over their shoulder, directly at him. The automatic lights then flickered on and off, off and on. The person pushed themselves off of the windowsill and stood upright, holding onto a bag.

Despite the adrenaline pumping through him, David didn't feel the need to run. The natural fight or flight response hadn't kicked in.

The lights clicked on, showing the figure for what it was. An expensive-looking, long, light grey overcoat covered the slim, short body of a woman. She wore black leather boots with a large, beige hat that hid her face from the angle it was tilted at. A handbag hung from their petite left hand.

David stepped closer.

The woman looked up at David, her hat lifting up above her face. She was wearing broad, tinted sunglasses that she quickly removed, along with her hat, to reveal her face. "I am sorry for intruding," she said in a soft, British-Italian accent. "I didn't mean to startle you."

David studied her.

I know that face.

Somewhat familiar brown eyes and amber-brown wavy hair that was tied back behind her head; a few strands left to dangle at the side of her face. Her skin was pale, only given the gentlest touches of makeup.

"Rose," David said.

She looked at him with a childlike vulnerability, her eyes downcast and her lips squeezed together.

"I don't think you should be here," he said, glancing behind him.

"Nobody knows I'm here. Please, David." She fumbled with the sunglasses in her hands. "I need to speak with you."

"Why?" He dug into his pockets to find his keys.

"Because I…" she stepped closer as she gulped, "want to help you. I'm not at all part of what Quentin does. It isn't me."

"And why should I believe that? I don't even know you."

"Because I hope, from the bottom of my heart I hope, that if I can help you, you can help me."

"Help you with what?" David asked before tentatively walking past her and unlocking the door. The subtle scent of her perfume hit him.

"Help me regain the life I once had. I didn't choose any of this and I'm trapped." Her eyes welled up, glistening from the lights directly above her.

David looked again around the corridor before setting back on her.

"Please."

He sighed. "Quentin doesn't know you're here?"

"No," Rose said with an emphatic shake of her head.

David hesitated. "Come in."

"Thank you," she whispered, following him into the apartment as David closed the door behind her.

Rose wandered inside, passing the bathroom, the spare bedroom and the kitchen, before stepping into the living room.

Wondering what sort of state he had left the place in, David followed her into the living room and scanned the room. Some documents lay scattered on the coffee table with several empty glasses. Two books sat across one of the sofas.

Rose looked around the room and then smiled at David. "You have a lovely home."

"It's, er," he said, tidying up the documents and forming a pile which he shoved under the coffee table. "It's sorta home. For now, I guess."

Rose nodded slowly as she placed her bag and hat down on the sofa. She took off her overcoat and placed it next to her bag before stepping towards one of the windows, looking out.

David picked up several of the empty glasses and took them to the kitchen, dumping them in the sink. He went back into the living room. "Can I get you a drink of anything? Water, tea, coffee?"

"A water would be nice, thank you."

"Sure," he said, disappearing once more. He grabbed two clean glasses from the cupboard and poured a chilled bottle of water into each of them. He returned to the living room and offered her a glass. As she reached out to accept it, he noticed the large diamond ring on her wedding finger. He moved around the table and sat on the opposite sofa across from her.

"I must apologise again for showing up like this," Rose began. "I understand it must have been very unsettling for you, given the circumstances."

"How did you know I live here?"

Rose avoided David's eyes. "I, er…" She cleared her throat. "I saw your address. In Quentin's notes."

"In what?"

"Quentin always keeps notes on people he's… speaking to. I happened to have five minutes alone in his office, and your name was there, along with this address and an address in," she looked up in thought, "East Horsley, is it?"

David didn't blink. "My god."

"I don't know how he knows the addresses, but I wanted to come and speak to you first. I wanted to see if we could help each other."

"You're sure Quentin doesn't know you're here?"

"I told him I was going shopping. That can usually last me the whole afternoon, so…" She quietened, looking down to the sleeve of her blouse. "I've been fortunate, actually. He usually orders someone go with me, everywhere. For *safety*, he says." She faked a laugh. "Thankfully Martin, the man who usually ushers me around, has recently contracted the shingles, and I've somehow managed to convince Quentin that until Martin is well enough to come back, I'll be fine on my own." She tried a smirk that turned into a semi-smile which faded quickly. "It's not often he listens to me, or then again, perhaps he just doesn't trust anyone else but Martin to accompany me."

David nodded, slowly.

"I've let him control me for all of these years. Let him turn me into his possession. My sad life has slipped through my fingers and

I have no means to stop it." She paused, letting out a loud exhale. She turned to her bag and started rummaging around.

David watched her.

She pulled out a pack of cigarettes and a lighter. "Do you mind?"

David looked at the living room's walls; contemplating the damage that smoking indoors does to an apartment. "Er, sure," he said, walking over to the window, clicking it open.

The sound of the hectic city below boomed into the apartment before settling in as background noise.

David looked around the room before taking a small plate from underneath a plant pot from the top of a cabinet and putting it on the coffee table in front of Rose. He sat back down opposite her as she lit the cigarette and took a deep drag. "I wouldn't have taken you as a smoker," he said.

"Three toxic years."

"I used to smoke myself," David said. "Haven't for a few years now, though. Not to sound cliché, but I decided to put my health first. You know how it is."

Rose nodded a few times, flicking the cigarette onto the plate in front of her. "Sure, smoking is bad, but I enjoy it. It's one of the few comforts I have. It gives me things."

"Thought about quitting?"

Rose smirked, looking back at him. "If you kill all of my demons, my angels might die too."

The outside noise seemed to get louder through the open window as the pair fell silent.

Rose shook her head and squashed the cigarette onto the plate, putting it out. "I'm sorry, I said I could help you."

"Yeah, um, can I ask a question?"

She nodded.

"Quentin, is he bluffing? Or does he really mean what he says with his threats?"

Rose closed her mouth and crinkled one of her eyes. "I've known Quentin for four years, been living with him here in London for three. He's an evil man, and whatever he has said to you he means. I'm sorry, David, but unfortunately nothing he says is a bluff."

He nodded in the knowledge that Alex Haynes was right, tapping his feet against the floor as the dread filled him. "He's trying to get money out of Down Dream. What am I supposed to do, just hand it over?"

"I've heard of him extorting other businesses and, as far as I'm aware, this is his first time he's targeted a charity. I don't know anything of what happens, but I sometimes overhear things. He doesn't involve me in anything, you see. But Quentin will want monthly payments to keep him satisfied."

David shook his head. "I don't know what to do. I don't know what I can do. I don't know who I can trust, or who I can even talk to. Is he gonna chase me? Come after my colleagues? I mean, can you talk to him for me? Persuade him to leave us alone?"

Rose glanced at her bag and then stood up. "I shouldn't have come here. I'm sorry, I have to go. I don't want him wondering where I am," she said as she threw on her overcoat. "I can't help you, and you can't help me."

"Wait, but what should I do? Won't the police be able to stop him?"

Rose secured the overcoat around her body and picked up her bag and hat. "The police might say they can do something, but they can't."

David also stood up. "What do you mean, *they can't?*"

"Quentin has contacts all over the place. He either pays them off or instils such fear in them that they bend to fit his mould. It's like he collects his own little team of corrupt people he can fall back on if he needs to." She gripped onto her hat tightly, her eyes cast to the floor. "I have to go. I can't believe I've been so stupid, he probably has someone watching your building."

David led her to the front door, opened it, and turned to face her. "Rose, you need help, I need help. If we can't help each other, maybe we could just be there for each other? It's all I'm asking."

Rose stepped out of the apartment and slowly moved her eyes off the floor and back to David. "I came to you thinking you could help me, and maybe I could help you." Her eyes flickered, her mouth almost pointed downward. "But I don't know."

"Whatever it is you need help with, if it's just talking to someone who'll listen, I can do that. Don't think you're all on your own."

Rose turned to look out of the corridor's window. "If anyone can help me, I think you might be the person."

David eyes were fixed on her, looking at her mouth, ears and eyelashes as her face was still turned to the side. "What makes you say that?"

"You used to be a psychiatrist," she said, turning back to face him. "Now you run a charity. I don't think I could find anyone more qualified to help me. I've met many people in my life, but none so seemingly genuine and kind-hearted as you. It's why I'm here."

David paused. "Can you meet me the day after tomorrow? Perhaps, somewhere public, somewhere busy?" His eyes wandered the walls. "Maybe…"

"The National Gallery, say, eleven o'clock?"

David nodded. "I'll be there."

Rose gave a muted smile. She popped her hat on her head and her sunglasses back on her nose. She walked down the corridor and entered the open elevator, as if it had been waiting for her.

David listened to the elevator doors close before he shut his own door. He leant against the wall and questioned why all of a sudden he felt a great sense of loss.

155

＜CHAPTER 20＞

"Kristian's running late. Should I give him a call? See where he is?" Stu asked as he sat at the circular table in the Down Dream offices, joined by Bev and David.

"Go ahead, there's no harm seein' how long he thinks he'll be," Bev said.

Stu picked up his mobile, flicked through his contacts, and dialled Kristian's number.

Bev leant over to David and sniffed. "Somethin' smells good," she said. She straightened her back and narrowed her eyes. "Who've ya been seein', eh?"

"What?" David asked with a laugh. "I've not been seeing anyone."

"I'm watching ya," Bev said before giving him a wink.

Stu pulled the phone away from his ear, looked at the two of them and shook his head. "He's not picking up."

David frowned. "He's not?"

The front door to the offices clicked open and Kristian stepped through.

"Ah, here he is. Took your time," Stu said, putting his phone down.

Kristian made his way to the table, took off his jacket, and sat down in a vacant seat between Bev and Stu. "Hi," he said, his eyes bouncing from one object to the next, his hands clinging on to each other.

"Right, now everybody's here," David started, "we need to go over this upcoming event for the Equal Opportunities. We need to agree on our angle and what we want to convey at the conference."

"This is gonna be a very important message that we need to get right," Bev said.

David nodded. He looked at Kristian whose focus seemed to be elsewhere, his attention distracted away from the conversation. "What do you reckon, Kristian?"

Kristian looked up at David. "I reckon this Quentin guy is pretty fucked up."

David grimaced at the name.

Stu leant forward. "What are you talking about?"

"We're in over our heads. He's gonna cause shit with us if we don't do as he says."

"Calm down, calm down," Bev said in a hushed voice, placing a hand on his shoulder. "What's happened?"

Kristian blinked repeatedly, his eyes finally settling on David. "Quentin called me. Yesterday." He looked around the table as he gulped, as if searching for his next sentence. "And there was a goddamn man in my apartment."

"There was what?" Stu asked with a raised voice of urgency.

"There was a man stood in my apartment, making sure I took the call from Quentin."

"Oh, Christ," Bev said, firmly holding Kristian.

David glared at Kristian. "What did he say to you?"

"The man didn't say anything, and Quentin wasn't on the phone long," Kristian said, his voice splintered. "He wanted me to give you a message."

David waited.

"He said you need to start listening to him and do what he tells you." He forced his legs to stop shaking up and down. "He said he's getting tired and everything would be easier if you just listened."

"Is that all he said? That he wants me to listen to him? To pay him the money he's after?"

"He wants twenty-five grand a month."

"He wants *what?*" David shouted.

Kristian flinched.

"I'm sorry," David said, reaching out his hand. "He honestly wants twenty-five thousand pounds a month?"

Kristian nodded.

Stu held a hand up in the air. "Wait, wait, wait. What for?"

Bev shook her head. "To keep us goin', probably. I can only assume he'll continue to threaten and disrupt us until we start payin'."

"He also told me to tell you that he knows about your apartment down the street, and your family home in East Horsley. He said you can't hide."

"I guess this guy showing up at Kristian's place proves that," Stu said. "But why would he get you to pass on a message for him? Wouldn't he just show up somewhere like he did at the shelter launch?"

"We should be thankful Quentin hasn't sent another message like he did with the offices and the security guard," Bev said. "Be thankful it was just a phone call and a random man, nothin' else."

An unmistakeable frown cast across Stu.

"Besides," Bev continued, "he'll know that if the message comes through one of us, it carries much more weight. I mean look at poor Kristian, he's shakin'."

"What's he going to do if we don't pay him something?" Kristian looked around the table. "What happens then? They're not going to stop. They'll take everything."

With Kristian's words looming in the air, all four of the group sat back in their seat with no answer to share.

Detective McField wasn't sure what was the right thing to do. As he drove in a steady flow of traffic on a quiet country lane, he felt it was his mind that was changing lanes, changing so quickly that it hindered his chances at ever keeping up. Based on the information he had gathered so far, as well as the information he was advised on a classified need-to-know basis, he was utterly torn.

His phone rang. He clicked the hands free, said, "Detective McField."

"Hi, Detective, it's David Dale. You recently spoke with me about my charity's offices being broken into?"

"Yeah, yeah. How are you? Is everything okay?"

"I'm fine, but one of my colleagues isn't. He had one of Quentin's men break into his apartment yesterday to threaten him. Kristian's really shook up."

"Woah, okay. Is he hurt at all?"

"No, thankfully he isn't."

McField rested an elbow on the car window, wiping his palm across his chin. "Right, okay. I'll have someone stop by and speak to him, try and get a description of the person and take a statement."

"Please do. As I'm sure you can appreciate, this is really getting to us all and we could do with some assurances. Have you found anything in your investigation?"

"I'm on a few leads, but I'm going to have to go now as I'm just arriving at one."

"All right. Please, keep us updated. We're getting pretty desperate."

"I will do. Thanks for the call, David." He clicked off the hands free and sighed, parking up outside of a rundown house buried deep in the countryside on the outskirts of the city. He stepped out, peering at the dilapidated structure.

Tiles hung off the roof, with the windows long deprived of warm, soapy water and a sponge.

He counted the steps from his car to the front door, before knocking as he reached it, half expecting no one to answer. Almost half a minute passed before it opened abruptly, revealing the tall, grey gentleman in a dressing gown. The man's unhealthy-looking pale skin was the first thing McField noticed.

"McField," the man said. "It's been a long time."

"Kevin Peters," McField said, smiling with an extended hand. "How are you?"

Kevin slowly outstretched a hand and squeezed the detective's. "Come in and I'll tell you how I am. It's too cold to be chatting in the doorway."

Not thinking it was too cold, McField stepped into the house. "I can't believe I've known you this long and I've never been to your home before," McField said, wiping his shoes on the doormat.

"I know," Kevin said, now with a roughness to his voice. He coughed. "It's sad how time passes by so quickly, isn't it?" He led McField through another doorway into a much warmer room. An open log fire burnt against the far wall. An armchair sat close by it, aimed towards the TV in the corner of the room. A smaller chair was positioned opposite the fire and closer to the TV. Kevin chose the armchair.

McField sat in the smaller chair. "Open fires are very comforting. You must have toasty winters in here."

Kevin laughed a singular, short laugh with minimal effort.

McField looked around the room. The walls were a bleak brown colour, decorated with a handful of, what looked like, family photographs and portraits. Opposite him, and next to the fire, stood a cabinet of drawers with a framed photograph of a much younger Kevin and an attractive brunette woman in a floral dress. Beside the photograph were prescribed bottles of pills, with small, folded pieces of paper, presumably his medication schedule. Glancing to his right-hand side, and behind Kevin, McField noticed a small black cat sat on a large cushion gawking at his presence.

"To answer your question, I am having a good day," Kevin said, holding back another cough.

McField nodded. "That's good to hear."

"But I suppose you didn't exactly come here to see how I am, or to give my cat the eye."

McField smirked.

"It's all right," he said. "I can help you though. I wouldn't have asked you here otherwise." He wiped his mouth.

McField looked to the fire and back to Kevin, now feeling slightly too warm.

"God," Kevin continued, "how I wish I was still at work. I wouldn't be letting that Christopher Forrest dictate the rules of the game." He tried a smile. "My goddamn kidneys have a lot to answer for."

McField pursed his lips together.

"Now, McField. Tell me what he told you. What exactly are you dealing with here?"

McField took a deep breath and began to outline exactly what he was dealing with. He spoke of David Dale, Down Dream, and the events that occurred at its offices. The pair discussed everything McField had been told about Quentin by the Detective Superintendent.

Kevin remained motionless throughout the explanation. Finally, once McField had finished, he prolonged his silence for a further minute.

"You can see why I've come to speak to you," McField said.

"Mhm," Kevin mumbled. "Everything Forrest has told you is correct."

McField faintly gasped, his mouth left hanging open. "It is?"

Kevin nodded. "And yes, I see how that puts you in a difficult position."

"What would you suggest I do? What *can* I do?"

"Well," Kevin began as he allowed his cat to jump up onto his lap, "you already know you have only two options."

McField waited for Kevin to continue.

"You can either act on this knowledge and almost certainty risk your career as you do so, or you can do as instructed and allow the higher-ups to command the battlefield and let it play its course."

"But not doing anything could put people at risk. How can they even contemplate this? People could get hurt."

Kevin looked at McField with glazed eyes. "You've been told what you must do. This is obviously a risk that they deem necessary."

When Quentin looks at someone, it isn't their face that he initially sees. Instead, its the physical size of their head and the shape of their skull. When Quentin looks at someone, he wonders how long their skull would hold up from a barrage of trauma.

That is what Quentin pondered as he looked at the grovelling man sat in front of him. From his comfortable red velvet sofa, he looked the man up and down. The man's trousers were soaked in urine, his shirt ripped open to display his sweaty torso. The man's hands were bound behind the chair he sat in, his long hair hanging over his forehead.

The bound man mumbled something inaudible. Saliva dribbled from his bust lower lip.

"Do I look like a fool?" Quentin asked, his voice carrying the heavy weight of authority. "You can't seriously expect me to believe that you weren't associating yourself with those bastards who want me dead."

Silence.

Quentin's eyes were rigidly locked on the man's skull. "Then I guess we continue," he said, signalling to the bald, gloved man that stood next to the victim.

Dressed in his typical black suit, Harold rushed towards the broken man from behind, grabbed a handful of his hair with one of his gigantic hands, and dragged him, along with the chair, out of the room.

Piercing screams bounced through the door, slowly fading from Quentin's ear. He shook his head with a sigh and removed his phone from his pocket, flicking through it.

Harold stepped back into the room, adjusting his suit jacket.

"I'll have a brandy, if you're going to offer," Quentin said without looking up from his phone's screen.

Harold walked over to a silver tray that sat on top of a short mahogany table in front of drawn curtains. Next to the tray and on the same table sat a long wooden box, resting against the wall. Harold picked up the half full decanter and poured the brandy into a crystal glass, passing it to Quentin.

He put his phone down on the vacant seat next to him and then immediately downed a mouthful of the brandy. "He'll crack, they always do," Quentin said, focusing on the glass that he held up in front of his face. "Part of the fun is chiselling away at them, isn't it?"

Harold stood by Quentin's side silently, his hands crossed below his stomach.

"And then, moving on to even more interesting things, we have Mr David Dale. The star in all of this. He's new, yes, and he's showing a lot more courage thus far than I was expecting. Respectable, but irritating." He looked at Harold, said, "Why don't people just pay up as soon as they're asked like they used to?" Quentin looked back to his glass. "Why must they always play the hero for as long as they think they can get away with?" Quentin nodded to himself. "Yes, we have threatened him plenty now. He must be getting a little worn down at least. Let's see how he responds to the Swede's message." He paused, slowly cracking a satanic smile. "Then I'll consider dishing out the real pain."

Quentin's mobile phone vibrated on the sofa. He picked it up, glanced at the caller ID, and then tapped the screen to accept the call. "All sorted?"

"Yes," the man said over the line.

"Good. Make your way to London tonight. I think I'm gonna need you very shortly."

CHAPTER 21

The morning started with a cold snap of trapped icy air that lingered from the overnight freezing temperatures. Sheets of frost settled on car windows, pavements and building tops. David had wrapped up in his favourite jumper, thick brown coat and dark grey scarf before venturing out of his inner-city apartment. He took the tube to Charing Cross, downed a small cappuccino from Caffè Nero, and approached The National Gallery at 10:53 a.m.

For a Wednesday morning, the entrance to the historic venue was unusually quiet, allowing David to climb the initial steps and walk into the entrance without delay. He stood in the vast hallway, with the wide stone staircase that led into the gallery directly in front of him. He scanned the thin crowds, looking for Rose's amber-brown hair and her innocent face. But the thought of Quentin confronted him.

The thought of a possible trap. An ambush.

As he searched the crowd, Quentin's face repeatedly flashed in his mind.

A group of more than thirty schoolchildren in navy uniforms and hi-vis jackets, guided by a handful of teachers, made their way from the glass doors next to the entrance and charged up the stairs.

David spotted an empty bench that faced the entranceway and so claimed a seat. He hunched over, rested his elbows on his knees, and pointed his chin up, moving his eyes across as many faces as he could see. As he sat there, waiting, it occurred to him exactly what he was doing. He instinctively brought his eyes to the floor as he searched for a good enough reason as to why he had put himself in such a precarious situation. Why he was risking his safety over a fifteen-minute, out-of-the-blue meeting with a criminal's wife he didn't know.

The constant streams of people entering The National Gallery, and the hustle and bustle they brought with them, seemed to louden with the pattering of footsteps and the swirling of chatter.

David couldn't seem to lift his eyes from the floor. His breathing had noticeably quickened, so he removed his scarf and loosened his coat and took a deep breath. His thoughts continued on Rose and Quentin, of Quentin's words and actions. The racing in his chest and the growing volume of his surroundings settled in. He rapidly tapped his foot before he managed to look up and take a final scan of the hallway.

No Rose, no Quentin.

David stood up and made his way past a couple that were speedily walking for the staircase leading into the gallery. He excused himself past a woman carrying what looked like a tray of pastries and cakes before arriving back at the entrance. As his arm extended to open the door, he spotted her outside, walking directly towards him.

That face.

Her windswept hair reflected a bright shine from the first glimpse of sunlight that David had seen all morning. She walked alone, wearing a long cream coat that was tightly wrapped around her body.

David found himself stuck on the spot.

Rose's eyes flicked up and connected with David's as she stepped up to the entrance.

David dropped his extended arm and mustered a smile.

She pushed the door open. "You're here."

"Hi," he managed to say as he picked up the smell of her perfume as it wafted into the hallway from the breeze behind her.

"I'm so pleased you came. I thought you might have changed your mind," she said, brushing her hair back into place with her fingers. Rose started walking. "It was tricky for me to get away. There were a lot of questions."

David caught up. "What did you say to him?"

"I usually say that I'm going to the spa when I want to break away for a bit, but he practically owns the one I go to, so I said I was going shopping for a new nightdress. My chaperone's still ill."

The pair stopped at the foot of the stone staircase.

Rose read David's expression. "Don't worry, I'm not with anyone and he won't know we're here. We're fine."

David gave a self-assuring nod. "All right."

She ascended the stairs. "Have you been here before?"

"Only once, a few years back. It's a big place," he said, climbing the staircase alongside her.

"It is, and it's a real favourite of mine. I come here sometimes to reflect and to get away from everything. I must say, this is the first time I've been accompanied by someone I can talk to, and not just followed," she said, glancing at the crowds. "It gets busy, but they have some stunning pieces." She looked at David. "I'm a big lover of art."

"I don't mind art. I appreciate it, but some works I just struggle to get. Do you know what I mean?"

Rose smirked. "I think you could say that some styles are an acquired taste."

They walked past magnificent bouquets of colourful lilies in oversized grey vases that sat next to towering marble pillars.

David followed the pillars with his eyes, observing the gold patterned ceiling and the giant glass dome. "I don't remember this."

They passed through an open double doorway and entered the massive Central Hall. Enormous peach walls hosted some three-dozen oil paintings, spread out in between three other doorways that led on to all corners of the gallery.

"Wow," David said, his eyes darting around the room.

Rose slowly moved her gaze across the walls. "Isn't it beautiful?"

"It is," he replied, walking towards the nearest painting.

"I don't think I've seen this one before," she said, following David and stepping up to the large canvas.

Placed in a golden, ridged frame, the painting depicted a young girl with a stern expression, flawless pale skin, and tied-back ginger hair. In a frumpy green and orange dress, the girl presented her sketch of a nude male figure.

David looked the girl up and down. "It does amaze me how they managed to paint so vividly hundreds of years ago. The precision and skill is—"

"It's fabulous."

The pair drifted toward the next painting and then the next, stopping to appreciate the styles, colours, and the possible stories behind them.

"Come, I want to show you my favourite piece," Rose said, gesturing for him to follow her.

"You have a favourite?" David asked, following her lead.

They exited the Central Hall through the left doorway, entering a smaller room with several huge artworks hanging from beige walls.

A small group of the visiting schoolchildren had gathered around one of the paintings, giggling and laughing at a half-naked mistress.

David forced his attention away from the playful kids to look at Rose. "Look, I wasn't sure when to mention this, but my colleague at Down Dream, Kristian, he had one of Quentin's men in his apartment the same day you paid me a visit."

Rose stopped walking. "What?"

David looked around. "It's okay, Kristian's okay. The man didn't assault him, but it really shook him scared. It shook us all scared."

"Oh my god, I'm so sorry," Rose said. She slowly started to walk again through the room. "David, he's turning up the pressure. It's what he does."

"You mean this is just another of the steps he takes when trying to extort people?"

The pair entered a second room, but kept walking.

"Yeah, it's his first tactic. He tries his best to scare people, it's what's easy."

"And what if it doesn't work?" David asked, noticing Rose's face had turned a little paler.

"You really don't want to get that far, David. You need to get help, or just get out of London. He won't stop until he gets what he wants."

David repeated Rose's words in his head.

"I wasn't aware that Kristian was going to be visited, I swear," Rose said.

"You didn't know?"

"No, of course not. I would've told you at your apartment if I knew. Quentin doesn't talk to me about what he does, I just overhear bits here and there."

Rose and David entered a third room, but still kept walking.

"Kristian said that the man was big, bulky, and bald. Does that at all sound familiar?"

"Sounds like Harold," Rose said.

"Harold?"

"He's pretty much Quentin's right-hand man."

David sighed. "It must have been terrifying for Kristian. Have you heard anything about what Quentin's going to do next?"

Rose shrugged. "He's been on the phone quite a lot over the last few weeks. More than usual. I don't know who he's speaking to, but in some conversations, he sounds softer, like he's trying to please. In other conversations, he sounds like he's barking orders, telling someone to do as they're instructed and *get on the good side*."

David looked to the floor, shaking his head.

"Ah, here's the room," Rose said, observing the turquoise marble doorway that they were approaching.

"Do you love him?" David asked, his eyes fixed on her.

Rose looked up at David with a scowl. "I hate him."

"Then can't you leave? Why are you with him?"

Rose gave the slightest of smiles as she looked up at the marble. "Unfortunately, things are never as simple as they seem." She sped up, walking into the large room on her own.

The room's walls were decorated in turquoise wallpaper and covered with Venetian oil paintings of different colours, sizes, and themes.

David trailed behind her, watching her body stride towards a medium-sized painting that hid in the far corner of the room with no one to admire it. He looked around before approaching Rose from behind. Her favourite painting slowly came into full view from behind her head.

A well-dressed woman in rich, colourful garments with jewels in her hair fled the violence on the hilltops behind her. Some metres away lay a dead man in torn, ragged clothes. Further from the corpse was a figure, covered in armour with a strip of pink cloth tucked by the waist, riding a horse in a battle-ready stance. The warrior was charging a cornered and cowering dragon at the foot of the hill, just steps away from the edges of a dark blue ocean. The fear in the dragon's eyes beautifully reflected the storm overhead, which was being brushed aside by a glowing, divine being.

"Saint George and the Dragon," Rose said in a whisper. "By Jacopo Tintoretto."

For a chunk of time, which neither of them noticed, the pair stood in silence observing the painting.

David spoke first. "I see why you like it so much."

"You do?"

"It's an incredible painting. The mood that it conjures. The fear and violence contrasted by the innocence of the dead and the fleeing woman. And then you have the skyline above," David said, pointing, "with the combination of colours and textures and depth."

Rose smiled, looking to him. "You aren't lying."

David gave her a knowing look. "Thanks for sharing it with me."

Rose pulled her attention to her sleeves, her fingers interlocked.

"What is it?" David asked.

"You've found yourself in an unfortunate predicament. I've been in mine for four years. If I can keep my eyes and ears open and help you in any way I can, David, then I will." She swallowed hard as a tear managed to escape. "But I feel it in my bones that unless I finally do something now, unless I finally fight for myself, then I'm going to waste my life trapped in a gilded cage with this dragon, with this man I do not love and who has taken me from the freedom I once had. I guess what I'm getting at is…" She looked up, squarely setting her eyes on David's. "I'm in desperate need to find my own Saint George and I can't help but feel that you're him."

CHAPTER 22

"How did you get in the building the other day?" David asked, scanning his resident card against the building's security keypad.

Rose laughed lightly. "I paced up and down just out here with a handful of cigarettes, smoking my way through, waiting for someone to come or go."

"You were lucky then," David said as they stepped into the elevator. He pressed the button for the 12th floor.

"For once in my life."

The elevator door soon opened and they walked down the corridor that led to David's apartment. He unlocked the door and stepped through. "Come on in," he said, before closing the door behind her. He led her into his living room where she claimed the same sofa as per her last visit. "Would you like a drink?"

Her eyebrows lifted. "What do you have?"

"Er," he said, glancing to and from the kitchen, as if it would help jog his memory. "I have coffee, tea, water, juice, wine—"

"A wine would be lovely."

David nodded and disappeared into his kitchen, the noise of glasses and bottles clanging behind him. He soon reappeared, placed two empty glasses onto the coffee table in front of Rose, and asked, "Do you mind if I join you?" He gestured to the bottle in his hand.

"You don't need to ask for permission to drink your own wine."

He poured the red wine into both glasses, handed Rose one, and sat down on the sofa opposite her.

"Thank you very much," she said, smelling the contents of her glass. A combination of red fruits, melded into hints of chocolate. "You have a good taste in wine."

"My sister, Sam, has a good taste in wine. This bottle's one of hers."

"You have a sister?"

"A younger sister, yeah. She lives not far from Manchester, though I don't get to see her as much as I should."

"You're very lucky." She gave David a look before diverting back to her delicately sweet drink. "You used to do psychiatry, didn't you?" She smiled. "A career devoted to other people, what does that say about you?"

David sipped his glass, unsure whether or not she was expecting an answer.

She wasn't. "Psychiatry is similar to therapy, isn't it?"

David nodded, said, "In some respects, yes, it is. As a psychiatrist, we specialise in psychological disorders that can, in cases, wreak havoc on people's lives. Psychiatrists can prescribe medication and support therapists, whose job is to talk through the issues that people are dealing with." He paused. "But you already know this, don't you?"

Rose coyly let out the slightest of smiles. "Yeah, and even though by the codes of conduct that, in your profession, you abide by with the utmost of importance, can I ask that we simply talk this evening? Just talk. I'm not wanting to be diagnosed with anything, or psychoanalysed in any way," she said with a laugh. "I just want a conversation with somebody genuine. Is that okay?"

"The involvement of wine alone is enough to break all ethical practices I used to adhere to when I worked in the field."

Rose smirked.

"I'm out of that profession now and solely work on Down Dream. If you are wanting just a chat, then I'm here."

"Thank you." She sipped from her glass. "You show such kindness to me when we have only just met. I'm the wife of a man who is threatening you and your charity, yet you still have time for me."

"You can't be blamed for what Quentin's doing. Why wouldn't I have time for you?"

"You really aren't like anyone I've ever met before," she said before a heavy gulp. "David, what must I do? I'm trapped with a man I hate. A man who sees me as an object to control and a possession to flaunt. To him, my personality, my wishes, and my dreams don't exist. He could've so easily replaced me over the years."

"Your life is your life. You have choices and you have dreams, make them and live them. Don't let anybody tell you otherwise."

"If I left him, he would kill me."

"Then we can think of something. Something to get you out safely. You can do anything."

Rose reflected a saddened smile, a faint teardrop slipping from her eye. "I haven't seen my family in four years," she said, wiping her cheek.

"Where are you from?" David asked, leaning down to the bottom of the coffee table and grabbing a small box of tissues from underneath, placing them onto the table in front of Rose.

"Thank you," she said, taking one. "I used to live in the town of Moncalieri, where I'm from." Her voice drowned in sadness. "In the north of Italy."

"I haven't heard of it before. Tell me about it."

Rose focused her gaze on her glass. "There isn't much to tell. It's famous for its grand, magnificent castle. It's a petite town, with not many stores or restaurants. Not much. The traditional buildings are tall, everywhere. The streets are cobbled and quaint. Near the centre of the town, there's a large tower with a giant clock, overlooking everyone. When I was young, my mother used to tell me that the clock was always watching. Always keeping its face on us kids to make sure we behaved."

David returned a comforting smile.

"My parents own a small farm on the outskirts. As a teenager, I'd get a bus into the town centre for school and then have to wait thirty minutes to get home again because the bus would usually drop me off last after every other kid. I used to moan and complain to my parents about this, but what did I know. I was getting an education, I was happy, really." She took another sip of her wine. "My parents grew tomatoes and olives; have done since I was a child. They have always had goats, too. Goats can be very friendly animals, you know. People think they're grumpy and unsociable, but if you actually spend time with them, you learn to appreciate their ways." Rose shook her head, laughing loudly. "What am I talking to you about?"

"Your town sounds amazing."

"It is a beautiful place. Beautiful."

"I see you returning to your home. Going back to those cobbled streets and letting that clock watch over you again."

Rose looked back to her glass. "Oh, I've been here too long now to go back. I'd like to go back, of course. I want to see my parents and my family. I want to know how they are, what they have been doing. To tell them I'm okay and that I love them."

"You will do."

Rose tapped her nails on her glass. "I was twenty-two when they took me. I was at a friend's birthday party when I met a very cute boy. Never had I seen him before. He said all of the right things and asked if I wanted to head to a bar just the two of us, as the party was getting loud."

David nodded as she spoke, his eyes watching the movement of her lips, hanging on to every word.

"I know I shouldn't have, but I left the party with him and we walked towards the town centre." Rose's face froze still, hiding all emotion. "He had a van waiting, which I was bundled into with a bloody nose and a dizzy head as someone hit me." She wavered, her voice gently cracking. "I found myself in a small room, tied to a mattress. When I was alone, there was enough leeway to stand up and bang on the door. Days passed and men came and went, some viewing me, as if I were a sheep at a market. Others abused me in that room. Touched me." She closed her eyes, rubbing them with her free hand, and fought for a deep breath. "I went from place to place for a few months, moving between vehicles and different rooms, sometimes small rooms like the one I originally found myself in, and sometimes in larger rooms, surrounded by other women. I was then picked, now I know by one of Quentin's men, and he moved me through Europe, in cars and trains. I must have been in France, or Belgium, before I saw Quentin, and he promised he'd save me from the hell I was in. In effect, that's what he did. He got me out of the situation and took me to London where he set me up in his mansion, bought me clothes and jewellery. I hadn't yet registered that I'd traded one form of hell for another." Rose drank a mouthful of her wine. "It was just over a week at his place until he started raping me. He was never overly violent, just very strict. And I've always been too scared to do anything about it. I just don't have the chance to turn him down. He used to say that I would end up in *their* hands again if he didn't look after me, and that I'd lose this *luxury* life. The clothes I didn't want, the jewellery I didn't want. The life I didn't want." A tear escaped from her eye, which she quickly swiped away, replaced by a brave smile. "Four years later, here we are."

David leant forward and passed her another tissue. "What happened to you was extraordinarily traumatic and a huge ordeal for someone to process and survive. You are such a brave woman to have gotten through it all and be how you are now. Anything could have happened before or after you met Quentin."

"Well, all of that is just a chapter in my life. I've done what I can to create a new one here given my circumstances and limited freedom." Rose dropped her used tissue onto the coffee table. "They say bad things happen to good people."

"They're right."

Rose chuckled. "Then I guess we're doomed," she said, shuffling in her seat to sit back upright. "Anyway, what are your plans? Long term."

David accepted the change of subject. "Er, good question," he said. "I hope to be running Down Dream for a very long time. There's so much work to be done and I know it'll take time, so I have a lot ahead of me."

"What kind of work do you want to get involved in? I know you're targeting homelessness at the minute, which is incredible."

"I want to open a few more homeless shelters up and down the country, especially in Edinburgh, Newcastle, and Manchester. I'd also like to get into providing assistance to food banks, maybe even within the year, we'll see. And I guess, for the long term, I would love to have some more interaction with the government, in helping their committees and various departments and agencies tackle the root causes of the many problems our society faces."

"You should have been a politician. You could change the world."

David couldn't hide his smile. "Thank you. But you don't have to be a politician to make things better in the world. Politicians deal with too much paperwork, anyway. And they take so long to get stuff done. When you're by yourself, you can just crack on."

"So true. You're an inspiration given everything you've also been through. How long ago was it since Maria passed? She would be so proud with what you've achieved."

David almost flinched as the surreal moment hit him. Despite it being three years, he now realised the bizarre situation he was in. In an unfamiliar apartment in the middle of London, chatting over wine to a woman he barely knew and whose husband was out to get him. The name of his late wife coming from her lips. David focused on the wall in front of him. His only reaction was to contrive a smile. He downed the remainder of his glass.

Rose broke the silence. "I'm sorry, I shouldn't have said anything."

"It's ok. How do you know about Maria?"

"Your name comes right up on Google. Everything about you is online. I'm sorry, I shouldn't have."

"Ah."

Rose sat silently.

"My little girls, too. They would be proud, wouldn't they? My Cassie and Sophie." David's attempts to hold back failed. Tears poured out of his eyes as his head collapsed into his hands.

Rose rushed around the coffee table and sat next to him, her arms wrapped around his body.

David quietly wept as Rose ran one hand across his head and through his hair.

"Shh," she whispered.

He slowly dried his eyes and attempted to compose himself, straightening his top with drawn-out breaths.

"Look at me," Rose whispered, pulling one of his hands away from his face and then pushing his chin up to her level. Their eyes met. "You are an incredible man, David Dale. Do not lose yourself in what has happened. They were with you back then and they are still with you now; throughout everything you do. How else do you think you've had the strength to achieve what you have so far? You've come out of the ashes and built an incredible charity that's helping so many people. Everyone is looking to you right now with respect. Continue your work and prove to everyone just what a hero you are."

David's eyes didn't flicker away from Rose's, but her eyes fell onto his lips and she slowly drifted closer towards him. Even though she had finished speaking, her voice continued in his ears; repeating words and phrases that she had just spoken. Her eyes closed as she etched even nearer to him, his throat now feeling full and heavy.

As Rose reached him, he pulled away. "I'm sorry," she said, instantly straightening her back with a snap, her lips hinged open and her eyes wide. "I'm so sorry."

David couldn't bring himself to look at anything but the floor. He cleared his throat and wiped his face. "It's fine, it's fine."

"I feel so silly. I shouldn't have done that."

David shook his head as he locked his hands together, squeezing his fingers down onto both of his hands.

Rose pushed herself from the sofa and moved around the table. "I should go," she said, picking up her coat and bag.

David climbed to his feet. "You don't have to. You can stay as long as you like."

"No, no. Thank you though," Rose said, sliding the coat onto her body. "I think it's time."

As the pair reached David's apartment door, he turned to her. "I don't know if I've made the right decision or not. Am I putting them in danger?"

"By not doing what Quentin wants?"

"Yeah. He's made several threats now and he's broken into Kristian's apartment. They're terrified. I'm not wanting to panic them, so I've not told them what I've learnt about him and his group."

"But what do they want to do? Pay him money?"

"Kristian's in a bad way after yesterday. Bev's worrying, so I think the two of them now want to try and pay him off. Get him out of our hair."

Rose delicately shook her head, as if being careful not to knock it off. "It doesn't work like that. You don't just pay Quentin off. He comes back for more. Every single month. He says you're paying a service; his *protection* and *respect.*"

David's lips parted. "I really don't know what we're going to do."

Rose leaned forward and pulled open the door, taking a single step into the corridor. "Tomorrow's Valentine's Day," she said quietly, peering out of the corridor's window. "The worst day of the year."

CHAPTER 23

"Blimey, you're in early," Stu said as he hurried into the homeless shelter's back office.

Bev looked up from the scattered papers that lay across her desk. She smiled, said, "Good mornin'. I didn't think anyone else would be comin' in at this time."

"I wanted to get a head start on the mid-month submissions for the shelter's progress." Stu pulled out a chair from another desk and sat down, still looking at Bev. "What's your excuse?"

"I'm just finishin' those submissions."

Stu raised his eyebrows. "*Finishing?* Jesus, what time did you come in?"

Bev shrugged and looked at her watch. "I dono, maybe an hour or two ago."

"Nobody can ever question your work ethic."

Bev couldn't help but giggle. She looked back down to the papers in front of her. "Have ya heard from David this mornin'?"

"No, not yet. He told me yesterday he was heading to the offices first thing and was going to be there until midday at the latest."

"Okay," she said, nodding.

Stu glanced around his desk and then across the room. "Well, I don't know what to do with myself now."

Bev finished reading the sentence she was on and then looked back up. "Ya could proofread the mid-month reports before I submit them." She stood up, bundled the papers into her hands and offered them to Stu.

"Sure," he said, scanning over the first page.

"I need to nip home anyway. I think I've left my folder that has all the government contacts in them."

"Okay. Don't worry, I'll correct all your grammar mistakes while you're out."

Bev threw on her coat and approached the door before letting out a deafening burst of laughter. "That's a good one."

Stu smirked as he listened to Bev continuously laugh as she walked out of the building.

With a pen in his hand and a pile of papers requiring his signature, David sat motionlessly at his desk in the offices of Down Dream, thinking of nothing but last night. Images of Rose's face in the light of his living room's lamp flashed across his mind. Visions of her walking into his office materialised, with her passing his desk, only to disappear by his side.

David shook himself and stared down at the piece of paper in front of him, his signature still vacant.

His mobile phone rang. Without hesitation he answered, "Hello?"

"Good morning, Mr Dale. How are you?" asked the all-too-familiar voice of Quentin.

David clenched his teeth and held his breath. "Stop calling me. I have nothing to say to you."

"That's fine. I'm not exactly looking for a heart-to-heart. I want paying, and I want paying now. The fun and games are over."

Quentin's statements repeated in his head. Rose entered his mind and he instantly realised Quentin would have said, or done, something more elaborate had he known of Rose's whereabouts last night.

He mustn't know.

"That's it," Quentin continued with a condescending tone, "there's no need for talking. Just meet with me now to pay your first instalment like a good, honourable man."

David swallowed the fear within him and clawed together an ounce of courage, forcing his tapping leg to stop moving in the process. "We've discussed this before and I'll tell you again for the final time. We're not paying you a penny. Nothing. We aren't going to be threatened by you. The police are already on to you."

Silence.

An almighty roar of laughter ripped into David's ear, making him pull the phone away.

Quentin attempted to speak as he continued laughing. "No one," he chuckled, "has ever. Ha ha ha! No one has ever spoken to me like that before." He shrieked a sinister cackle. "Especially with such a fairy tale touch to it. I like it."

David clenched his fist.

"I do like you, Mr Dale. I like you a lot."

"Fuck you and stop calling us," David said before hanging up and turning his mobile phone off. He jumped to his feet but held onto the desk to steady his trembling hands.

Quentin clicked off his phone and momentarily let it dangle as he sat on his sofa, joined by Harold and two other men. Harold stood to the side of the sofa in Quentin's immediate presence, his hands folded across his abdomen. The other two stood against the walls of the room, as if just another object in the bustling room of antique furniture and fittings.

Without warning, Quentin rapidly raised his arm and launched his mobile phone at the fireplace in front of him. The device smashed into the upper stone slabs and broke into countless pieces that scattered across the floor. The two men against the walls looked down at the broken phone, before resuming their default expression. Harold raised an eyebrow for a moment, but then swiftly reined it back in.

Quentin lurched forward spontaneously, kicking the table in front of him, launching it half a metre away from the sofa. "That fucking smug piece of shit!" Quentin shouted furiously, his face burned in anger and his hands moulded into tight fists. He looked up at Harold and kept his voice loud. "This is why I can't give people chances! You give them a little leeway and they expect to be able to take more and more. No wonder we live in a world of dictatorships and violence." He took a deep breath, glancing around the room. "That fucking weasel. That motherfucking weasel." He shook his head. "We've offered him enough. We have offered him too fucking much." Standing up and straightening his sleeves, he glanced at the men against the walls, still standing in waiting. He changed his focus back to Harold, said, "The security is beefed up at the charity offices, but I reckon you'll have no resistance at the shelter."

Harold's eyes fixed on Quentin, but his lips didn't move.

"Head over there now." He paused, breaking a little smile. "And make him sorry."

"Now is it *Yours sincerely*, or is it *Yours faithfully*?" Stu asked himself as he typed the question into Google. Without moving an inch since he sat down just over two hours ago, he had finished his proofreading of Bev's mid-month reports and kicked himself for being unable to identify any mistakes in her grammar. He had moved on to email correspondence on behalf of the charity, bringing him to the question of how to end his mail to someone he knows the name of, but has never met or spoken to before. The search engine instantly beamed back the answer he was looking for. "I bloody knew it."

An unexpected thud sounded from the corridor leading to the office door. Frowning, Stu glanced at his watch and thought that Kylie and Jordan, the maids, don't start their shifts for another twenty minutes. He resumed his focus on the computer monitor and closed the Google page to finalise his email.

Few moments passed before another, unexpected sound startled him. A distinctive footstep; as if someone was entering the corridor from the rear door.

"Kylie?" Stu asked, his voice unsure.

No response.

Stu rose from his seat and slowly approached the door to the office and opened it, looking out to the dark corridor; poorly lit from the lack of windows. "Jordan?" he asked, keeping a grip on the door's handle. A possibility, he thought, that it could just be Lauren, one of the many volunteers scheduled to help out today. They always head straight to the office when they get in though, to inform whoever's in the building that they've arrived.

What looked like a black trouser leg, footed with a man's steel toe-capped boot, lurched around the corridor's corner. "Hello?" he asked, his voice now almost feeble. "Who's there?"

Silence.

Stu stepped through the doorway and entered the corridor.

Bev pulled up in front of the homeless shelter. "Now who owns this lovely beast of a car?" she asked herself as she laid her eyes on the monstrous Range Rover that was dominating two parking bays. She parked up and stepped out, carrying her thin, leather briefcase in one hand and a small paper bag in the other. She opened the exterior rear door of the building and pushed through into the corridor.

"Sorry I took a while. City drivin' and all that," Bev said, slowly making her way toward the office door. "I've brought fresh bagels though. Us early birds need feedin'."

She stopped short of opening the office door that stood ajar. Looking closer, she noticed two small holes that had punctured the door, enabling beams of light from the office windows to reach her in the corridor. "Stu, do ya know how these have come about?" she asked, pushing open the door. As her eyes made their way across the office, she screamed a piercing shriek.

CHAPTER 24

Just under two hours after his unwanted phone call, David left the Down Dream office and drove the twenty-five-minute drive to the homeless shelter. His attempts to think about work instead of Quentin were limited, as the man had quickly manifested himself into David's consciousness. Instead, he found slight comfort in the thought of Bev's current work within Down Dream and the positive influences she has already brought since the charity's inception. The achievements that the four of them, as a collective group, had managed to achieve in such a short space of time was astonishing.

As he turned the corner onto the shelter's street, David couldn't escape the flashing blue lights. He slowed down his car as he approached the shelter, taking in the sight of the small crowd of people that had gathered outside.

Parking on the road, behind the spectators that lined the police cordon, David leaped out of his car and ran towards the guarding officers. "What's happened?"

"I'm sorry, I can't say anything just yet," the officer said.

"Can I get past? I run this shelter," David said, noticing one of his volunteers, Lauren, being interviewed behind the cordon. With his focus centred on her glossy eyes and the tissue gripped tightly in her hand, a voice bellowed from near the shelter's entrance.

"David!" Detective Thomas McField shouted, stepping out from the building and hurriedly walking towards the police cordon.

The name and the familiar face grabbed the attention of the spectators as the quiet mixture of chatter simmered; their whispers and speculation beginning to swirl.

McField looked to the officer next to David. "Let him through, it's his property."

David stepped under the cordoned tape and met the detective. He tried to find his voice.

Detective McField beat him to it. "Where have you been? We've been trying to call you for almost half an hour."

"My…" He gulped. "My phone's off. I turned it off an hour or two ago. What's happened?" He glanced back at Lauren, a mere twenty metres away but still being interviewed; her face expressing a renewed sense of sadness as her eyes connected with his.

McField spotted a van parking up across the street with a local news station's logo printed on its side. He gestured for David to follow him, leading him away from the police cordon and behind one of the two parked ambulances.

David couldn't concentrate or focus on any one thing. "Who's in there? Tell me what's happened."

McField exhaled, struggling to lift his heavy eyes. "David, I'm so sorry to tell you this, but Stu Jackson is dead."

David's sight of the detective in front of him seemed to fade as everything turned grey. His pupils shook side to side. He brought his hands to his mouth, unable to look away from McField.

"He had been shot."

Regardless of anything or anyone around him, David fell onto the inside step of the open ambulance door. His body swayed, as if trying to balance itself. He arched his back, elbows dug into his knees, and lowered his head. "I don't understand." He paused, breathless. "Shot?" David tentatively raised his head, clocking the second ambulance. "There's two ambulances?"

McField's eyebrows somehow fell even further, his eyes glazed. "Why are there two ambulances?"

"There's no easy way to say this," McField started, "but Bev has also been hurt."

David recoiled as if a bullet had pierced his heart. His stomach contracted in shock. "What?" he managed in a whisper.

In a hushed voice, McField said, "The paramedics are preparing to take her to the hospital now. Your volunteer, Lauren, found the pair of them in the offices at the rear of the building, about thirty, forty minutes ago. Stu was pronounced dead when the paramedics arrived. Bev's in a pretty serious condition. She was stabbed, David."

David couldn't muster a response.

McField pursed his lips together. "She was impaled against the wall."

For the third time in three years, and for the second time in three minutes, David felt the world dissolve beneath his feet. His eyes fell to the floor, tears starting to flow.

McField stood, silently, observing David.

David buried his face in his hands and sobbed. He raised his head to say something but caught the sound of movement from the shelter's entrance and, soon enough, activity came pouring out of it. Standing up and wiping his cheeks, David recognised paramedics in their dark green uniform wheeling a moving stretcher towards the steps and lifting it down attentively. He stepped closer, reaching them as they hit the ground. He spotted Bev's bloodied face. Her body was strapped to the stretcher, holding her in a sturdy position. "Bev?"

"She's drifting in and out of consciousness. It's best she doesn't speak to retain her energy," said the female paramedic without slowing her hastened pace.

"Bev, it's David. Don't worry, you'll be all right," David said, wiping away a stream of tears. "I'm here with you." He turned to the paramedic. "Can I join you in the ambulance? To stay with her?"

The paramedic shook her head. "Unfortunately not. Given the circumstances, we have to travel with a police officer. For her protection."

David now noticed a police officer in waiting, stood next to Detective McField. Before he knew it, Bev was rolled into the ambulance, the officer and paramedics jumped in after her, and the doors slammed shut in David's face. The sirens blared as it drove through the parting crowd and down the road. With the ambulance gone, the crowd of spectators re-gathered, joined by journalists and photographers who began to shout David's name.

"David Dale! What happened?"

"Who got hurt?"

Cameras clicked and their flashing lights lit up the area.

McField gently pushed David towards the shelter and led him inside to the corner of the entrance hallway away from prying eyes. "Can I get you anything, David? A glass of water? Do you want to call anybody?"

David shook his head as he sniffled and cleared his eyes. "No, no. I'll call Kristian shortly, when I pull myself together."

"David, I know this is a hugely stressful time for you, but I want you to know that we're doing everything we can to get to the bottom of this and to find those responsible. A witness has already come forward with a description of the men that she saw enter the building, as well as a description of a car they were driving. My colleague has already spoken to Lauren, your volunteer, and we'll be offering all of the support we can to her and everyone at the shelter."

"I know who's responsible. You can arrest Quentin now, before anyone else gets hurt."

"I wish it was that simple." McField cleared his throat. "We have nothing on him. Everything apart from his few verbal threats, it appears he's had other people do his dirty work for him. We actually hold no evidence in connection to him and anything that's been done against you or Down Dream."

David could feel his face redden. "You're telling me that a very close, good friend and colleague of mine is now dead, and another could very well die soon, yet you can't lock up the man who's behind it all? The man who's orchestrating everything?"

McField's eyes looked to the floor.

"That's bullshit."

"It could turn out that Quentin himself came to the shelter to attack Stu and Bev, and evidence might be found to prove this, but until then we have nothing on him and can't do anything."

David rigorously shook his head.

"In response, we're upping the security around the charity and yourself as we deem you to be a high-risk target. We'll be placing two twenty-four-seven police officers to guard the shelter, as well as personnel to watch over your home, Kristian's home, and with Bev at the hospital at all times. In the meantime, we'll do everything we can to stop this guy and the people working with him."

David stepped away from McField and towards the shelter's entranceway, as if to leave. Before reaching the doorway, he turned back around. "Before you can find a shred of evidence to put this man away, we all might be dead."

McField didn't respond.

"A week ago today it was my therapist who happened to fall to his death. Today Stu's been murdered…" His voice cracked. "Bev…." He vigorously shook his head. "Contact a man called Alex Haynes, a journalist. He knows more about Quentin than you obviously do."

CHAPTER 25

Indicating left and turning onto Cable Street, McField identified the building and parked in a vacant spot one street away. Despite the fresh breeze bringing a form of much needed respite, Quentin was still there, in the back of his mind, as if he were slowly chiselling away at his head. Through his twenty-four years in the force, McField had never encountered such a character, which he could confidently say without having yet met him. From what he'd heard so far, from those in and out of the police force, and from what he'd read in old case notes, McField knew Quentin wasn't the regular suspect. A cloud of mystery surrounded him, as if he were a ghost that everyone had bumped into, but nobody wanted to talk about. But David Dale was a different victim, unequivocally pointing the finger of blame at Quentin like he was the man about to singlehandedly destroy the planet.

Now approaching the apartment block of David's journalist contact, McField found himself going over the information his superintendent had given him, and the information his retired colleague had confirmed. Whether or not McField already knew what he would soon be told by the journalist was unclear, but one can have faith.

After counting his sixteenth step, McField buzzed the intercom for the first floor.

The intercom beeped. "Yes?" a voice asked.

"My name is Detective Thomas McField. I'm meeting Alex."

"What's the code?"

McField tapped his mobile phone, checking the message he had earlier received from Alex. "58291".

The door buzzed open. McField stepped inside the cold, dull hallway and ascended the winding staircase to the first floor. He glanced around the neglected landing with frayed carpet and stained walls before catching sight of one of the many doors creaking open.

A man's head peered out of the doorway. "Can I check your ID?" asked Alex Haynes, propping up the circular glasses that perched upon his nose.

"Of course," McField said, sliding out his ID and flipping it open with an extended arm.

Alex studied the card for several moments, before giving a slight nod. He pushed the door wide open. "Nice to meet you."

"Afternoon," McField said, offering his hand.

Alex shook his hand. "Please," he said, gesturing into his flat. "Come in."

"Thank you," McField said, stepping into the apartment's corridor.

Alex shut the door behind them and squeezed past the detective, leading the way into his box of a living room. The tiny room was dim with the only window darkened by drawn blinds. Am old, dusty-brown sofa sat in the centre, facing a cluttered table and flanked by a single armchair that matched the sofa in colour and age. One of the room's walls was plastered with paper clippings of newspaper articles, magazine stories, and website pages that had been taped and pinned up, creating an expansive collage of both his own work and others' articles detailing the events of various crimes. "Please, take a seat," Alex said as he sat in the armchair, crossing one leg over the other.

McField sat down on the far side of the sofa, leaving an awkward gap in between the pair.

Alex spoke again. "David messaged and told me that he passed you my details. He should really have run it past me first but given the circumstances I understand why he didn't."

"I imagine it's been pretty traumatic for him; he's lost a good friend and a partner in Down Dream."

"How's Bev doing? Do you know?"

"She's in a critical but stable condition. The doctors said that the first night was the most crucial."

Alex hesitated a silent nod.

"All the best to her," McField said, counting the number of pictures on the wall. He pulled his eyes back to Alex. "Anyway, thank you for agreeing to see me. David said that you know a lot about Quentin and that you might be able to assist in the investigation? Any information at all would be greatly appreciated."

Alex's eyes narrowed behind his glasses. "Well, Detective, I don't mean to disrespect your authority, or to hinder your investigation into Quentin, as, of course he deserves everything he gets, but I'm a journalist and I have bills to pay. This story I'm working on about Quentin and everything involved with him is my big ticket out of this shitty apartment. So, surely, you can see my point of view in that if I divulge all of this information to you now, how do I know that my scoop isn't going to end up being a handful of cat piss?"

McField smirked. "I appreciate your work, Alex, and any information you provide may just get this man sent down. Any information you have will still be your story, provided you don't leave it too late."

"But if you charge him before I'm ready to go to press, all of the information I provide will already be in the public domain. My scoop *would* turn into cat piss."

"Then I advise you work quickly."

Alex shook his head, leaving a lengthy silence. "Right," he finally said. He moved his hands together and cracked a knuckle. "Where do I begin? I, er, contacted David four or five days ago and spoke to him about Quentin. I thought it was important that he was fully clued up with what he's dealing with."

McField nodded enthusiastically.

"And before I get into the nitty-gritty, I do have all the media articles from all the cases involved to support what happened and when."

"Go on."

Alex uncrossed his legs and leant forward, resting his elbows on his knees, and began to retell everything he knew of Quentin and his operations.

Nine minutes passed before Alex spoke of something that caught McField's attention. Something he wasn't aware of.

"And this is where the MP, Duncan Chiles, comes in," Alex said in the midst of his professor-like lecturing.

McField's ears sprung up.

"He's obviously playing a part at some point or another. A cog in a large-scale operation."

"What makes you say that?"

Alex smirked.

"Bev's daughter is boarding a flight for London tomorrow morning," Kristian said, sat down in the corner of the private hospital room as he looked towards Bev, lying motionless in a pastel, checked gown under a thin bed sheet. A life-support machine continuously beeped, wired up to Bev from next to her bed. The room itself was a generous size compared to other private wards, assigned to Bev due to the security fears. Fresh flowers stood in a vase next to a small TV on top of a coloured chest of drawers beside Kristian.

Hunched over as he sat next to Bev, David pulled his face out of his hands, revealing his red and stuffy eyes. "That's good. It'll be a nice surprise for Bev when she wakes up."

Kristian chewed his cheek as he restlessly tapped his feet. "Are we not gonna address this, David?"

"What do you mean?"

Kristian forced his lips together, crinkled his forehead, and threw out an open palm towards Bev. "What do you think I mean? Look at her. Look at what happened to Stu."

"I know, I know," David whispered, holding his head up with his hands.

"I'm scared for my life, David. This isn't what I signed up for. One of us has just been murdered, the other brutally attacked. What's going to happen next?"

David stared at Bev. He turned to Kristian, said, "If you need time, I understand. If you want out, I understand. But I can't let this charity down. I've made a promise that I can't break."

"Even if it means it'll break us?"

"Don't make me feel worse than I already do. I'm doing everything I can to try and protect us. I'm working with the police alongside the investigation, speaking to Alex about Quentin—"

"Who's Alex?"

"He's a journalist, someone who's been investigating Quentin since the beginning. He's gonna help the police."

"Hm. Something needs to be done quickly. This guy needs locking up, or we need to go into hiding or something."

"Look, Kristian, I absolutely get where you're coming from and why you're worried, but you have to understand that I can't let this charity down. I really believe the police are going to resolve this. Look at the security they've stepped up."

Kristian's focus drifted from David to Bev, then from Bev to the life-support machine. He shifted his focus again from the machine to the door, and then from the door back to David. "I didn't sign up for this, David. None of us did. This is too much. It's gone too far." He released a deep sigh. "I'll help wrap things up, but I need to distance myself from all of this. From everything."

David silently nodded. "I get it. I'm so sorry to have put you in this position."

Kristian chewed his cheek once more. "Why don't you get yourself off home," he said. "You've been here all evening. I can stay with her. Have a shower and a sleep."

David's eyes flickered at the thought of sleep, yet they were still fixed on Bev.

"Go on, David. I need you at your best. We all need to be at our best right now."

Closing his eyes, David nodded once. "Okay," he said. "Okay. I'll go home for a few hours." He picked up his jacket from behind his chair and stood up. "See you soon, Bev," he said, leaning down and planting a kiss on her forehead. He looked at Kristian as he headed for the door, said, "Take care of her."

Kristian shifted towards the TV and clicked it on. "Of course I will."

David turned the handle of the door and pulled it open before stopping suddenly. He looked at the TV as the news coverage began.

"The manhunt for the three suspects from yesterday's attack on a homeless shelter in central London has now been widened, a Scotland Yard spokesperson has confirmed this morning.

Yesterday's attack was said to have targeted Down Dream personnel who were at the shelter, which was opened earlier this week. Stu Jackson and Bev Walcott, both founders of the charity, were working at the shelter at the time of the attack. Mr Jackson was pronounced dead at the scene and Miss Walcott was rushed to hospital, where she remains in a critical condition. Police are looking through CCTV footage of the shelter for clues as to the identity of the three suspects."

Without saying a word, David turned the handle of the door once more and opened it, stepping outside. He closed the door behind him and glanced at the police officer guarding Bev's room. He started walking down the hospital corridor, the newsreader's words repeating in his head.

Mr Jackson was pronounced dead at the scene.

A passing nurse stopped and stared at him expectantly. "Sir," she seemed to repeat.

David looked at the woman. "Pardon?"

"Your phone," she said. "It's ringing."

David looked down to his pockets, only now realising that his phone was indeed ringing. He hurriedly dug into his pocket, took it out, and answered. "Hello?"

"David, oh my god. I've heard what's happened," a panicked Eva said. "I can't believe it."

"Eva, hi." He continued to walk down the hospital corridor. "I can't believe it myself."

"You must be in a state of shock. Are you okay? Were you there when it happened?"

"No, no. That seems to be a recurring theme, really. People are threatened or hurt, and I'm nowhere to be seen."

"Don't blame yourself. There's nothing you could have done."

David felt pressure in his throat and couldn't fathom the words.

"I'm worried about you," Eva continued. "What are you doing now? Where are you?"

He found his breath. "I'm just leaving the hospital."

"Look, I'll send a car for you. You shouldn't be on your own after something like this."

"Oh, no, I'll be fine. It's okay, I'm just going home and to bed."

"Are you sure?"

The exit's automatic doors opened as David stepped up to them. "Yeah, I think I just need to sleep and be by myself."

"All right. I'll check in with you another time then."

"Cheers, Eva."

The phone clicked off.

Standing in the hospital car park, David followed the hospital's external walls, his right-hand scraping across the rough brick as he walked. He turned round a darkened corner, a shadow now cast over him, and leant against the wall. He fell to the floor, covered his face from view, and cried.

CHAPTER 26

Nothing was in the way of David and his bed, but a heavy heart and a guilty conscience was preventing him from sleeping. Given the length of time that had passed since his last shower, David opted for a soaking beforehand. Even then, despite the comfort of the warm water and sweet-smelling shampoo, his mind was in overtime.

He took a melatonin tablet before lowering his bedroom's blinds and slumping onto his bed, burying his face into the pillows. His hair was still damp as he wriggled into the most comfortable position, tossing and turning his body, pulling and pushing the pillows.

His eyes twitched as his mind slowly began to quieten.

Pushing himself from his bed, David rubbed his forehead and stood up. He picked up a navy wool jumper and brought it up over his head and down across his chest, shielding his body from the winter-like cold air. He left his legs bare; only his grey boxers protecting his modesty. Moving to his bedroom window, he parted the blinds to see that it was dark outside. He shuffled back to his bed and picked up his mobile phone from the bedside drawer, tapping it to check the time, but the screen remained black and refused to turn on. He dropped it back down and stepped into the narrow, pitch-black corridor. At the end of the corridor, David could see a flickering orange light that conjured an uneasy feeling in the pit of his stomach. Timidly moving forward, he reached the corridor opening and his eyes made their way around the room.

The sofas and coffee table that once sat in the centre of the room were gone. In their place, a square glass table with two opposing chairs tucked underneath it were the only pieces of furniture in the dark-filled room. On top of the table was a long, thin candle, flickering its orange glow onto David's face. He instinctively pulled out a chair and sat down. The candle, now inches from him, felt warm and somewhat comforting. As he looked around, all he could see was darkness.

Footsteps from the other side of the table echoed. Step by step, the sounds grew louder and closer. He sat, waiting.

Rose's face appeared from the shadows and into the glow of the candle, radiating her beauty. Her smile instantly added to the candle's warmth. She pulled out the vacant chair and sat down opposite David, still smiling, and looked him up and down, from his wool jumper to his overgrown stubble. "How are you, David?" she asked.

The surreal scenario unfazed him. "I'm okay. How are you?"

"I'm fine," she said. "I'm wanting to check on you though."

"Why? I'm okay."

"I wanted to make sure you were all right. You know when someone asks if they're okay, and they just say that they are, but really they're hurting inside? It's like that."

"I'm hurting for Stu, and for Bev."

"And for Maria."

David's lips parted as he sucked in a sharp breath.

"It's Valentine's Day," Rose started, her smile still evident, "of course you're going to be hurting for your wife. You're always hurting for Maria."

David placed his elbows onto the table and raised his hands to his face, rubbing his eyes. "I hurt for her every day. It being Valentine's Day doesn't make a difference."

"But this day, just like her birthday and your anniversary, brings all of the memories and emotions to the surface, doesn't it? It brings it all back." Rose pushed a hand across the table and opened it. "It's okay, David. We all hurt," she whispered.

Tears formed in David's eyes. A long silence filled the air and David's heavy breathing blew on the candle. He looked down to Rose's hand and placed one of his own onto hers.

Muted footsteps crept up on the pair, reaching the table without either of them glancing up. A third chair, one that David hadn't noticed earlier, was pulled out from underneath the table. David jolted his head backward with his mouth hanging open as he watched Maria sit down.

Looking exactly like she did three years ago, Maria sat on the seat next to David, not one foot away from him. Her brunette hair wavy and long, flowing down to her shoulders. Her cheeks rosy, her skin perfect. "Hello, David," Maria said with a sombre smile, her eyes sparkling in the candlelight. "It's me."

"Maria?" David asked, his voice quaking.

"Hello from the other side, my darling," she said, scrunching her face in an act of masking her emotions. She forced a smile past the first set of tears.

A tear streamed down David's face. He moved his spare hand in a gesture for Maria to take it. "Maria," he managed. "I've missed you so, so much."

She moved to accept his hand, holding it tightly. "I've missed you the world over."

"Please come back," he said in a cracked voice. "Please come back, I need you."

Maria shook her head, her lips pursed together. "I can't, my dear. I can't come back." She glanced at Rose and then back at David, composing herself. "I know you're struggling right now. I know that. But even when it feels like every light in your world is going out, know that there is always one light burning for you." She looked at Rose again. "And I know you have another light that's starting to shine." She looked back at David with another brave smile. "Let that light shine."

"I'm so sorry," David said. "I'm so sorry I didn't—"

"No, no," Maria said. "You don't need to say anything, my dear. Your purpose is to help others now." She slowly stood from her seat, releasing her hand from his, and stroked his cheek delicately. "Shine that light," she whispered before leaning down to kiss him.

David embraced the feeling of her lips on his skin, clinging onto the moment for as long as he could.

Maria pulled away and turned her body, stepping back into the shadows.

"Maria," David said, trembling. "Maria." Tears rolled off his cheeks. He tightened his grip of Rose's hand.

"David," Rose whispered.

His eyes were still scanning the darkness.

"David," Rose repeated.

He turned his head and looked at her.

"I'm calling you."

He wiped his cheeks. "What?"

"You need to wake up. I'm calling you."

*

David's wet eyes snapped open. The light from the bright room seeped into his vision as he woke from his deep slumber. Lying under his duvet, he looked up from his bed and saw the navy wool jumper on the floor. Now, as he sat up, the noise emitting from his mobile phone registered with his ears. He moved to the bedside table and picked up the phone.

Rose.

He wiped his eyes and then answered the call. "Hi." He cleared his throat.

"David, I'm so, so sorry for what Quentin's done. What he's done to Stu and Bev. I just, I can't believe it."

David looked to the window as the recent events filled his head.

"I wish I could stop him. I really do," she said.

"So do I."

"Perhaps we will stop him. Maybe we'll be able to bring an end to all of this, if the cops help."

"I don't know."

"Look, Quentin's meeting somebody tonight. Someone important."

"What do you mean?"

"For months now, I've been overhearing him speak to somebody over the phone in his office. He always goes in there to have his important conversations. This morning, he was speaking to somebody who sounds like they play a big role in what he does. He's meeting with them tonight at six o'clock at a building he owns in the city centre to go over their progress, or so he said. I've got the address written down."

"Hold on," David said, looking around for a pen and a piece of paper. He tore a corner off the back page of a magazine and found a blunt pencil in a drawer. "What's the address?"

Rose told him, spelling out the street name.

David scribbled it down. "Thanks."

"How are you? You don't sound good."

He sighed. "I'm fine."

"Can I come and see you?"

"I don't know," he said, bringing his hand up to his head, running his fingers through his hair. "I was going to take a few hours out to myself. I think it's about time I go and see my old family home."

"The home you shared with Maria and—"

"Yeah."

"That sounds nice. That'll be good for you."

David looked back at the navy jumper on the floor. "Would you like to come?"

"What?"

"It sounds a little odd, I know, but could you come? I've not been to the house since I lost them, so it'd be nice to have somebody with me. Don't worry if you're busy, or can't—"

"Yes, I can come with you."

"Okay. What time is it now?"

"Just after quarter past three."

"Jesus, I really slept in. Erm, shall I pick you up somewhere, or do you want to meet at my apartment?"

"I'm in a phone box outside Fortnum and Mason now. It'd only take me ten minutes to walk to The National Gallery. You could pick me up there?"

"Okay, that sounds fine. Is Quentin not with you?"

"No. He never comes shopping with me. Besides, with this meeting tonight, he'll most likely be out for most of the day."

"Great, I'll see you shortly then. Meet me on the corner outside the gallery." Clicking the phone off, David typed a short text with the address of Quentin's meeting location, time, and a short description of how the information came about and sent it to Alex Haynes with the instruction of informing Detective Thomas McField.

Mounting the kerb and parking up against the winding road to the side of The National Gallery, David turned off the engine and looked around. The overhanging trees cast a shadow, assisting his desired objective of laying low. He took out his mobile and sent a quick text off to Kristian, asking how Bev was getting on and letting him know that he would visit later in the day. David put the phone back into his pocket and continued his lookout for Rose, quickly noticing a well-dressed woman walking directly towards his car.

Wearing a long overcoat and oversized sunglasses that concealed a large portion of her face, she stepped closer and closer to the car. Upon reaching it, she opened the passenger door, tipped her hat, and climbed into the vehicle. She removed her glasses and looked to David with a smile. "Hi."

"Thanks for calling. I'm glad you could come." He started the car's engine and pulled off into the road.

"Have you had any update on Bev?"

David began to fill Rose in on the details since their last meeting.

Unbeknownst to the pair, a car pulled out of a nearby junction and began to follow them to David's East Horsley home.

CHAPTER 27

As he pulled a handful of dead leaves from the Bonsai tree, his mobile vibrated against his keyboard. The name on the screen made him quickly throw the dead foliage into the bin under his desk and answer the phone. "Detective Thomas McField."

"Hello, Detective. I'm wanting to inform you of a possible significant development in the case of David and Quentin," Alex Haynes said.

McField lent forward onto his desk. "I'm listening."

"David's gathered information that Quentin is meeting somebody that he thinks is significant to Quentin's operations. Meeting them this evening, that is."

"Do you know who?"

"No, but I'm going to hang around the building and find out."

"And why do you, or David, think that this is in any way important?"

"Because the source is Rose Zicela."

McField raised an eyebrow. "Why would we trust anything that comes from her?"

"Well, it appears Rose has struck quite the relationship with David and, for some reason, he trusts her."

McField pushed back in his chair, slouching. "I don't like the sound of this." He sighed. "What time is Quentin meeting this person?"

"At six p.m. In just over an hour's time."

McField's eyes darted for the clock, hung high on the office wall. "Where did you say they were meeting?"

A medley of corn yellows and pumpkin oranges hovered over the horizon, as if the sun were giving its final gift to the earth before bedding down. The endless fields that led David and Rose to his old family home shone a golden reflection in the afternoon's light. Memories of the local area engulfed David. The nights he would drive home from the nearby train station after spending hours at a time on his commute to and from London. The countryside pubs he would visit with his girls for a treat meal out.

After driving past the meadows for almost five minutes, David drove round a small bend and into an estate. The entrance had large brick walls on either side of the road, accompanied by the amber glow of lanterns. The grass was freshly cut, the hedges neatly pruned. Spotless pavements lined the road, blending into the picket-fenced front gardens of extensive, detached homes. Their car strolled past several houses before the car tentatively crawled up the driveway of his East Horsley home.

Rose peered up at the windows and brick. "Is this the house?"

"This is it."

The house looked untouched after all of the time that had separated him from his last visit. The white walls stood clean as if just washed for his return. The light blue window shutters unmoved with their delightful charm intact. The driveway sat directly in front of an adjoining garage. The house had two towering bay windows which were separated by the front door, each with a wooden raised flower bed beneath. A handful of delicate lilacs were still hanging on to their limited space which was increasingly becoming overgrown by weeds. Directly above the front door, on the first floor, a large open window gave natural light to what was the staircase.

"Are you ready?" Rose asked.

He blew out a stream of air, then took another deep breath. "Yeah."

"Are you still sure you'd like me to come in with you? I can wait in the car."

David opened his car door to step out. "No. Please, come in."

The pair approached the front door of the five-bedroom house and looked up at its gigantic stature. David took a single key from his pocket, holding it in his palm. He slid it into the keyhole, slowly turning it, then pushed down the handle and, with a creek, the door opened.

David took a moment to himself before pushing the door wide open and taking his first step inside the house. Inside, he flicked on the nearest light and looked around the hallway. The sideboard hosting the key bowl looked dusty and tired, but the hallway was tidy. He peered through the open doorway to one of the reception rooms that led on to the kitchen. The wide staircase sat directly in front of him, bringing the thought of his children's bedroom screaming to the front of his mind. He pulled himself away and entered the first reception room, adjacent to the hallway. Rose quietly followed him inside, closing the front door behind her.

A long, dark coffee table sat in the centre of the reception room, positioned on top of a coral rug. On either side of the table lay grey sofas, joined by multiple square cushions in a variety of colours. They moved through the room and into the kitchen, where David and Rose looked around at the tidiness that the family had left it in all those years ago. The surfaces of the kitchen countertops had a sprinkle of dust, though were empty of clutter and junk. The American-sized fridge-freezer was adorned with magnets from zoos, Disney theme parks, and inspirational life quotes. They walked past the breakfast bar and the island counter, ignoring the conservatory, and glided through the dining room and into the second, spacious reception room that the family often used as their main living room.

The walls were decorated with photographs of Cassie and Sophie as young girls, laughing and smiling to the camera; their faces covered in paint and their arms flailing in the air. Cassie's brunette hair waving in the wind, capturing her mother's very essence. Sophie's blonde, curly locks frizzed into the picture, making her cheeky smile absolutely adorable.

Looking at the pictures, David felt his throat close up. He forced a hard swallow and smiled to them. He changed his focus to the disused stone fireplace and accompanying sofas.

"They're beautiful," Rose said, her concentration still on the children's photographs.

David didn't reply, his eyes set on the door that led back to the hallway and the staircase. "I'll be right back," he said, leaving the room without waiting for a response. He stepped out of the lounge and pulled the door behind him ajar, finding himself at the foot of the staircase.

After watching David leave the room, Rose wandered around the living room, admiring the charming ornament pieces that adorned the many sideboards and the fireplace mantel. She returned to the photographs on the wall, appreciating their beauty for a second time. She imagined the moment that the pictures were taken, smiling to herself as the girls' giggles of laughter entered her head. Rose moved across the room to a long oak cabinet and leant down, looking at more framed photographs that sat in between small elephant figurines.

The first photograph again had the two sisters with their arms wrapped around each other at the foot of a bouncy castle.

Rose's smile held up as she moved across the various photos of beaming faces and beautiful holiday locations. But then her eyes stopped on the last photograph in a small silver frame. She leant closer, seeing David planting a delicate kiss on Maria's cheek, her eyes set on the camera and her smile unable to be any brighter.

Rose straightened her back and stepped up to the large window at the rear wall. She looked outside, noticing how big the back garden was and how much land had come with the property. Close to the conservatory doors outside, she spotted a small, pink slide that the girls must have once enjoyed. She let out a brief smile and then turned, wandering back over to the sofas where she took a seat and waited.

McField watched from the corner of the building as Alex Haynes crossed the road, seemingly quickening his pace after he had caught sight of the detective. As he waited for Alex to join him, he flicked his eyes back to the target building where Quentin was holding his meeting, only a few hundred metres away.

"Why don't we wait in the car on the street, surely we can get a good view from there?" Alex asked as he made his last step up to McField.

"Because," McField said, turning his back and unlocking a side door to the building, "if we wait in a room on the second floor of this building, we'll have a direct viewpoint of everyone who enters or leaves that building."

"Oh," Alex said, following McField inside. "What is this place? How do you have access?"

McField locked the door behind them and led the way down a wide corridor. "It's a commercial property that's been shut down by the Metropolitan Police. I managed to swipe a key to it as it was raided two weeks ago. The owners were using the upper floors as a cannabis factory. Until the investigation concludes, we have access."

"Crikey."

They took an elevator to the second floor, where the duo entered several rooms looking for the best vantage point over the adjacent building and its entranceway.

"Got it," McField said with a raised voice, shouting to Alex who was one room away.

Alex made his way into the room and stood by McField at the window in the corner room. They looked out across the road to the building where the entrance was positioned, a flight of stone steps leading up to it. "Fingers crossed whoever is showing up tonight will stop just in our line of sight right there," Alex said, pointing to the bottom of the building's steps. He dug into a small bag that was latched around his neck and pulled out a camera and a voice recorder. "Let's stake this shit *out*!"

McField frowned. "Remember we're here for a very serious matter."

"Remember that David told me about this meeting. He didn't text you about it, did he? He told me first because if it was the other way round, you'd be here on your own without me, and I'd be missing out on expanding my scoop. So be thankful I've brought you along."

"Remember there's so much more to this than your scoop."

"Yeah, sure, there's national interest in the underground criminal world that's controlling society more than people realise. My story's going to uncover a large chunk of it for millions of people, and I'll be the one to draw the curtain on it all."

Rose checked her watch after ten minutes had passed before standing up and venturing out of the door that David had left through. She looked around the hallway, noticing a light was on upstairs. "David?" she called out.

No response.

"David?" Rose repeated as she slowly started to ascend the staircase. She reached the landing, looking down its spacious walkway with seven doors. She stepped closer to one, noticing an open door on the other side of the landing with a light on inside. She approached, making out the room's purple wallpaper and the pink carpet. "David?" she asked for the third time, pushing the door open gently. In the corner lay a small, single bed with a bright pink duvet and an abundance of cuddly bears. The room had numerous posters and pictures, consisting of Disney and Pixar characters.

The door hit a wardrobe, having been pushed open as far as possible, and Rose stuck her head inside. David sat on the floor in front of a chest of drawers, facing Rose, clutching on to two large cuddly toys and silently sobbing. A child's colourful painting lay in front of him, showing the family next to their home with a gigantic sun above, each matchstick person labelled: *Mummy*, *Daddy*, *Cassie* and *Me*.

CHAPTER 28

Perched on one of the sofas, Rose stared at the enchanting stone fireplace, its amber flames flickering in an animated dance. The fire celebrated being brought back to life after such a long period of neglect with a burst of loud crackles. She slipped off her high heels, pushed herself back into the sofa, and curled up her legs.

"Here," David said as he walked back into the room from the dining room, pushing closed the door behind him with a tap of his leg. He carried two small glasses of wine, offering one to Rose.

"Thank you," she said, taking one of the glasses. "How are you feeling now?"

David inflated his cheeks before exhaling the air sharply. He sat down on the sofa opposite Rose. "I honestly don't know. I feel incredibly drained, like every ounce of energy has left my body."

Rose raised her body slightly, straightening her back to be at eye level with David.

"I feel like I'm slowly losing everything, and I don't know what to do. I thought I was ready to come back here, to give me some perspective." He glanced around the room. "But I don't know if it's helped."

"You've been carrying a lot on your shoulders. Not just recently, but for some time."

"It all happened three years ago, I know, but coming back to our house. Our home. It's all just…" He gulped. "With everything that's happening at the minute with Down Dream. With Quentin, Stu and Bev." He exhaled another burst of air. "It's all just overwhelming." His eyes darted around the walls. They finally settled back on Rose. "And I'm struggling, Rose. I think for three years I've been falling apart, and now I'm beginning to finally crumble."

"Do you want to talk about it? About anything?"

David's focus retracted to the glass in his hands. He took a sip. "I've not spoken about it properly in such a long, long time," he said. "I've never properly spoken to my sister about it. Only to my therapist when it all happened." He rubbed his eyes, lowering his head. "About that day in South Carolina."

"And that doesn't need to change now. Just do whatever you feel comfortable doing."

David looked up at Rose. "I think it's time."

Rose nodded silently.

"Three years ago. We just went over for a holiday. Maria always had this idea of spending Christmas at home, then going on a holiday straight after. We were supposed to be back the day after New Year's Day." He tapped the wine glass with his fingertips. "But on our sixth day, we got into an argument, Maria and I. She hated the fact we were on holiday, but I was still taking work phone calls. Disappearing to the hotel lobby for Wi-Fi so I could manage situations that were happening at the office." He shook his head. "We were on a family holiday and I thought it was more important to make sure my psychiatry practice was running smoothly."

Rose offered a comforting smile.

"After a bit of a cooling down, we spoke and made up. I apologised and said I'd stop." His eyes suddenly glazed over, if only made more noticeable from the reflection of the fire. He took a deep breath. "Then we got in the car and headed for a restaurant on James Island, near where we were staying. Sophie and Casie in the back, Maria by my side. It was only meant to be a short five or ten-minute drive." A single tear dropped from his eye. "But close to the island crossing, my phone rang, and I knew it was only supposed to ring in an emergency." His voice broke. "I was too busy looking at my phone when I let the car drift onto the other side of the road. We hit the corner of a truck at an angle that sent us spinning, then rolling. My girls didn't have a chance." More tears dropped before he could wipe his cheek, his eyes now overcome. "Every day I spend my life in regret that I didn't put my family first. I failed them."

Rose caught the first few tears that fell from her eyes. She brushed her face dry with two fingers and shook herself. Nudging herself to the end of her seat, Rose reached out a hand to David. As she began to move her lips to speak, she found herself breathless by an intense thud, as if it had originated within the house.

Both Rose and David turned their heads instinctively to face the closed door that led into the dining room and onwards to the kitchen and conservatory.

"W-what was that?" she whispered.

David's body stiffened with the fear of the unknown. Rose's voice resonated through him, bringing him to his feet. Stood still and silently for several moments, listening, he bent down to place his glass of wine on the table next to him and took one step towards the door. He wiped his eyes dry.

"Where are you going?" she asked, still in a hushed voice.

David took another step closer to the door.

"David?"

Another step forwards and David turned his head, pointing his ear at the door. He listened.

Absolute silence.

As he turned his head to face Rose with shrugging shoulders, David suddenly pulled his arms up to his chest in a protective stance as a loud crash hurled the door open, barging it against the wall.

Rose screamed as she jumped in her seat, turning her body away.

David re-opened his eyes from his braced, defensive position, seeing the unknown man, wearing a tight, black, padded vest with black pants. For only a millisecond, his eyes connected with the intruder's; his body prepared for fight or flight, his hands clenched and his toes braced against the soles of his shoes. With the sound of Rose's scream ringing through the room, David instinctively launched his body towards the man, forcefully grabbing his arms.

The well-built man responded by grappling with David, both attempting to gain the better grip of the other. The man took hold of David's left bicep, digging his fingers into the muscle. Using his right hand, he attempted to strike the left side of David's head.

David saw the man's right-hand rise, so rapidly brought down his head to face the oncoming fist.

The man struck the top of David's head as a loud crack of a finger rung out. He instantly softened his grip, moaning in pain as he shook his hand.

Rose fell to the floor by the sofa, scrambling behind it.

Dazed, David managed to pull away from the man and shook his head, the room seemingly spinning around him. As he watched the man clench his right hand once more, David franticly glanced over to the sofa where Rose was sat.

Empty. Where is she?

Quickly stepping backwards as the man launched himself forwards once more, David ran for the door that led to the hallway. As he ran, he heard the man behind him give chase. David sprinted through the hallway and through the first reception room, entering the kitchen and running behind the island counter. He desperately searched the kitchen counters for obstacles as he heard the man's booming footsteps grow louder.

The man closed the gap as he lunged around the island counter.

Grabbing the kettle from the corner of the kitchen, David held it firmly in his hand, swaying it through the air in aggressive, swift motions.

The man clipped David's arm, grabbing him by pinch of his sleeve. He barrelled over the corner of the island counter and into David, taking a firm hold of his wrist to restrict the use of the kettle, and pushed him back against the kitchen cupboards.

As David watched the man's head draw back, as if he were about to head-butt, David promptly brought up his knee towards the man's crotch.

The man released David and knelt down, gripping his groin as he winced.

Rose appeared in David's head, and so he dropped the kettle and vigorously shoved the man away from him, throwing him to the floor. He ran out of the kitchen, through the dining room, and back into the living room, scouring the room for her. He noticed Rose cowering behind the sofa and next to the fireplace. "Rose," he said, running up to her and leaning down, offering her his hand. "We need to go."

Before Rose could get to her feet, the man bolted back into the room and wrapped his arms around David from behind, picking him up and chucking him to the floor in one swift, brutal movement.

David landed with an almighty thump, causing an uncontrollable wheezing for air. Disorientated, he looked around the room, his vision blurred.

The man stood over David and moved his hand behind his back. Something clicked. As the man moved his hand back to his side,

David could now make out the shape of a gun. The intruder raised his hand and pointed it towards David, taking aim.

Abruptly, David witnessed the man scream out in pain as his mouth widened and his face looked up to the ceiling.

Having silently crawled from behind the sofa, Rose had picked up one of her high heels and used the thin heel of the shoe as a blade, banging it into the centre of the man's lower leg, just above the ankle. Rose released it, leaving the heel lodged inside him.

Looking down to his leg, the man turned to face Rose and aimed his gun, shooting several times. "You fucking bitch!"

Rose scuttled back behind the sofa as the shots fired out, hitting the floor inches from her.

David seized his chance to pull himself to his feet and focus every piece of energy into a tackle, driving his body at the man. He watched as the man flew across the table and land in front of the fireplace, smacking his head on a stone slab.

Searching for breath, David looked down at the lifeless man. Rose timidly lifted her head up from behind the sofa, her eyes red and teary. David moved around the man carefully, reaching Rose where he squeezed her into his embrace.

Crouched by the window in the corner room of the empty building, McField and Alex kept their eyes firmly on the entrance of the building across the road.

McField looked at his watch. "It's almost twenty past six."

"They'll come any minute now I reckon," Alex said.

"They must be running bloody late then." McField looked up to the overcast sky. "Looks like it's going to start raining."

The pair waited a further four minutes as tiny specs of drizzle started to fall, landing on the window.

McField edged his body upwards and towards the glass, spotting an approaching vehicle. "Is this someone?" He watched the black Mercedes roll up to the target building and stop at the bottom of the steps leading to its entrance.

"Here we go," Alex said, raising his camera into position.

The vehicle remained in place without any further motion for half a minute before one of the rear passenger doors opened and outstepped a man.

"Know who this fella is?" McField asked.

Alex repeatedly clicked the camera. "One of Quentin's men, it would seem."

The pair watched as the man walked around the back of the vehicle and opened the other rear passenger door. Stepping out of the vehicle and looking up to the building, Quentin slicked back his hair with the palm of his hand and sprinted up the steps to the entrance. The other passenger followed him up the stairs.

The driver of the Mercedes drove off, replaced with another car a moment later. Stopping, three men got out and joined Quentin in the building.

"More of his men," Alex confirmed.

"A well-guarded man."

After the second vehicle drove off, McField and Alex were left slightly disappointed with no other activity occurring.

"Unless his guest is also late," McField started, "then we're not actually going to get much out of this surveillance apart from the faces of a few of his employees." He changed his focus back to the clouds, watching as their colour darkened the more they moved overhead.

"Don't speak too soon," Alex said with a grin on his face.

McField looked back to the building's entrance and watched a Bentley SUV roll up to the foot of the steps just as the clouds opened and rain began to fall. The front passenger door opened and outstepped a suited, young-looking man. He walked to the rear of the car and pushed up the boot. Seconds later, he pushed the boot back down with a long object in his hand. The man was now joined by a second passenger that had emerged from one of the rear passenger doors.

"This is it," Alex said, holding his camera in position, his finger poised on the button.

The second man opened the remaining rear passenger door and the young-looking man opened up the object in his hand.

A large, black umbrella covered the car door, blocking Alex and McField's view.

The car door closed and the two men escorted somebody up the steps towards the entrance, their feet barely visible as they shuffled one step at a time. As they reached the doors, and still just in view of McField and Alex, the young man pulled the umbrella away, closing it to the side of him.

McField gasped as he caught sight of the guest.

"Holy shit," whispered Alex, clicking his camera as quickly as it would allow.

With the umbrella removed, Alex and McField could now clearly see the figure dressed in all red, from the shoes to the shoulders. A slim figure, wearing expensive, designer clothing and large, darkened sunglasses. Her blonde hair tied behind her head in a discreet ponytail.

Stepping into the building with her two security personnel, Eva Shields removed her sunglasses.

CHAPTER 29

Rose's eyes were transfixed on the immobile man lying on the floor of the living room as she clung onto David. "Is he alive?" Rose asked, breaking the long silence.

"I don't know. He hit his head hard," David said. "If he is alive, we need to restrain him until the police arrive." David moved closer to the man, gently stepping on the ground around him. He manoeuvred to the side of the man's head before leaning down and extending his arm, placing two fingers against his neck.

Rose, still stood in her original position, crossed her arms around her chest and braced herself.

David reined in his hand and stood up, slowly taking a step back. "He's alive, but his pulse is faint."

Rose glanced back and forth between David and the man.

"We need to call the police."

"I have my phone, I can call them," she said.

"Okay, you do that. I should have some rope in a cupboard."

Taking out her mobile, Rose dialled 999.

David left the room and entered the hallway, bending down to a small cupboard next to a set of drawers. Opening it, he rummaged through several boxes, cartons, and packages in search for the bundle of rope he remembered once owning.

"I can't get any service," Rose said, entering the hallway with her mobile in her hands and her eyebrows tilted in worry. "Shit, you're bleeding," she said, inspecting the top left side of David's temple.

David placed a hand on the top of his head, feeling a patch of blood. He wiped it onto his jeans. "The neighbourhood is renowned for shit service," he said. "Try the conservatory, I managed to get it in there all the time."

Re-entering the living room, Rose let out a deafening scream that sunk to the bottom of David's stomach. He abandoned the cupboard in the hallway and ran back into the living room, stopping beside Rose.

The man was gone.

Rose quickly closed the door behind them. David stepped forward, observing the area where the man had been lying in front of the fireplace. A spot of blood stained the carpet where his leg had rested, as well as a small sign of blood on the stone slab where his head had hit. Looking closely, David made out several droplets of a blood trail heading for the door, through the dining room and then into the kitchen. David followed the trail through the kitchen, but stopped as he looked into the conservatory and noticed the smashed window where the man must have entered and then escaped. David dashed back into the living room to a speechless Rose. "We're leaving," he said, before closing the door between the conservatory and the kitchen, creating a temporary barrier between Mother Nature and the contents of his home. The pair left through the hallway, out of the front door, and locked it behind them.

"What are we going to do now?" Rose asked in a hasty breath, jumping into the passenger seat of the car.

David slammed the door behind him and whipped the seatbelt across his chest. "We need to put some distance between us and him. He could easily still be in the area, or in the house." He started the engine, reversed out of the driveway, and spun the car 180 degrees, driving out of East Horsley.

As the night had finished its descent on the town, Rose could no longer take comfort from the meadows and idyllic scenery. She stared out of the passenger window mindlessly, searching for some sort of escape amongst the darkness and shadows.

David hit 40 mph on the country lanes that held the typical 30 mph speed limit. He headed towards the A24, racing past signs for London. As he tackled the sharp turns and bumpy roads, he took out his mobile phone from his pocket and connected it to the car's Bluetooth, dialling Kristian in the process.

The car speakers rang with the Swedish accent. "Hello? Is anyone there? David?"

"I'm here, I'm here," David said as he dodged a mini roundabout.

"What's going on? What's that background noise?"

"I'm driving. Look, Kristian, I haven't got long, I need to make another call, but are you okay?"

"Yes, I'm fine, why? What's happened?"

"Is Bev okay?"

"As far as I'm aware she is. David, what's happened?"

"I can't speak now, I'm sorry. Please call the hospital and have them check on Bev. Don't go anywhere on your own, Kristian."

"I can text Olivia and ask her about Bev, she's with her now."

"Who the hell is Olivia?"

"Bev's daughter, the one from New York?"

"Right, of course. Listen, Kristian, just make sure Bev is okay and look out for yourself." He hung up.

Rose kept her focus on the outside world that flowed past.

Flicking through his contacts, David tapped the mobile screen, choosing a name. They merged onto the A24, heading straight to London's city centre.

"Detective Thomas McField," he answered.

"Thomas, we've been attacked. Rose and I. We were—"

"Whoa, whoa," McField interrupted. "Slow down. You've been attacked?"

"Rose and I must have been followed to my house in East Horsley, or he knew where we were going to be, I don't know. A man broke in and attacked us."

"Are you hurt?"

"I'm pretty banged up, but I'm fine. Rose is fine. We're heading back to my apartment now."

"Okay, er, I'll send a car round to the house now and have it checked out. What's the address?"

David shared the address with McField. "Rose managed to stab him in the leg, so he might not have gotten far."

"If he's still there, they'll find him. I'll drive to your apartment now and meet you when you get there, make sure you're all right and get a statement."

"Okay," David said, preparing to hang up the phone. "Oh, Detective, how did tonight go? Did you and Alex go to Quentin's meeting place?"

McField hesitated. "Yeah, we, er. We went."

David narrowed his eyes. "And?"

Rose turned and looked at David.

McField didn't respond.

"What happened at the meeting?" David asked again, slowing down the car. "Who was there?"

"Eva. We saw Eva Shields meet with Quentin at the address."

David's hands trembled against the steering wheel. His eyes widened and his breathing quickened. He stepped off the car's accelerator and onto the brake pedal, turning into a layby and came to a halt. He felt the beating of his heart, each thump knocking against his heavy chest.

"David?" McField asked. "Are you still there?"

Silence.

"David?" McField snapped with a noticeable frustrated tone.

"I'm here," he finally said.

"How could that be?" Rose asked.

"Alex is with me," McField said. "And although he's also surprised, he says that he isn't overly shocked."

Rose shook her head. "Who's Alex?"

"A journalist."

"Eva?" David asked. "Eva Shields?"

"David, meet me at your apartment. I want to make sure you're both all right and I need a statement after your attack. We can go over the repercussions of what Eva's involvement means."

More silence.

"Is that okay?" McField asked.

"Her arriving at a building doesn't mean anything," David said. "It could easily be a misunderstanding. You can't draw such rapid conclusions based off one tiny detail."

"Alex seems pretty certain. Listen, are you okay meeting us at your apartment, as soon as you can? We can go over it all."

"Yeah," David said.

"I'll be there in thirty minutes. I'll wait outside if you're any longer."

David and Rose heard the phone click off. Allowing the car to fill with silence, their multitude of questions hanging in the air.

*

227

Parking in David's allocated bay beside his apartment building, the pair silently walked around the corner of the building towards its entrance. With the waiting police car sat close to the doorway, the patient policemen perked up as they spotted David approaching.

David glanced at them from afar as he and Rose stepped up to the entrance of the building with Detective McField and Alex Haynes there to greet them. The group took the elevator up to the 12th floor and stepped up to David's apartment door, where he ushered them inside with a motion of his hand. Still, with little words exchanged, they all instinctively agreed to sit down in the living room without a drink.

McField opened the discussion. "How are you both?"

David answered. "Shaken, but we're okay."

"Are you hurt at all?"

"Scrapes, bruises, and a banged head, but I'm alive."

Rose held her head downward.

"Can you tell me exactly what happened?" McField asked.

David began to relay the story of their night. Rose added minor details to David's story, describing how she hid behind the sofa as David and the intruder raced through the house and fought in the kitchen.

McField nodded. "So he seemed professional? Like he knew what he was doing?"

"He was definitely dressed like a professional," David said. "He seemed to know what he was doing as he crept up on us very bloody well, and he was armed. I don't know how we managed to fight him off."

"Well a heel in the ankle sounds extremely painful," Alex said.

"Yes, you did well to prevent his advances. Both of you," McField said.

"So, tell me before I drop with anticipation," David said. "Eva Shields?"

Alex, seemingly clearing his mouth of a bad taste, nodded several times before pushing his glasses closer to his eyes. "The detective and I both saw Eva this evening entering the building that you gave us the address to earlier today. She arrived just minutes after Quentin and his men did, and I have photographs of this," he said, leaving a brief moment for anyone to request to see the pictures.

Nobody did.

"After seeing her," Alex continued, "it just confirmed everything that my research had been leading to. It was the final nail in the coffin, so to speak."

"What are you talking about?" David asked.

Both McField and Rose joined David in looking towards Alex.

Alex gulped as subtly as he could. "I didn't quite tell you everything when we first met, David. I've had my suspicions for some time, but since yourself and Miss Shields seemed to develop some sort of relationship, I thought I would hold off on my theory."

Rose briefly glanced at David.

David noticed and looked back at Rose, his eyebrows raised. He focused back on Alex. "What do you mean? She catapulted Down Dream into the limelight and made it an overnight success. She raised a quarter of a million for us on the first evening. Since then, we've become friends, yeah, but why would all of that happen if she were in on what Quentin's doing? Why would she go to the trouble?"

"Maybe it was her intention to get you into the limelight. To get Down Dream popular. It's clear Eva's struggled with her reputation over the past couple of years. Controversies have followed her very publicly. Having her name closely linked to the launch of a new charity goes some way to combatting that. And, when you think of the financial element to all of this, if Down Dream becomes popular, you get a lot of donations, right? And if a charity is in the limelight, how long does it take to get further funding from the government?" He paused. "David, to criminals, you're a cash cow."

"It all still doesn't add up. Why would she work with Quentin on all of this? She's an international businesswoman. What ties them together?"

Alex sighed. "I'm not one hundred per cent certain on that just yet, but I have my theory which I would like to keep to myself for now, if you don't mind."

McField gave Alex a glare.

"I have my report and scoop, and all of that to think about," Alex said. "Anyway, there's still a few avenues I have to dig down before I can confirm anything."

"This is bullshit," David said. "All of it." He stood up and paced the living room.

"David, please keep calm," McField said. "We need to keep a level head on all of this. We can't let them get to you."

"Without actual evidence to her links with Quentin, I'm struggling to believe this," David said, still pacing.

"Aren't witnesses of her meeting Quentin enough? Pictures of her arrival, in fact?" Alex asked.

David shook his head. "No."

Alex stood up and held out his open palms. "David, listen. I know you're incredibly stressed about everything, but I promise you, we are getting to the bottom of this. But if we're going to do that, you have to trust both myself and the Detective."

David couldn't think of anything to say.

"David," Alex continued, "that car that was following you last week, do you remember? Last Saturday night. You sent me the license plate and asked if I could look into it?"

David stood still, recalling the night he met Eva for dinner. He nodded.

"That car is registered to an unknown entity that I've not been able to trace, but it's been photographed in many articles and associated as being used by the Shields Corporation."

"I was on my way to meet with Eva at a restaurant that night, so why would she send a car to follow me? It doesn't make sense."

"To make sure you weren't meeting up with anybody on your way? Journalists, police? David, I'm more than certain that the car belongs to Eva, and it was her that has been following you. How many other times has she had someone follow you without you noticing? Was the man who attacked you this evening sent by Quentin, or by Eva?"

CHAPTER 30

As light slowly intruded into her senses, Rose forcefully opened her eyes and looked around the unfamiliar bedroom. She pulled the top half of her body up out of the sheets and sat upright, looking to the undisturbed other side of the bed. The clinking of glasses could be heard from the apartment's kitchen.

"David?" Rose asked openly, holding her breath for an answer.

"Yeah?" he replied from the other room with a muffled voice, as if in the middle of eating something.

Rose exhaled, throwing herself back down onto the bed. As her head hit the pillow, she stared up to the ceiling and let the moment consume her. She rolled onto her side and clocked her bag leaning against the bedside table. She pulled up her hand and took a long look at the wedding ring on her finger. Its white gold band still as shiny as the day she was gifted it. The ring had numerous white diamonds paved into the metal, all leading to a large oval diamond which glimmered with every fraction of light. To Rose, the ring symbolised nothing more than a ball and chain. The smallest of shackles ever forged, it bound not her wrists but her entire future. She slid it off with a gentle tug and dropped it into her bag.

"Are you decent?" David asked from behind the door, open by a crack.

Rose glanced down at the sheets covering her. She nudged herself up the bed's headrest, pulling them close. "Yep."

David bumped the door open and slid through the gap. "Coffee and crumpets?"

With a smile, she watched him stand there, waiting for her response, with a cup in one hand and a plate with two buttered crumpets in the other. "You are too kind."

"I thought that despite everything that's going on right now," David started, "we could take twenty minutes just now, at the start of the day, to forget it all and pretend we're just like everybody else out there." He sat down on the bed next to her.

"Oh, your head looks really bruised," she said, looking at the black and blue splodge at the top of his temple, a clean cut at its centre.

"That's not forgetting it all," David said.

She shook her head, accepting the plate of crumpets. "Thank you. I've not had these in years."

"Do you not want the coffee?"

"I don't like coffee."

"What?" he said. "You don't like this black bitter liquid? How could you?"

Rose laughed. "Thanks for the bed. How was the sofa? I feel bad."

"Don't worry about it, the sofa's surprisingly comfy."

Rose took a small bite out of the crumpet. "I keep thinking, we don't even know who that man from last night worked for. If it's Quentin, which I'm confident it will be, then he's going to tell him that I was there with you, at your home. Quentin's going to know."

"That's what I was saying last night. You did right by stopping here. It's too dangerous for you to go back to Quentin now."

"But if I don't go back to him, he'll come looking for me. He's not the type to let someone depart quietly. Especially his wife. I mean nothing to him but sex and to be a trophy that he can show off on his arm, but he'd hunt me just out of principle."

"I'm sorry," David said, casting his eyes down. "But you can't go back to him. Not now."

Rose took several nibbles of the crumpet whilst David drank the unwanted coffee.

"Oh," David started, "I've had a text from Kristian. He's heard from Bev's daughter. Bev's still unconscious, but the doctors are positive about her progress. Things are looking promising."

"That's great news."

David nodded before the room fell silent. He let out a sigh. "So much has happened. I've let the charity get out of my sight for too long. I need to concentrate on it; make sure my neglect isn't affecting its operations." His mobile phone rang from the living room. Putting his coffee down on the bedside table next to Rose, David left the bedroom to find it. He found it tucked down the side of the sofa and checked the caller ID. He answered, said, "Morning, Detective."

Rose climbed out of bed and started to dress herself.

"Yes, she is. We're fine. I'm not sure on her plans just yet, but I know I need to get back to work. Down Dream hasn't been my priority over the past few days, so I need to check in and make sure everything's going smoothly," David said.

Rose slid on her socks and brushed some fluff off her trousers.

"Yeah, I think that was the man's way in and out. How long will they need access to the house for?"

Rose pulled up her trousers and threw on her blouse.

David paced the living room. "Okay, just that I need to get someone over there to board up the broken window."

Rose approached the bedroom door.

"Thank you, Detective," David said, watching as Rose joined him in the living room. He sat down on the sofa.

Rose perched next to David with a concerned expression; now sat close enough to overhear the full conversation.

"I can't just ignore Eva. What if she calls? Or wants to meet?" David said.

"Yes, you can just ignore her, David. And you're going to have to. It's far too dangerous to play with fire like that. You can't let them play with your mind," McField said. "Working out who the man was from last night will also help, so give me some time to crack on with this and we'll settle it as soon as possible."

"Is it safe for us to go out like normal people?" David asked, looking to Rose.

"Until we know Quentin's next moves, we can't assume anything. Don't answer any calls from him and avoid busy places where you're likely to be spotted. It's all we can do for now."

David slowly nodded. "Fine. Thank you for the update."

"Do you and Rose have somewhere you could go for the time being? Somewhere you'd consider safe?"

"Well I thought my home in East Horsley was safe." He quietly gasped, his eyes widening. "Oh, we can go to my house by the lake, in Wanstead."

"Okay?" McField said.

"Quentin threatened Kristian days ago, and he told him to give me a message about having to cooperate with him, and that I couldn't hide. Not in my *London apartment or my East Horsley home*. Quentin doesn't know about my Wanstead house by the lake, he didn't mention it. I go there when I need to get out of the city. He has no idea it exists, so we can stay there, completely out of his way."

"Brilliant, that's settled then. Listen, David, before I go." He cleared his throat. "I didn't want to mention this in front of her last night, but, are you being wise getting close to Rose? What's that all about?"

David looked straight at her. Her eyes let him know she heard. "She needs our help. We need to arrange for her to safely leave Quentin where she's being forced to live. I don't want to go into detail now, it's not my place, but we have to help her. I have to help her."

"Right, it's your judgement on the Rose situation, but once we've sorted Quentin I'll definitely speak to her and get her side of the story. I'll also speak to my superintendent about getting something done now in the short term."

David nodded, his eyes out of sight from Rose's. "Okay, thanks."

"I'll speak to you soon. Just look after yourselves and call me if you need anything."

David clicked off his phone. "They didn't find anything at my house apart from the guy's blood on the floor. They've taken samples and they're gonna see if they can find a match."

"So the guy is still out there then."

"Yeah," he said, giving out a deep sigh. "Look, nothing going on is safe right now. I know they're targeting me because I have money, Down Dream has money, but you're associated with me now. You can't go back to Quentin."

"Then what can I do? I can't just sit around here all day, hoping they don't come knocking."

"No, we'll go to my house in Wanstead."

"I have no clothes, no nothing. It's all at his place."

"You don't need any of it. All of it can be replaced. Your life can't. We just need to lie low until Quentin's sorted out."

Staring into his eyes, Rose processed David's suggestion. Reluctantly, she nodded, said, "Okay."

David took hold of her hands. "Thank you. You're gonna be safe. If you can go there this morning, I'll join you later."

Rose flinched at the soft touch of David's hands. Her eyes flicked at them, before returning to meet his gaze. "Why? What are you doing?"

"I need to make sure everything with Down Dream is going well. I can't just abandon it. As soon as I've checked in, I'll speak to Kristian and maybe visit Bev before I drive to join you."

"But that's far too—"

"It has to be done," David said, letting go of her hands. He walked into the kitchen, picked up a set of keys, and slid a single silver key off the keyring, offering it to Rose. "The Wanstead house key. Forty-seven Northumberland Avenue. Can you remember that?"

"Forty-seven Northumberland Avenue," she repeated.

"I'll be a matter of hours."

Rose hesitatingly accepted the key, placing it into her pocket.

David looked around the room. "Ah, just thought. Eva's invited me to the Shields Corporation's ten-year anniversary party tonight. I'll certainly be skipping that now. I'll come straight to Wanstead and meet you after visiting Bev at the hospital."

The door to the beautifully decorated room opened and a middle-aged man with a sharp beard stepped in. "He's arrived," he said before stepping aside for a second man to enter the room.

Wearing a dirty and tight, black padded vest with scuffed black pants, the man in his late thirties stepped into the room with a limp.

Sat comfortably on the velvet sofa with a cup of tea in his right hand, Quentin glanced downwards to the man's trousers and noted the dried blood covering the lower third of one leg. He narrowed his eyes at him and allowed the silence to create his desired atmosphere.

Harold stood motionless at the side of Quentin, his eyes also focused on the man's leg.

Quentin finally spoke. "Well, your news isn't what I wanted."

The wounded man, struggling to stay stood in the same spot, said, "Sir, I—"

"Ah, ah, ah," Quentin hushed, raising a finger to his lips.

The man gulped, glancing at Harold and then back at Quentin.

"You successfully follow him to his lovely, family home in that shithole of a town, and yet you somehow fail to carry out what was asked of you?" Quentin sipped his tea. "How can you possibly explain that?" He tilted his head dramatically. "You had the element of surprise and the experience of combat, yet you couldn't take out a pansy, little psychiatrist? Ha!"

Harold held his stare on the man.

"Well?" Quentin snapped.

"I wasn't expecting him to fight back as well as he did."

"You *weren't expecting him to fight back as well as he did?*" Quentin mimicked. "Pathetic." He leant forward to place his cup of tea onto the table that separated him and the man. "I don't think you tried as hard as you could have. You were armed, weren't you? So how could a dweeb of a man who attends to the scum of society fight you off? Please do enlighten me before I reach the end of my tether."

The man glanced once more to and from Harold.

"Speak!" Quentin shouted.

The man shook. "He wasn't alone," he said, forcing a swallow as to take a deep breath.

"And whom was he with?" Quentin asked in another sarcastic mimicking.

"Rose," he managed with bated breath. "David was with Rose."

Quentin's curiosity instantly drained from his face as his cheeks deflated and his eyes steeled. "Rose?"

The man stood silently, but the confidence behind his answer rung out unmistakeably.

Quentin analysed his expression and body language, attempting to identify any signal of a lie. "*My* Rose?"

The man hesitated, his eyes looking at the several men staring back at him. He nodded.

"My Rose was with the dickhead psychiatrist at his home? Did she not come home last night when I was with Eva?"

"They were drinking together and talking about David's life," the man said, fulfilled by a renewed sense of courage. "They came across as quite close."

Quentin shifted in his seat. "She wouldn't do that."

"It was Rose that stabbed me in my leg with her shoe. She was defending him."

Quentin looked up at the man. A wave of heat flushed into his cheeks as his anger erupted. He furiously launched himself onto his feet and pulled a gun from inside his jacket. The pistol pointed towards the man's chest not two metres from him.

The wounded man instantly took a step back with an open jaw. "Please!"

With a twitch of his eyebrow, Quentin roared at the top of his lungs, twice squeezing the trigger.

CHAPTER 31

Rose reached the ground floor and stepped out of the building and into a gust of wind that blew her hair out of its arrangement. As she walked towards the waiting taxi, she glanced towards the stationary police vehicle at the side of the building, brushing her hair out of her face. "Tintoretto?" she asked the driver after opening the rear passenger side door.

"Something like that," replied the slightly overweight driver with a noticeable receding hairline.

She pulled the door open further, stepped in and sat down, closing the door behind her.

"Where to again?"

"Northumberland Avenue, Wanstead, please."

"Rightyio," the driver said as he pulled out onto the road.

Rose looked up towards David's apartment, unable to rid herself of the doubts that tumbled through her mind.

David stood with his temple pressed against the window as he tried to achieve the best angle of watching Rose leave the building. With his breath creating a sizeable patch of condensation against the glass, his eyes focused on her tiny legs that darted across the pavement and towards the waiting taxi. Her brown hair swayed in the wind, wafting strands across her face. As the taxi pulled away, he found himself wondering why he was watching her drive down the road.

Taking a moment to contemplate these thoughts, David stared at the turn of the road where her taxi had just disappeared. He pulled himself away, turning to face his empty living room. He picked up his mobile and decided to check his emails before contacting Kristian. As he flicked through the list, scrolling through the never-ending pile of messages sent to Down Dream, he wondered where he would find the time to get up to speed with the charity and how Stu and Bev's absence would impact their work.

David stopped flicking through the emails as he caught a glimpse of several messages from national news stations and journalists. One after the other, he speed-read their propositions for interviews and TV appearances to discuss the recent events surrounding Down Dream and the attacks on both Stu and Bev. As he almost reached the end of one email, requesting written answers to pre-written questions for a national newspaper, he noticed a segment of it dedicated to the charity's current popularity with the general public.

David closed his emails and brought up Google, typing in *Down Dream* and clicking on the search button. His eyebrows jumped as he sifted through the numerous articles detailing the charity's boost in popularity and the acclaimed status it had garnered through its resistance to violence and extortion. Blogs and user comments debated the charity and David himself, detailing their thoughts and sympathies. Reading on, he found himself shaking his head.

TROUBLED CHARITY DOWN DREAM SURGES TO THE TOP WITH PUBLIC SUPPORT

Published: 07:29 GMT, 15 February 2026

Charity newcomer, Down Dream, has lately been the target of unexplainable attacks since its launch earlier this month. The non-profit organisation, founded by entrepreneur and psychiatrist David Dale, has so far aimed at tackling city homelessness in central London but has suffered two separate attacks, with its offices broken into and vandalised whilst founding member Stu Jackson has been murdered and Bev Walcott, also a founding member, has been left in a critical condition.

Despite these criminal violations, and the on-going investigation into the perpetrators behind them, the public support for Down Dream has surged. A recent poll ranked the charity as the most talked about non-profit organisation in the UK. An impressive 28% of those asked have donated to Down Dream.

Luke Elliot, a spokesperson from the Charity Commission, has said, "Down Dream has done exceptionally well to gain so much popularity in such a short space of time. I can imagine that the recent events surrounding the charity have been exceptionally difficult, but the support from the public is staggering. Mr Dale really has mastered the skill in getting the public on board with his agenda for issues he feels passionately about. Despite these criminals that are seemingly targeting Down Dream, I really feel they'll go from strength to strength."

David Dale and the fourth founding member of Down Dream, Swedish-born Kristian Sinason, have not yet released a statement regarding the death of Mr Jackson or the recovery of Miss Walcott.

Clicking off his phone, David brought himself back into his living room, attempting to drone out the journalist's voice in his head. He looked around the room for answers before he brought his phone back to life with another touch, flicking through his contacts to Kristian's name and dialling the number.

Four rings later, Kristian answered. "Hi, David."

"Hey Kristian, I'm only just catching up on everything, and apparently, we've gained a ton of support. Have you seen the articles about us?"

"Yeah, it's been insane. Over the last two or three days, the support has been pouring in. We're only small, but we have people queuing to volunteer and the phones at the office have been non-stop. I've had to divert helpers from our shelter to manage the calls."

"Insane," David said, taken aback by the thought.

"If you've got the time free, head over to the offices and get stuck in, we need all the manpower we can get. And," Kristian paused, "it'll be nice to have you back around. It's not been pleasant with everyone missing."

"I know, I know. We can just hope that Bev makes a speedy recovery. I miss having her around. I'll head over to the offices now and catch up on everything."

"I'll be there, too, shortly. I'll see you there."

Hanging up the phone, David rushed to put on his shoes and a jacket and then left the apartment.

The Saturday traffic was appallingly slow, gridlocked up and down the city. It took twenty-five minutes for David to drive half a mile, costing him even more time to finally reach the offices that are only two miles away as the crow flies. As he finally reached his destination, he parked up and approached the building's entrance, passing the tightened security that instantly recognised him and permitted access. He took the elevator up to the third floor and then punched in the door's code, stepping into the office.

David inhaled sharply as he witnessed the office buzzing with activity, with at least ten volunteers answering phone calls, tapping away on keyboards, and clicking through their computer screens. With his presence making its way through the office's residents, the volunteers all peered up from behind their monitors and desks to look at the philanthropist who had an ever-growing celebrity profile.

Cracking a small, shy smile, David nodded towards the group and thought only of Bev and Stu.

From his desk on the other side of the room, McField watched as Detective Superintendent Christopher Forrest re-entered his office, closing the door behind him. He looked back to the open brown file that sat on his desk, filled with the CCTV images taken from the night of Down Dream's office break-in and of the homeless shelter attack. None of the images had provided any tangible leads with all of the suspects having hidden faces and zero unique attributes. The only other contents of the folder was a written report on the generic findings of the purported S and F Insurance that contacted Bev on the night of the office break-in, a statement from Kristian after a man broke into his apartment, a statement from the volunteer who found Stu and Bev at the shelter, and a statement from David after the attack at his East Horsley home. As McField looked down at all of the supposed evidence he had on the David Dale and Down Dream case, McField let out a hefty sigh. He pushed back his chair, stood up, and walked up to the superintendent's door, knocking twice before entering.

Christopher was stood behind his desk, his body facing the window, and with his mobile phone pushed against his ear. He looked over his shoulder at McField and raised his index finger. "Yeah, I can't talk now, but it's getting done. I'll call you back," he said. "All right, thanks for calling." He clicked off his phone and slotted it into his pocket, turning to face McField. "Can I help?"

McField closed the door behind him. "Sorry for walking in like this, I hope I wasn't interrupting."

The superintendent sat down at his desk and shook his mouse to bring his PC back to life. "It's fine. What is it you want?"

McField stepped forward. "It's, erm. It's about the Down Dream case, and about Quentin."

Christopher's eyes narrowed in on McField. "I told you to drop the case and move on to something else. It's being dealt with."

"I know what you said, Sir, but someone's died now. The stakes have changed. David was attacked last night, and things aren't adding up. I need to keep working on it a bit longer."

"I told you, no. It'll breach what the NCA are working on, and you know how they get when we fuck things up for them. Trust me, McField, you have to back off on this one. Now."

McField interlocked his fingers, pressing them together. "Well I need to speak to you about Quentin's wife then."

"What about her?"

"She's alleging she's being forced to live with Quentin and needs help escaping his abuse. What options can I give her?"

Christopher threw his head back and laughed. "McField, that is a domestic issue for the couple to sort out. I'm insulted you've even asked."

"But she's being held against her will," McField said, the lines on his forehead unmistakeable.

"If that's true, the NCA will have it sorted when they decide the time is right. I don't want to hear any more about it."

McField restrained himself from shaking his head, stood up, and said, "Thanks for your time." He left the office, tugging the door closed behind him, and walked back to his desk and threw himself into his chair, kicking the bin underneath. His mobile phone that rested next to the brown folder vibrated. He checked the caller ID and picked up. "McField."

"Thomas, it's Alex Haynes," he said. "I need you to look into somebody for me."

"I haven't got time for this."

"It's related to Quentin and Down Dream."

"And?"

"And I'm convinced this person is somehow connected to Quentin and everything he does, but I'm not yet sure how. If you could run his name for me, it might give me a lead."

McField reached for a pen and his notepad. "Fire away."

"The name is Christopher Forrest."

McField loosened his grip on the pen and froze.

"Did you get that?" Alex asked. "Do you want me to spell it?"

McField placed the pen back onto his desk and attempted to shake off the stunned expression that plastered his face. "No, no. I got it."

"What's wrong? Do you know him?"

McField looked back over at the office across the room. In a lowered tone, he said, "Christopher Forrest is my superior. He's Detective Superintendent."

As the taxi approached the outskirts of London, Rose appreciated the change of scenery as her eyes adjusted from the concrete towers to the low-lying houses.

She managed to shift David off her mind but had replaced him with the telephone conversation he just had with Detective Thomas McField of which she managed to overhear some of. Unsure as to why, something kept niggling at the back of her mind, unsettling her. She repeated as much of the conversation as she could remember but soon turned her attention to two key statements the detective had said.

"Working out who the man was will help," she whispered to herself in the back of the taxi.

The driver glanced in Rose's direction through the rear-view mirror.

"What are Quentin's next moves? Can't assume anything."

The taxi driver slowly pulled the vehicle to a stop on Northumberland Avenue. "We're here."

Rose looked out of the window, taking in the sight of the unfamiliar, secluded property covered by overhanging trees in the corner of the street. She pictured David coming here, to his reclusive hideaway, to get away from it all. To be by himself. At peace.

But Quentin came roaring back into her mind. The resources and power available to him; able to find people and do what he wants with them. For a dark moment, the thought of David succumbing to Quentin's men took hold.

"He took a chance on me," she whispered again to herself. "He's protected me."

"Er, hello," the driver said.

Rose changed her focus back to the driver. "Take me back to the city centre."

"What? We've just arrived where you wanted to go."

"I've changed my mind. I need to go to Walton Street in Knightsbridge. I will pay you in full for both journeys. Please!"

CHAPTER 32

By the time the taxi arrived at its second destination, the clouds had gathered above, unleashing relentless thrashes of rain onto the city. From the back of the car, Rose took several deep breaths as she looked up at the property that was her gilded cage. Never before had she thought she would be given a real opportunity to never see Quentin again; to run away to some hideaway home in Wanstead. But then never before had she thought she would risk that opportunity for the sake of another person.

Rose dug into a hidden compartment of her purse, taking out several £50 notes. She paid the driver his substantial fee and stepped out of the taxi, slamming the door shut behind her. She hurriedly opened the property's black metal gate and jogged up the few steps that led to the front door until she stood next to the adjacent Greek-styled beams that held up the sheltered open porch. Without the need to knock, the large oak door unlocked with a loud click and swung open.

A suited man stood behind it. "Welcome home," he said without a smile.

Rose walked into the grand hallway. Its high-reaching ceiling was adorned with an ornate golden rose which always made an impression on her no matter how many times she stepped underneath it. In one corner of the hallway lay a wide mahogany staircase with a freshly polished, shiny handrail. In the other corner lay an open door leading to the rear of the property that was dominated by a huge, open-plan kitchen, private dining room, reception room, and a conservatory. Either side of Rose lay more doors; to her right, the first and most formal reception room, and to her left a small library which was Rose's favourite room of the house.

After closing the door behind her, the man held out a hand. Rose gave a smile, removed her jacket, and handed it, along with her bag, to him. "Thank you," she said, before she watched him carry them away.

"Ah, you're finally home," Quentin said.

Rose jolted at the sound of his voice. Looking up to the staircase, she watched as he descended in an open white shirt, his eyes transfixed without a single blink. Rose contrived a bright smile. "Darling, I'm so sorry if you've been waiting for me, that wasn't my intention," she said, skipping up to Quentin as he reached the ground floor. As she leant forward to kiss him, Quentin grabbed hold of her arms. Before she had time to react, he landed an open-mouthed kiss on her.

Quentin pulled away. "I *have* been waiting for you," he said, releasing his grip on her arms. "Where did you get to? You didn't come home."

For a moment, Rose had nothing to say and so found herself simply staring into his eyes. "Gosh, after I did all of my shopping yesterday afternoon, I got a phone call from The Dorchester Hotel. Do you remember, darling, how on our last stay with them, they promised me a free evening at their spa because of the mix-up with the bookings?"

Quentin narrowed his eyes, but then slowly began to nod. "That was a while back."

"Well, they said that my offer was going to expire and that I had to use it that evening, so I ended up going straight there." She paused, unable to resist the urge to gulp. "The staff were just as lovely."

Quentin's eyes were still narrowed, looking her face up and down.

Rose held her breath, unsure how else to hide her racing heart.

"That's the second night this week you've not come home."

"I'm sorry."

"Ah, ah," he said, waving his hand in the air. "And why is it you didn't contact me last night? Give me a quick call to tell me you were at The Dorchester?"

"I tried to reach you, so you could maybe join me, but for some reason my phone kept crashing. For some reason it turns itself off and then freezes on the start-up screen. It might need looked at."

"Right," he said. He turned around and walked through the door in the corner of the hallway.

"Please. I'm sorry, you know I am," she said, following him through the hallway and into the reception room at the rear of the property.

"You know what happens when you have to say sorry to me," Quentin said as he walked past the red velvet sofa and stood next to the long wooden box that sat against the silver tray and decanter of brandy. "Close the door behind you."

Rose stood in the doorway, looking at Quentin standing next to the box. Her eyes glazed and her chest heavy, she tried to swallow the lump in her throat. Slowly, she reached for the double doors and pulled them closed.

Quentin rested his hand on the box.

Rose watched his every move. "Please, it was an honest mistake. I should have done more to tell you, I'm sorry."

His fingers slid across the box's surface. He tilted his head before brushing his fingers away from the box. "This one time then," he said with a smirk. He stepped around to the sofa and opened his arms. "Come here."

Rose couldn't mask her relief as she looked to the floor, concentrating on her breathing. She placed a hand on her chest and tried to smile, then stepped up to him.

"You'll have to make it up to me," he said, taking hold of her and pulling her close.

Rose managed a single, fabricated laugh as his arms wrapped around her body. "How was your evening?"

Quentin brushed his tongue across his upper teeth, parting his lips in the process. "Semi-eventful. Bit of business here and there, but you're not interested in that."

"Oh? Have you got much coming up?"

Quentin smirked.

Rose waited.

"Well, if you insist," Quentin said before pushing her down onto the sofa, vigorously kissing her.

Rose panicked, her eyes wide and her hands clutching at the sofa and his shirt. Quentin overtook her whole body as he began to grab and pull at her clothes and her breasts.

"Wa– Wait," she managed.

He brought himself to a rare pause, looking down at her with a frown. "What?"

"We, er, we should have a drink first. Would you like a brandy?" Rose asked, squeezing out from under Quentin and stumbling to her feet. "Take it slow with a brandy first, and then fun." She adjusted her skirt and walked over to the silver tray at the side of the room, her eyes unable to avoid the long wooden box. She picked up the decanter of brandy with a shaking hand and poured some into a glass, clearing her throat. She took hold of her wrist, trying to stabilise its movement as she realised how unsettled she had become.

From behind Rose's line of sight, Quentin stood up from the sofa, straightened his shirt, and smoothed-over his hair with his palm. "Where are all of your clothes?"

Rose's heart dropped as she clung onto the air in her lungs, temporarily feeling as if she couldn't breathe. She quickly glanced over her shoulder and said in a near-quaking voice, "Pardon?"

Quentin repeated himself, emphasising each word elaborately. "If you went shopping yesterday, where are all the clothes you bought?"

She took hold of the glass of brandy and turned around, now facing him. "Oh, you're right," she said, steadying her hand. "I must have left them at The Dorchester. I can be so clumsy," she said, slowly stepping towards him. "I'll give them a call and ask if they have my bags." She offered him the drink.

"You're shaking."

Rose couldn't help but wrinkle her forehead as she plastered a brave, fictitious smile on her face.

Quentin took hold of the glass but wrapped his tight grip around her fingers in the process.

Tempted to look down at her hand that was now pinned to the glass, Rose kept her focus on his eyes.

Without moving the rest of his body, Quentin gradually leant his face closer to hers until his mouth was inches away from her ear. "I rescued you from a life of slavery and abuse," he whispered. "And you now lie to my face about purposefully staying in a hotel without me? I could smell him on you the moment you stepped back into my house." He moved his body around hers, bringing her arm up around her head until he was pressing his chest against her back, his face now looking in the same direction as hers and his mouth now centimetres from her ear. "At least put your wedding ring back on if you're going to try and pull that shit with me."

The gasp that escaped her lips was audible, her hand physically shaking.

With one hand still holding the glass of brandy and pinning her fingers along with it, Quentin clicked his fingers using his free hand.

The pair faced the doorway that they had entered from and Rose watched Harold enter the room, carrying a large object in a transparent plastic bag over his shoulder.

"I know where you really were last night," Quentin whispered.

Harold threw down the object in front of their feet.

Looking down at it, it took Rose a few seconds to realise what it was. The details were blurry at first, until she was able to make out one small feature, before another, and another. Then the realisation hit her. She was making eye contact with a dead man, his eyes still open, looking up at her like a suffocated fish. She immediately closed her eyes and screamed.

Quentin moved his free hand up to Rose's chin, grabbing it and holding it in place so that she couldn't look away. "My employee here wasn't very lucky last night. He wasn't able to give our mutual friend the message he was supposed to get."

Rose kept her eyes closed, feeling the wet trickle of tears on her face.

"Before I shot him, he told me a little something, and rumour has it, dearest Rose, that you and David are rather fucking friendly. To add insult to injury, you even helped defend David, didn't you, eh?" He shook her face. "A little heel to the leg, does that sound familiar?"

Rose attempted to resist Quentin, pulling away with as much strength as she could muster.

Quentin immediately tightened his grip, digging his fingers into her mouth and hand. "Ah, ah" he started, "wouldn't want to spill my drink, would we? Because that really would send me over the fucking edge."

Her body uncontrollably trembled, her spare hand grabbing on to his shirt.

Quentin exchanged a glance with Harold who then lifted the dead body up over his shoulder and left the room, closing the door behind him.

"Please," Rose muffled with her squashed mouth, Quentin's hand restricting her actions.

"Don't give me that," he urged as he viciously threw her as hard as he could with his empty hand.

Rose struck the ground hard, sliding on the herringbone floor. With her legs and hands grazed, she lay there, thinking what was to become of her. What was to become of David. She turned her body and looked up at Quentin.

Quentin walked back over to the silver tray where he downed his remaining drink. He put the empty glass onto the tray and then placed both of his hands onto the long wooden box, sliding off its lid. "I normally quite like you choosing your poison at this point, but for such a day like today, I'm going to have to make the executive decision," he said with a smirk. He flexed his fingers and placed one hand in the box.

Rose couldn't find the energy to bring herself to her feet. The thought of doing so wasn't even there. The one thing that was now consuming Rose was the sight of Quentin rummaging in the wooden box, and the thought of the coming pain.

Quentin lifted his hand out of the box, brandishing a thin metal object that reflected a sparkling shine. As he stepped closer towards Rose, the pointed object became clearer to see. A small wheel was attached to a metal hilt, with needle-like sharp blades sticking out that rotated as he walked.

"Please," she begged, shaking her head with streams of tears covering her face.

Quentin stepped closer to Rose with a spring in his step, aggressively swiping the device down upon her.

CHAPTER 33

"Thank you so much," David said down the phone, sat behind his desk in the charity's bustling office; his door closed to block out the constant ringing of phones and chatter of volunteers. "We honestly can't wait. We'll see you there." He nodded, listening to the voice on the other line. "Goodbye," he said, hanging up.

Kristian opened the door and poked his head inside. "Hey, how'd it go?"

"Come in, come in," David said, gesturing into his office. "After everything that's going on, they've moved our presentation slot to midday, which is when *everyone* will be there."

Kristian closed the office door behind him and sat down, nodding eagerly.

"They think we're going to be inundated with questions, so thought it best we had the prime slot."

"Brilliant," Kristian beamed. The twinkle in his eye didn't last long. "God, I can't help but keep thinking of Stu and Bev. They're missing out on all of this."

"I know," David said, placing an elbow onto the arm of his chair and resting his face in his palm. "When she wakes up, Bev will be proud."

Kristian smiled without parting his lips.

"I'm going to go and see her in a minute," David started, "after I finish up here. I haven't met Olivia yet."

"She's really nice. Obviously sick with worry, but she's lovely."

"Being Bev's daughter, that's kind of a given."

Kristian laughed.

Two sharp knocks landed on the office door before swinging open for a second time. A young volunteer, whom David had barely had the chance to speak with, squeezed her face into the tiny gap that she had dared to create. "Erm," she began timidly, "there's a phone call for you, Mr Dale. It's your sister."

"Oh, great."

"I've parked her on line two."

"Thank you very much."

The girl shyly retreated back behind the door, closing it with a click.

"Sorry, one minute, Kristian," David said as he leaned to pick up the phone, tapping on a flashing button to connect the call. "Hello you."

"David, what the hell is happening?" Sam asked. "I've been completely in my own little bubble for that past few days and I haven't had the time or chance to look at the news, but Stu's been killed, and Bev's in hospital?"

"Sam, calm down, calm down. Our homeless shelter was broken into two days ago and, yeah. They were attacked." He looked at Kristian with a dented cheek.

Kristian returned a knowing look before he stood up and left the office.

Sam gasped as if it she had just found out the news for the first time.

"I wasn't there, so I wasn't involved," David said.

"Oh my god. David, what's actually going on? Who's doing this? Why?"

"The police are looking into it, but we know they're after money."

"Haven't the police caught anyone? It's been days."

"No, they haven't yet, but they're spreading their net wide. The detective who's heading the investigation is really down to earth, so I have faith in him."

"Jesus, David. They've killed someone and an elderly woman is fighting for her life, and you're telling me you have *faith*?"

David closed his eyes. "Look, Sam, I really don't need this right now. I've got a whole heap of stuff on my plate with Down Dream and everything. Can you please just be supportive instead of being on my case?"

"I am supportive, but sorry I don't sound so cheery after finding out second-hand from my colleagues that my brother's charity has been targeted by criminals."

"I've been a shitty brother, I'm sorry." He opened his eyes and looked around the office. "I've been carried away with Down Dream and wanting to really make something of it that I've stopped communicating with you, and that's not right. I'm sorry."

"That's not quite true, you came down and had lunch last week."

"But how often do I make an effort out of the blue? Even after I lost Maria and the girls, I put distance between us. I isolated myself and I shouldn't have."

"Don't talk like that, David. You reacted in the best way you could. There's no normal way to deal with things like that, so don't you dare start blaming yourself."

David turned in his chair and looked out of the window at the grey clouds that hung over the city. "Yeah."

"Look, David, I'm just wanting to make sure you're okay, and that everything's going to be sorted out. You know how I worry."

David nodded, trying to find the words in the clouds. He fought back a wobbling lip.

"Richard keeps asking about you and how you're doing. I think you both hit it off last week, so we need to make some plans and have another get-together. I know Ben would love that, too. Ah, Richard's actually working in London at the minute, I almost forgot."

David wiped his dry eyes. "Oh?"

"Yeah, he got pulled down there at the start of the week and I was hoping he'd be back home by now really."

"That's no good."

"Nope. David, before I go…" She paused. "Can you please just tell me everything's going to be all right? Tell me you'll be all right?"

The corners of David's mouth turned upwards. "I'm going to be just fine, Sam. Look, I'm going to go now and visit Bev; her daughter's flown over from America so I'm going to meet her, too. After that I'm going to lie low outside of the city for a while, just to let the investigation crack on."

"That sounds like a good idea. Do you want to come and stay with us? You can keep us company until Richard gets back."

"Thanks for offering, but I'm gonna stay in Wanstead."

"Wanstead? Why there of all places?"

"Because I have a place there."

"Gosh, I didn't know that. You keep far too many things from me."

David sighed. "I'm sorry, Sam. I am."

"It's fine. Look, I just need to know you're gonna be safe wherever you go or whatever you do. I'm really worried."

"Look, my address is forty-seven Northumberland Avenue in Wanstead, that's where I'll be. You can look it up on Google, it's quiet and out of the way, I'm gonna be absolutely fine there."

"Well take care of yourself and keep me updated on everything. I'll give Richard a quick call now and let him know you're okay; he really has been as worried as me."

"That's nice of him. Take care, Sam, and thanks for the call."

"Take care. See you soon," she said, hanging up.

David rested the phone on his desk and took a moment to breathe. He closed down his PC and organised all of the documents and bits of papers in front of him into neat and tidy piles.

The door opened and Kristian stuck his head into the room once again. The noise of a thriving office behind him swept in. "Everything okay?"

"Yeah, everything's fine. It was just Sam calling to check up on me."

Kristian entered, closing the door behind him.

"Bless her. I haven't spoken to her for a few days, so she was really worried."

Kristian offered a comforting smile as he watched David gather his belongings. "I'm sorry to say, but I've just got off the phone to Olivia. You won't be able to go and visit Bev at the minute as she's being reviewed by the doctor and it's likely to last several hours."

"What do you mean, *reviewed?*"

"Olivia said the doctor's looking over her condition and seeing if she needs any further treatment or if she's best how she currently is. I don't know the details."

"All right. Well I guess I'll unpack my things again," he said, switching the PC back on. "I'll stay for a couple extra hours before heading off."

"You sure?"

"Yeah. It'll be nice to get the first leg of work for our presentation planned anyway."

Kristian stepped back toward the office door. "Let me grab my notepad, I've also been making some notes on that which might help. One second."

Five hours had passed, and the city's grey clouds had drifted north, leaving a trail of clear sky behind them. Darkness had descended with the streetlights now guiding David out of London as he made his way to Wanstead.

David and Kristian had managed to use their extra time productively, having put together an initial draft of the presentation and speech for next week's event. As they worked through their plan, their fears and worries dropped away, with only enthusiasm and passion left standing.

Kristian hadn't yet repeated what he'd told David two days ago; that he wanted out. The danger and threats would be too much for most people. Nobody could be expected to stay on. Yet, David hoped the situation would quickly improve and Kristian would change his mind. There was still time.

David parked up on the driveway to his Wanstead home. The house was tucked into a corner of the street, with another detached house on one side and a wall of trees on the other. A tree in the front garden dangled its branches over the driveway, making the house feel secluded and private. He stepped out of his car and could see a single light was on in the front room of the house with the curtains drawn. He locked his car and knocked on the front door.

No response.

David knocked again before trying the handle. The handle turned, opening the door with a metallic click. He pushed it open and stepped through. "Rose? You left the door open."

The corridor and staircase were in complete darkness, with the only source of light coming from the front living room, its door ajar.

"Rose, it's David," he said as he stepped into the room. A single lamp, perched on a side table against the window, was lit, with both sofas unoccupied. He looked around the room as if he was going to spot Rose hidden behind the sofa, or her toes sticking out from behind the curtains. Just as David turned his body to walk to the kitchen, he felt an almighty blow land against the back of his head, throwing him to the floor. He shouted in pain, quickly pressing a hand against his head as he tried to regain his composure. From the floor, David turned and looked up.

Two men stood in the doorway, wearing thick, black jackets. One of the men held a gun in his gloved hand, pointed directly at David.

"Who are you? Where's Rose?" David asked, his face wrinkled in pain.

The armed man stepped forward and hit David over the head for a second time with the handle of his weapon.

David's upper body fell against the floor in a daze. He slipped in and out of consciousness, slowly rotating his head against the floor, quietly grumbling.

"Bag him," the armed man said.

David looked up in his blurred vision, watching a figure approach him and put something over his head. He urged his body to do something; for his arms to lift up and push the man away, or his legs to kick back the intruder, but his body failed him.

"We're ready," a voice said.

David's hands were then grabbed and pulled together, as were his feet, and he was lifted into the air. His head bopped up and down, his eyes opening and closing to the same darkness. The outdoor cool air hit David as he picked up the sound of the distant vehicle engine. Only a few moments passed before the vehicle's brakes squeaked their way to a stop next to him. The men started moving again, carrying him further away from his house.

"Easy," one of the men said.

Vehicle doors opened and David was pushed down onto a hard floor, clipping his knee on something sturdy and sharp in the process. The doors closed behind him with a snap.

CHAPTER 34

The phone connected. "Detective McField."

"Hi, erm, this is Kristian Sinason. I work with David Dale in Down Dream."

"Hi Kristian, is everything all right?"

"I don't know, I don't think so. David left our office over two hours ago, said he was going to his house in Wanstead and that he'd call me when he got there, but I haven't heard from him."

"Have you tried calling him?"

"Of course, but his phone's off. No one's seen him at the hospital so he's not visited Bev either."

"Okay. Where are you now?"

"I'm still at our office."

"Stay where you are just in case he comes back. I'll arrange a car to check out his house. In the meantime, try and think of anywhere else he might have gone. If you think of anything, give me a call back."

"All right, will do. Thanks."

McField clicked off his phone and rested it against his chin. Looking around, he could only think of one person. He dialled the number.

A voice answered. "Hello?"

"Alex, it's Detective Thomas McField."

"Ah, hello. I'm not far off finalising my report now. Should have it ready for release in the morning."

"I'm not calling about that. Kristian from Down Dream has phoned and said that David's gone silent."

"Shit."

"He said that David left the office two hours ago to drive to his house in Wanstead. He's since tried to call him, but his phone's switched off, meaning I can only assume he's gone to meet Quentin or they've got him." He cleared his throat. "Listen, I don't have access to Quentin's file. Permission is being withheld from me. I need you to tell me all the listed buildings you know that Quentin, or even Eva, own. Do you know where they frequently go?"

Alex blew down the phone as he sighed. "Right, let's start with Quentin."

The back of Quentin's hand landed against Rose's bloody cheek, a deep gash from the top of her cheekbone to her lower jaw dripping with blood. The room that they occupied was dark and dingy, stripped bare with exposed wooden studs and brick walls. A handful of doorways surrounded the room, some stripped of a doorframe and others with tired oak doors. Pallets of bricks lay next to stacks of concrete blocks and bags of construction materials.

With her hands tied to an uncomfortable, poky chair, Rose cowered as she held her chin close to her chest; her eyes screwed shut in an attempt to prevent the release of her tears.

"And you really thought you'd get away with it?" Quentin shouted inches from her.

Rose's tears found a way out as she whimpered.

"After all I've given you. After all I've done for you." Quentin shook his head frantically. "I didn't think you had the guts to mock me like this."

Rose opened her eyes and, for the first time since she was at Quentin's home, looked at him.

Quentin stood still, returning the gaze.

She opened her mouth to speak, but found her voice shattered. "You've given me the life of a prisoner. You didn't save me, you just bought me for your own abuse."

Quentin leaned closer, pressing both of his hands down onto her tied arms. "I've given you a good life, haven't I? Filled with clothes, expensive jewellery. Why are you so ungrateful? Why have you rejected me?"

"I'd rather be dead than be your bitch."

Quentin's eyebrows twitched into an unmistakeable glare, his face reddening in anger. "You whore!" he shouted, landing another blow to Rose's cheek, shunning her face away from him.

One of the old side doors to the room creaked open, allowing in a blend of faint crowd chatter and music. Quentin straightened himself up and looked over.

Two men carried a hooded man into the room, a brown bag covering his head.

Quentin laughed. "Ah, he has finally joined us."

Having been pushed down onto a chair placed beside Rose, the bag was removed from his head, revealing David's face with a dark blue bruise covering the corner of his temple and a bloody, wet nose. A man strapped cable ties around David's wrists and the arms of the chair, securing him into position. David immediately noticed Rose tied to the chair next to him, looking at her flaming, dripping cheeks. At least half a dozen men surrounded Quentin, stood against the walls in a guarded stance. David glanced at the tall, bald man, stood only a few metres behind Quentin, of whom he recognised from the casino and the launch of the homeless shelter. From an open doorway at the other side of the room, David could see a flight of bare brick stairs, covered in dust and cobwebs, and what seemed to be disused, open elevator shafts taped off with bright-yellow warning signs.

Rose and David shared a glance, each analysing the state of the other, but didn't dare speak up.

A man closed the doorway that David had arrived through, blocking off the faint noise.

"The *great* David Dale," Quentin said as he dug into one of his pockets. "Widower, psychiatrist, entrepreneur, philanthropist." His pocketed hand fidgeted. "And now wife-stealer."

David stared at Quentin, his breathing heavy.

"Hello again, and my apologies for the secrecy of getting you to our little meeting point. I hope they weren't too gentle with you." Quentin glanced around the room with a smirk and then looked back at David. "And, as well, my apologies for my treatment of Rose today. Although, after all of her poisonous words towards the man that has given her everything, I'm not at all sorry." He leaned down from where he stood, facing Rose. "How's your pretty little face?" He smirked once more and stood up, looking back at David. "All this fuss over a few little payments. My, my." He formed a grin. "Poor little Bev. She's still in hospital, isn't she? Someone should put the old girl out of her misery."

David pulled his arms at the cable ties, unable to move. "You fucking—"

Quentin pulled his hand out of his pocket, revealing the brass knuckle dusters wrapped around his fingers, and landed a devastating blow to David's face.

David shouted in pain as he and his chair fell to the ground with a loud thud. Blood profusely poured from his lips.

"That's gotta hurt!" Quentin shouted. He shook the pain from his hand and then removed the knuckle dusters, placing them back into his pocket. He locked his eyes onto David and watched him as he tried to regain himself. "What's the matter, David? Are you having a *down dream*?" he asked, releasing a boisterous laugh.

Rose sobbed as she helplessly watched. "Stop it!"

"Shush, woman," Quentin said as he paced in front of her. "You don't have to worry just yet. I'll only kill him if, after all of this, he yet again refuses to pay me the money I'm rightfully owed."

"Well, that means Quentin is a dead end," McField said down the phone. "What about Eva? Surely there's something, somewhere."

"Hold on, hold on," Alex insisted as he tapped away at his computer.

"We need to move a bit faster here. This is taking too long." McField looked around the office. "I might have to try and get on someone else's account to attempt accessing Quentin's file on the database."

"Bear with me, it's around this section somewhere." Alex scrolled through his documents. "Ah, here we are," he said, starting to read through the contents he had uncovered. "Under the umbrella of the Shields Corporation, Eva Shields has acquired countless brands, businesses and premises across Europe."

"But we're looking at the UK specifically."

"I know, but there's just so many," he said with a sigh. "Some businesses she seems to buy and keep hold of, whilst others she buys to then re-sell. Erm, if I narrow it down to all of the premises that she purchased in the UK and has not re-sold, and then I narrow it down further to those limited to London, then we may have our potential locations."

"Do it."

"Give me a minute."

McField patiently waited on the other end of the line, contemplating the current goings on of David and Quentin. His phone buzzed. "There's somebody on the other line, Alex. One second," he said, switching lines without waiting for an answer. "McField."

"Detective, we've just had a phone in from a member of the public about a man being bundled into a white Ford Transit van on Northumberland Avenue in Wanstead."

"David's street. Did they get the registration plate?"

"Yep."

"And?"

"And we've tracked it via CCTV arriving at Shields Tower twenty-five minutes ago."

David slouched, his body unable to keep him sat upright. One of his black eyes started to show signs of severe swelling and both of his lips had been bust open with blood dribbling down onto his chest.

"You've been such a disappointment, David," Quentin said, wiping his hands with a cloth. He shook his head. "Silly, very silly." He rolled the cloth into a ball and threw it across the room.

Another door to the room opened behind David and Rose, releasing the distant medley of chatter and music.

Rose moved her head around in different angles to see if she could catch a glimpse of who was entering.

Several pairs of feet could be heard scuttling around the open door.

David held his breath as the unmistakeable footsteps of high heel shoes stepped closer and closer, growing louder and louder.

As the swelling of David's wounded eye began to take hold, his vision was restricted to just one eye. He could hear the footsteps now approaching his side and quickly walking past him. He looked up towards Quentin, now seeing her in a pearl white dress that reminded him of all those nights ago in the casino. He lost his breath as everything came full circle.

Stood at Quentin's side, Eva was wearing a long, sleeveless dress that flowed to the floor. Her hair was slicked back over her head and ran down her back.

David watched as Eva gently kissed Quentin on the cheek. Quentin responded by turning his head and passionately kissing her back.

Eva pulled herself away and turned to David. She stepped towards him and leant down so that her face was clear to see. "Good evening, David," she said with a slim smile. "I might have lied about that metaphorical milk that I mentioned to you all that time ago." Her smile widened into a grin. "Maybe it was poisoned."

CHAPTER 35

"Leave him alone!" Rose yelled, staring at Eva.

"You better listen to her, she seems pissed," Quentin said with a smirk.

Eva straightened her back and stepped towards Rose. "Oh, you don't like me being near David? Is he all yours now?" Eva asked, stepping around Rose's chair to stand directly behind her. Eva leant down and wrapped her arms around Rose's neck and chest, resting her chin on Rose's shoulder. "Bless you. Caught up in all of this. You should never have involved yourself, you know. You could have kept the lovely lifestyle that Quentin was so generous to give you. Although," she paused, turning her voice into a whisper, "you need to work on your technique. The man's been deprived of a real woman's touch, but I helped him with that."

Quentin shrugged with a proud nod.

The bleeding from David's lips had subsided, but the swelling in his eye forced it completely shut. He looked over at Rose and could just make out Eva leaning over her. He changed his focus to the room, looking for any sign of hope.

"And I didn't take over the Shields Corporation to have a little bitch like you try and derail my operations with your boyfriend,"

Eva said before sliding her hands off Rose and walking back around to Quentin.

David looked up in Eva's direction. "Screw someone for it, did ya?" he said wincing as his lips moved.

"Oh, David, you really don't know me at all, do you? The Shields Corporation was actually the invention of my father. He had such low ambitions for it." She paused, as if re-living a memory. "But pay some high-up police enough money and they'll make any evidence disappear."

David looked away.

"How better to remember one's father than to continue his work and take it further than he ever imagined," Eva said. "Everybody was so sympathetic and helpful, it was a real boost for me."

Quentin laughed. "We really must move on to the purpose of you two being here." He took a step closer.

Rose looked to David for comfort but found nothing but the striking visuals of his bloody, bashed face.

Eva watched Rose, pouting out her lower lip and quickly placing a hand on her chest.

"Now," Quentin started, "after all of this shit, I'm hoping that once and for all we can settle our little disagreement and turn it into an agreement. Well, in fact, more of a contract. I'd hate for you to again deny me the money that I'm owed." He changed his focus to Rose. "Otherwise, the pair of you might end up in a small, plastic bag, eh, Rose?"

Rose avoided his eyes.

"Well," Eva said, running a hand through her hair. "I best leave you boys to business. I've been missing from my own party for long enough. Oh, David. It is a real shame you couldn't have joined me tonight for our tenth birthday party. But I guess you kind of are here, in a satisfying kind of way."

Quentin pulled Eva to him and gave her a prolonged kiss. "Enjoy yourself," he said. "I'll be down later."

Eva turned to David, said, "I really did start to like you." She leant down and kissed him on the forehead. "I was hoping for a proper kiss on the lips, but he's mucked them up good, hasn't he? He's a clever man." Eva walked past David and towards the side door that she had entered from.

David and Rose listened to the bundles of feet that started moving as Eva left the room.

"Anyway," Quentin continued, "let's get down to business, shall we?" He glanced over to his right and walked towards another chair. He picked it up and placed it directly in front of David, sitting down. "Your face looks a little nasty. Would you like a cloth for that?"

David kept his eyes on the ground.

"Suit yourself," Quentin said, raising an eyebrow. He leant back in his chair and rested an ankle on his other knee. "Okay. I take it you'd be interested in knowing why you. Why out of everyone in the world are you the one sat here right now?"

"Because you know I have money." David whispered slowly, his lips trembling. He looked up at Quentin. "Because Down Dream has money."

Quentin shook his head. "Wrong. Would you like to try again?"

David didn't respond.

"I thought that would stump you. Okay, okay. What if I told you, it all comes down to your little family holiday in South Carolina."

David recoiled as his lips quickly parted, making way for the sudden intake of air. A cold tremor lashed its way across his body.

"Your woman popped her clogs along with your two daughters there three years ago, didn't they? That mustn't have been a nice holiday for you." He rested his elbows on his knees and placed his face in his palms. "Some sort of traffic accident, wasn't it? But in your little brain, did you ever stop and wonder who else was hurt in your crash?"

David stared blankly at Quentin. Although his guilt and grief had always been focused on his family, he had always been well aware of the additional casualty. Another dagger of guilt David had been carrying in his side for all these years.

Quentin exhaled sharply in laughter. "You either didn't know or didn't care enough to think about it, did you? Too busy thinking about your wife and kids to think about anybody else."

Rose frowned as she listened, hanging on to Quentin's every word.

"You know, David, I told you this when I met you, and it's true. You remind me of my selfless brother. He was twenty-eight when he moved to America, and he was just thirty-six when he was involved in the accident that day. The same accident you caused." He pinched his lower lip with his fingers, his eyes set on David, waiting for his reaction.

David looked up with a slack jaw.

"My brother was seventeen when I last spoke to him. All my fault, of course. The good kid didn't want anythin' to do with me or what I was doin' round here, so he fucked off. And rightly so. But to find out on the goddamn Internet that you had crashed into him because you were too busy, too distracted. You didn't give a fuck about him, did you? He wasn't even a thought in your head." He swung his shoulders from side to side energetically, his face reddened. "He had broken his back in the accident, and over the next four months underwent two operations to try and save the use of his legs. He couldn't take it. He was too young, too damaged, too alone. He ended up topping himself, you know."

David buried his head in his chest, tears and subdued whimpers followed.

"I guess the pain of his operations and the high chance of being permanently disabled was too much. No one gave a shit about him then and no one gives a shit about him now." He pushed his body back against the chair. "You had to drive like a fucking prick, didn't you? My brother had to go through all that shit for nothing. Is it hard to understand, David? I wanted to track you down years ago and sort you out then, but you became a recluse and were difficult to find. You sold your psychiatry practice, and it was like you disappeared. Until recently."

Rose's eyes flicked back and forth between Quentin and David.

"When you came back onto the scene with your charity, Eva was quite right that you'd be very worthwhile. A vulnerable man like you with bags of cash at your disposal, ripe for the picking. Instead of just sorting you out down an alleyway, or in a car accident of your own, Eva came up with the ingenious plan, I must give her credit." He exaggerated a swallow with the smacking of his lips. "Help thrust you into the spotlight and make Down Dream as big as it can be. As popular and as rich as it can be. To help with this, yeah, we've made a few calls and made a couple of things happen. Do you really think the charity would be where it is now if we didn't get you the public's sympathy? I mean without Eva's attention-seeking at your launch event, no one would know what Down Dream is. Without your phone-in on Shields Radio, no one would give a damn about you. And then we had to up the ante just a little more, to really convince the public that you're worth their sympathy."

David clenched his fists against the chair.

"Once you were on your pedestal, I wanted to wear you down to your rawest form, you see. We started by wrecking your office to put you on edge, which also helped with the public sympathy, but I thought it'd be a good idea to give this whole thing a bit of a kick-start. I know that even doctors speak to therapists."

David looked up.

"Your therapist… Allen, was it? He certainly helped with the kick-start I was looking for. Poor guy didn't see it coming at all." Quentin displayed a proud grin.

"You fucking bastard."

"Ah, ah," Quentin said with a raised hand. "We then moved on to your colleagues, didn't we? Poor Bev and Stu, eh?" He inched closer to David. "I hope I made you feel weak and indefensible; just how my brother would have felt." He straightened his back. "The money that's been pouring into the charity is just the cherry on top."

David forced his eyes closed.

"We dug up some real, juicy info on you, David." Quentin removed his mobile phone from his pocket and scrolled through it. "I have all of the details here, because I was so interested, and because some of it is now going to become mine." He looked at Rose. "Listen up, Rose, you'll find this interesting." He stopped scrolling and cleared his throat. "Ah, here we are. David, you and your late wife had one hundred and sixty thousand pounds in savings before she died, didn't you?" He cleared his throat for a second time. "And then you have your big, fancy, family house in that shitty town."

David didn't respond, his eyes to the floor.

"Look at me when I'm speaking to you, goddamn it," Quentin shouted as he leant forward and slapped David in the face.

David's head was thrust to his shoulder, the slap stinging as he groaned. Reluctantly raising his head, he slowly shifted his eye to Quentin.

"The family house in East Horsley. You bought that for almost six hundred thousand, didn't you? Boy, you were rolling in it even before you sold your psychiatry practice." Quentin looked at Rose, said, "No wonder you gravitated towards him, you gold-digging bitch." He looked back at his phone. "The house should be around one point seven mill right now. Then you sold your business for five point nine million dollars, which was about four point eight million pounds at the time. But you also managed to get some of their stock in the deal, you good little negotiator, you. You received stock worth eight hundred thousand pounds. And I took the liberty, a few days ago, to look up the price of your stock now and see how it's performed since then, because, you know, some of it's mine now." He paused, raising his voice. "And isn't Wall Street on fucking fire! The stock is now valued at one point two mill. We'll sell those shares later." He smirked, catching David's eye. "So, after you were done and dusted with your psychiatry shit, you then launched Down Dream. I have it written down here that you transferred three million pounds into the charity. That's quite a tasty lump sum for any charity to start off with, isn't it? You obviously weren't planning to have poxy little charity shops, operated by old grannies, were you?" He laughed, glancing to Rose and then back to David.

Rose scowled.

"You used some of the money to buy that scummy shelter, too, didn't ya? And then," Quentin said with an uplifting voice, as if he were about to announce an award, "Eva's sprinkle of magic really took effect. You were the new kid on the block with your fancy little charity. Being the good guy that you are." He rolled his eyes. "Eva kick-started Down Dream and launched it into the spotlight, and then, what do you know? You get money pouring in by the bucket load. And to date, Mr Dale, I can tell you that Down Dream has raised over four point six million pounds by public donations and the odd government grant."

Rose kept on glancing between David and Quentin, the information not even entering her head.

"Now if we total all of that up, it's one heck of a number." Quentin glanced to his phone. "I'm not including your cosy apartment down the road, the one that has the police car constantly outside of it. I'm also not including your little hideaway house in, Wanstead, is it? You bought those with the proceeds of your business. So that brings us to your net worth, combined with Down Dream's. If you haven't wasted much of it, which, by your records you haven't, then you're looking at over twelve million pounds." He stopped, letting out a stretched laugh. "Boy's done good!"

David didn't respond.

"What? Aren't you going to say anything?"

David raised his head and looked at Quentin. "Fuck yourself."

Quentin smiled. "You can speak, that's great. I was beginning to worry I'd broken your jaw."

"You're sick," Rose said in a hushed voice.

Quentin leant forward, looking at Rose. "Pardon?"

"You're a sick bastard," David added.

Quentin laughed. He placed a single finger under David's chin and pushed his head upwards. "Your penalty, Mr Dale, if you'd like to make it out of here alive, is a big payment here and now. I think that's fair."

David blinked with his one eye.

"Let's say… two million. We don't have to shut down your shitty charity or kill anyone else. We can settle all of this now by you paying what I want."

Rose shook her head.

"And then after your very kind payment, I expect a hundred grand to be wired to me at the start of every month, without delay. Sell your properties or dip into the charity's donations, I don't give a shit, but I want that money."

David closed his eyes.

"I'll take your sorry-ass face as an agreement," Quentin said as he held out an open palm.

Harold appeared from behind Quentin, passing him a small notebook laptop from his gloved hands.

David raised his head again and looked up at the tall bald man.

Quentin opened the notebook, tapping several buttons. "Now, David. I need you to work with me here. I know you have your stash in your National Savings and Investments account. I need you to log into your account for me and authorise the transfer." He rotated the notebook around on his lap, showing David the screen.

David looked down at the notebook, viewing the National Savings and Investments login page. As he looked closer, he could see his account username had already been entered.

How could he possibly know that?

"All I need is your password and PIN," Quentin said, staring down at David.

David shook his head. "No."

Quentin widened his eyes and crinkled his forehead. "What did you say?"

"Fuck you."

As his eyebrows raised and the redness in his face returned, Quentin jumped from his seat, knocking the notebook to the floor in the process, and punched David, splitting open his lip once more.

Rose screamed.

David and his chair were knocked back onto its two back legs, for a second dangling mid-air. The chair then dropped back down onto its four legs. David shook his frail head as the room spun, his one able eye twitching to stay open.

Quentin rushed to Rose and tugged on the cable ties that bound her to the chair. One of the watching security men stepped forward and cut her free. Quentin then snatched Rose's arm and yanked her onto her feet as he pulled a gun from behind his back and clicked it into action. He dragged her into David's line of sight, wrapped an arm around her neck, standing behind her. He pushed the gun into Rose's temple.

David watched as Rose struggled against Quentin's grasp, her face frozen in fear.

"Are you playing games with me? Are you fucking testing me?" Quentin roared with raging eyes, further pressing the gun against Rose's head. "I don't have time for this. Tell me the password and PIN now!"

CHAPTER 36

David's head spun with the traumatic sight of Rose pleading with her tearful eyes and Quentin screaming in his face. David's wounded head, swollen eye, and bloody lips stung from the pain that radiated through him. Quentin stared down at him with furious red eyes. David bowed his head and closed his eye. He forced his lips to move to say his password, but found his fragile voice lost in the faint music that was again seeping into the room along with the bustling of dozens of feet.

Quentin's eyes darted towards the moving door. With his hand poised on the gun, he firmly held Rose against his body. The men in the room all looked towards the door.

It flung open. "Police!" a uniformed man shouted as he flew through the doorway, gun in hand.

One of Quentin's men, stood just metres away from the door, immediately pulled his gun and shot the policeman.

The officer fell, hitting the ground with a thump. All of the other men in the room dived into the cover of open doorways and tucked behind pallets of bricks.

Quentin instinctively swung his armed hand at David, cracking him over the head with the handle of the gun. The impact hit David squarely on his temple, throwing him and the chair to the floor.

As his head bounced off the ground, David fell unconscious.

With Rose still in Quentin's forceful grip, he tugged her body close to his and quickly pulled her through the doorway behind him.

Detective McField, reinforced by almost a dozen policemen and women, stormed the room, returning the ensuing hail of bullets that shot in their direction. Officers stormed the closest doorways, shooting Quentin's men in the process, while others dove behind the construction materials sprinkled around the floor. One officer covered his colleague who dragged the wounded officer out of sight.

Bullets blitzed through the room, cementing themselves into the brick walls and tore through limbs that found themselves without cover. Two of Quentin's men were shot to the ground by bullets piercing through the thin, exposed parts of the walls.

Without drawing a weapon, Harold shifted through a side doorway unnoticed, observing the gunfire from both sides.

"Help!" Rose screamed as she was aggressively pulled away from the commotion and dragged towards the set of exposed staircases.

McField pushed forwards, watching Quentin flee to the rear of the building. His sight of Quentin was cut off as an officer attempted to sprint across the open room that had become a temporary no-man's land. Three gunshots rang out, and the officer collapsed next to David who lay motionless in the middle of the room. McField made eye contact with another officer who had made his way to a doorway on the other side of the room. Using his hands, he communicated several gestures.

The officer nodded and immediately started firing from his cover, drawing the attention of the opposing gunmen. McField sprang from his crouched position and shot down two of the men. Other officers gradually pushed forwards, closing the gap. McField watched as the remaining officers pushed the rest of the armed men into a corridor that shot off from the main room. He ran to David and checked for a pulse, placing his hand on his neck. "Parson," McField shouted to one of the officers closest to him. "We need medical attention now."

The officer started talking into his radio requesting urgent assistance before approaching David and cutting him loose from the chair.

McField ran through the doorway and climbed the flight of stairs that he saw Quentin approaching earlier, taking two steps at a time. The dusty stairs were dirty and unfinished, as if progress on the renovation had stalled. He clutched onto his gun with his sweaty hands, pointing it in multiple directions as he reached the first landing with a single door.

Locked.

McField turned back to the stairs and pushed onwards, climbing another flight. Another locked door greeted him before he took the final set of stairs to the very last landing. A single metal door was ajar. He took several deep breaths and cautiously inched it open. He slipped through the small gap with his gun raised in front of him. The landing was small and barren; its air thick with soot and dust.

"Don't fucking move!" Quentin shouted from behind him.

McField turned his body and looked behind him, noticing Quentin squeezing Rose against his chest, standing directly against one of the open elevator doorways.

"I said don't move!" he shouted, pressing the gun against Rose's cheeks.

Rose wept, shaking uncontrollably as a draught from the elevator shaft behind them blew her hair across her eyes. She looked at McField and shook her head.

"Okay, okay," McField said, stood still in front of the metal door.

Quentin put on a laugh, said, "You dickheads, you shouldn't be here. You shouldn't be here!"

McField gently nudged closer. "Easy."

"Ah, ah, ah!" Quentin blared, moving the gun from Rose's face and aiming it directly at the detective.

McField froze, holding his hands in sight, the gun still firmly in his palm.

"Drop it."

McField glanced at his gun and then back to Quentin, before slowly leaning down and placing it on the floor.

Rose watched McField as he put down his only defence. She stared at him with an open mouth. "No," she whispered.

"You're surrounded," McField said in an authority-like manner. "The party's over. There's no one left downstairs to fight your corner."

Quentin kept his unyielding gaze on McField. "There might not be anybody left downstairs, but there's so many more out there who'll come to my call. You have no idea how many people work for me."

"We know about your group and we know about your affiliation with Eva. She's already in custody."

Quentin's head involuntarily jerked. His confident expression drained from his face, replaced by a sceptical scowl.

"Give it up, Quentin," McField said, glancing to and from Rose.

"Fuck you!" he shouted, waving the gun towards Rose and then back to McField. He took a quick glance at the open drop behind him.

McField heard a muted shuffling of footsteps close behind the door next to him. Beginning to hear the whispers of his colleagues, he motioned with an open palm for them to stand down.

Quentin replenished his grip on Rose by flexing his hand that held her tight, square against his body. "You have no idea who you're dealing with or what the repercussions will be. I need you to arrange my safe passage out of this building, or you'll have her life on your conscience until the day you die and, by God, will my men not rest until they find you and everyone you've ever loved."

McField moved one arm forwards, showing his empty, open palm. "Give yourself up and we can talk." He glanced again to and from Rose. "Cooperate with us, Quentin. You'd be an incredibly valuable asset to the NCA, they'd cut you a deal."

Quentin smirked. "You have hugely misjudged me if you think that I'd give myself up or cooperate with you." He poised his finger on the trigger and braced his arm. He lightly adjusted his aim, pointing the gun at McField's head. "Thank you for trying though."

McField held his breath.

Just as Quentin squeezed the trigger, Rose outstretched her elbow and forcefully bashed it down into his ribs. Quentin instinctively hunched over, gasping for breath as the shot rang out; the bullet managing to fly past McField who ducked to the floor. Rose pulled away from Quentin with a strong tug, but was unable to break from his relentless, iron-like grip. As she threw herself back at him, punching and slapping his face to break free, Quentin forced himself to straighten his back and brought in his armed hand, grappling with her for control. In the commotion, he squeezed the trigger a second time, shooting the ceiling of uncovered concrete that rained down a gravelly powder.

For the few seconds that had passed, McField froze in the same spot just metres away from the pair as they tugged and pulled at each other. But then he noticed the direction in which they were edging, prompting him to sprint towards them.

Rose kneed Quentin in the crotch, and he stumbled two steps backwards. One foot dropped over the ledge of the open elevator door, bringing his whole body tumbling down after him. Rose watched as Quentin began to fall. Her eyes looked down in horror; his fingers still tightly wrapped around her wrist.

McField raced forward as he watched both Quentin and Rose plummet down the dark elevator shaft.

CHAPTER 37

"But what happened to the big bad wolf, Daddy?" Sophie asked, looking up from her dining table chair. Cassie joined her sister in spinning her head to face David, her eyes hopeful.

"What did happen, Daddy?" Maria asked with a coy smile, picking up the empty plates from the table.

Sat at the same table, David raised an eyebrow. "Well, some people say that the big bad wolf was so frustrated, so angry, that he couldn't blow down the house of bricks, that he climbed on top of it."

Sophie enthusiastically dropped her lower jaw.

"Yeah, some people say that he climbed up onto the roof of the brick house and jumped down the chimney."

"But what about the three little pigs?" Cassie asked.

"Well, when the big bad wolf jumped down the chimney, people say he landed into a big pot of boiling water, and the three pigs slammed the lid on top of him, locking him in."

Both Sophie and Cassie gasped.

David leant forward. "Then the three little pigs ate him!"

"Ew!" Sophie shouted.

Maria shook her head. "Don't believe everything your father tells you. Of course they didn't eat the nasty wolf."

"That's what some people say," he said with a shrug. "Other people say that the big bad wolf didn't climb onto the house and, instead of trying to get the three little pigs, he just gave up and ran away, never to be seen again."

Cassie looked on in thought.

Sophie brought a hand up to her forehead. "And the three little pigs lived happily ever after?"

Maria approached Sophie and lent over her from behind, hugging her. "Yes, happily ever after."

David couldn't help but let out a smile. "I've missed you all so, so much."

Maria raised her head from her daughter's shoulder. "It's not your time yet, my love."

The sound of a repetitive beep abruptly appeared. Slowly, its presence seeped into existence with its increasing volume, growing ever louder and louder. Light was next, emerging into reality. A strong glow of white developed into colours and shapes.

David painfully opened his eyes. As his sight stabilised, he looked around the room he was in. A tall machine sat next to him, the culprit of the beeping. Wires connected the machine to the plug socket in the wall, whilst tubes ran up onto the bed he was in, leading to a patch on his hand. He looked down at his bedding, realising he was in a private hospital ward. The far wall had a closed door and a large window with its blinds drawn across it. Tentatively, he turned his head to the other side of the room and saw her.

Slouched in an armchair with her eyes glued to her mobile phone, his sister Sam was patiently waiting.

David pushed himself to sit up in his bed, groaning in the process.

"David," Sam said, shifting her focus off of her phone and rushing to his bedside. "Oh my god, you're awake."

David made himself somewhat comfortable in his new posture. "Hi," he muffled, his voice weak. He rested back down on two bulky pillows.

"Are you okay? How are you feeling?"

David rubbed his eyes, suddenly experiencing a sharp pain around one of his eye sockets. He flinched. "Jesus, that hurts."

"Hey, take it easy," Sam said, resting her hand on his. "You're pretty beaten up."

"What are you doing here? Where's Ben?"

"Judy from work's looking after him. I had to come and see you as soon as I could, make sure you're okay. Can you remember what happened?"

David fixed his eyes on the bed sheets. "Quentin," he whispered. Sam nodded.

"He hit me," he said, moving his hand to touch his forehead, delicately feeling fresh bandaging.

Sam squeezed his hand. "You've been out for almost twenty-four hours, David. The doctors said you had severe concussion."

"What happened?"

"The police found you just in time."

"Rose," he said, looking up to Sam. "What happened to Rose?"

The door to the room opened with a click. Detective McField popped his head through the doorway. "Ah, you're awake," he said, pushing the door open further and stepping inside. "We've been worrying about you."

David kept his hand on his head, his face wrinkled in pain.

"I'm sorry, have you just woken up? Would you like to see a nurse?" McField asked. "Or am I interrupting something?"

Sam kept a hold of David's hand.

"Where's Rose?" David asked.

McField took a step towards the bed. "You don't need to worry, David. Rose is down the hall."

"Is she all right?"

McField pursed his lips together, exhaling sharply. "She's broken both of her legs."

David ripped up his bed sheets and pushed himself forward. "I have to see her."

Both Sam and McField raised their hands to form a barrier. "Whoa, whoa. You're not going anywhere until a doctor checks on you," Sam said.

McField raised his eyebrows at David.

David reluctantly lay back down onto the pillows and pulled the bed sheets back over his body.

"I'll go and see if I can find someone to see how you're doing," Sam said as she let go of David's hand and exited the room. "I'll be one minute."

McField nodded. "I'll let you get some rest. Just know that I'm really sorry things turned out how they did. We should have done more. I should have done more," he said, before turning his back.

"Wait," David said.

McField stopped and faced David.

"What happened? Did you arrest Quentin?"

After releasing a short sigh, McField stepped back towards the bed. "Quentin's dead."

"*Dead?*"

"You were taken to Shields Tower and held in an off-limits section on the building's east side. This was all while Eva held her ten-year anniversary party for the corporation on the floor below. When we entered the room where you and Rose were being held, Quentin knocked you clean out. His men slowed us down and he managed to climb up a few floors with Rose, trying to use her as leverage to escape. He was cornered and had nowhere to go. Then Rose tried to fight him off." McField paused, blowing out his cheeks. "They both grappled and fell before I could reach them. They fell down an unfinished elevator shaft. It must have been fifty or sixty feet."

"Christ."

"Quentin was pronounced dead at the scene after hitting his head. Rose broke both of her legs and fractured a collarbone. I don't know how serious her breakages are. Quentin must have at least cushioned her fall."

David looked away from the detective. "He got what he deserved."

"Yes, well. We could have used him for valuable information. There's a lot of people out there who would have liked to have seen him on trial."

David didn't respond.

"Luckily we managed to get to Eva just in time," McField said.

David looked back at him. "You did?"

"Just. Our arrival at Shields Tower wasn't in any way discreet, so she had some time to make a move. We caught her trying to slip out of a side exit with a handful of her personnel. She's in custody and I think there's a strong chance she'll negotiate for a plea deal. We're working on it. Although there's an incredible amount of information in Alex's report on the Shields Corporation and Quentin's organisation, there's still a lot to learn."

"Alex published?"

Sam re-emerged into the room, pushing the door closed behind her. "Somebody's gonna come and see you in a minute," she said, reclaiming her spot next to David and retaking his hand.

David tried a smile until it hurt.

McField smirked at David. "He published this morning, and the whole country is in uproar. Shields Corporation is in absolute meltdown. Scotland Yard has shut it down, preventing all of its businesses from operating until a thorough investigation has taken place. As you can imagine, the BBC is lapping it up."

"Have you read Alex's report? What does he actually say?"

"Of course. I think everyone's actually been caught off guard by it. It's pretty phenomenal. The whole situation goes deeper than even I thought it would. The Shields Corporation has been illegally buying out foreign businesses, which we deem to be shell companies; completely fictitious, created by Quentin and his associates abroad in order to launder money across Europe. Alex thinks that for the majority of the time, Eva was using this method to pay off criminals who had been dealing with Quentin. It involved widespread crimes, from drug and human trafficking, bribery, and extortion. The influence and power behind the Shields Corporation, Eva, and Quentin's organisation let this go on undetected for so long."

"Oh my god."

"It's why I think they chose to target you. To get you and Down Dream under their wing so they had more options to launder money through a legal front. Who'd suspect a charity?"

David was expressionless. The thought of Quentin's brother entered his head.

"The NCA has made twenty-six arrests this morning. A long-serving government minister, Duncan Chiles, has been arrested for perverting the course of justice by covering up Quentin's actions and withholding information from various governmental bodies. Similarly, Detective Superintendent Christopher Forrest who led my department has also been arrested for the same offence."

David shook his head.

"As Alex investigated Duncan Chiles, he encountered communications between the pair, with Duncan and Christopher discussing Quentin and current investigations and cases against him. Alex spoke to me about this and I looked into my superintendent. Christopher was interacting and scheming with Duncan, plotting obstacles and diversions away from Quentin. It's how he's gone so long without being investigated or taken down. Christopher even tried to get me to drop your case because he said the NCA was watching Quentin, waiting to build up a pool of intel before making their move. All bullshit, I now know."

"Bastards."

"Yes, well," McField said, glancing around the room. He looked back at David. "I'm disappointed it all practically happened under my nose and I knew nothing of it. I had even contacted an old colleague of mine, a superior who Christopher Forrest replaced. He retired early due to kidney failure, but I trusted him. Turns out he used to be one of Quentin's pawns, too. Terribly ill and he was still lying for him. Covering up for Quentin." He shook his head. "The NCA have also arrested him and are launching a corruption investigation into the force."

"How could you have possibly known? Both you and Alex have done an insane job. You've saved Down Dream," he said in a lowered voice, instantly thinking of Bev and Stu.

"I spoke to Kristian last night," McField said. "He'll hopefully be seeing you later. He said there's been another outpouring of public support for Down Dream." He laughed, said, "He needs you to get back on your feet as soon as possible so you can help him with the shit ton of work he's got."

David tried to smile, thinking of the renewed focus he can commit to the charity. He looked at Sam. "Are you okay?"

"Me? I'm fine. Why do you ask?"

"How long have you been here?"

Sam shrugged her shoulders. "I don't know, since this morning."

"You must be knackered. Go and have a breather. Meet up with Richard. You said he's working in London."

"I'm hoping to, but I've not heard from him for a few days." Sam tried to hide a disappointed expression. "Might have scared another one off. Another fleeting, failed romance."

David frowned.

"Before I go," McField started, "I know you've only just woken up, but I'd like to have a proper discussion with you about the events which led up to what happened at Shields Tower. Anything Quentin or Eva might have said to you that we don't have on record which might help. When you feel up to it, of course."

David sat silently for a moment. He looked at Sam and squeezed her hand. "He told me his brother was also in the traffic accident in South Carolina."

Sam leant forward. "What?"

"Quentin's brother was the person I crashed into three years ago. I knew someone else was hurt, but I never even bothered to look into who, or how seriously. Quentin said his brother had to go through so many operations to try and save his legs." David fought his trembling lips. "He ended up killing himself and Quentin rightly blamed me."

"Oh my god," Sam said. "So Quentin targeted you because his brother was also affected in the same accident as Maria and the girls?"

"That's part of the reason, and I think because they knew I had money from my psychiatry practice and I was launching a charity."

McField raised an eyebrow at the revelation, then slowly nodded. "Personal motive, financial incentive, and the goal of using Down Dream as a new legal front. The perfect victim."

CHAPTER 38

David was discharged shortly before midday after the doctor signed the required paperwork and prescriptions. The bandaging that was wrapped around David's head had been replaced with a fresh dressing that barely covered the great black gash in the side of his head. The fringes of the heavily bruised skin ran out from underneath the dressing, like a disease slowly taking over. David was under strict orders to take it easy over the next few days but was assured that he'd fully recover. He peeked through the dull curtains that surrounded the silent bed in the middle of a shared ward.

Rose's eyes instantly flicked up to meet David's as she sat upright but tucked under the bed sheets, resting on a wall of pillows. Her left arm hung in a sling and her lower legs, wrapped in plaster, stuck out from the bed sheets.

David let a gradual smile slowly form, but his sad eyes reflected the hurt he saw from Rose's condition. He stepped through the curtains, making sure they closed behind him, and approached her, leaning down to her level.

She pushed her body forward and landed her chin onto his shoulder, wrapping her able arm around him with a tight grip.

David held her tightly. As he pulled away, he pushed strands of her hair out of her eyes, moving them behind her ears. "I'm so relieved you're okay."

Rose placed a hand on his chest. "I didn't think we were going to make it. I didn't think we were going to make it out of that building."

"Neither did I," David whispered, swallowing hard. "How are you feeling?"

"I'm okay. I was in a lot of pain this morning, but they think I'll be fine. Just knocked about, really." She looked at the bandaging on David's head. "How's your head?"

"I'll survive. I've been prescribed some strong painkillers, and I've just been discharged. Nothing more than a concussion, thankfully."

Rose sighed loudly as her eyes welled up. "I was so scared, David. He hit you so hard," she said as she cried.

"Hey, don't cry. You don't need to cry now." He wiped her cheeks with his thumbs. "You have your life back."

Rose fought for her composure and wiped clear her eyes. "I'll never be able to thank you enough for everything you've done for me."

"You don't have to thank me for anything," he said. "You've helped take me to a place in my life where I feel like a new man, no longer stuck in the events of my past."

"I will forever be infatuated with you, Mr David Dale," Rose said with a broken voice, the slightest droplets of tears breaking out from her eyes.

David's expression shifted. The faintest of frowns appeared.

"It doesn't matter where I am, or what little I have. I have my life back, and I can build it into what I want it to become. Only you've given me that." She gulped. "I owe you everything."

David exhaled emphatically, unable to conjure the words. His eyes floated to the arm resting in the sturdy sling, before moving down to the plastered legs at the end of the bed. With his head turned, he squeezed his eyes shut and breathed.

Rose lurched her head forwards. "What?"

David shook himself before facing her. "I've been living in the past for three years. I've held on to the pain and the regret, and it's not something I'm ever going to be able to live without." He fought for a breath as he clutched onto her hand. "I'm going to be there for you whilst you sort everything out. You have clothes to collect. You have your family in Italy to contact." He couldn't hold back the smile. "My, how they'll be elated to hear from you." He felt Rose squeeze his hands. "But I can't be anything more than your friend, Rose," he said, squeezing back. "At this juncture in your life, you don't need a reason to stay here. But you have *every* reason to go to your village, to your family. To live the life you were meant to live. As much as I've come to care for you so quickly, so deeply…" He caught himself by the thought, hesitating. "I can't be there for you in that way." A tear trickled its way down his face and ran off his chin, landing onto the bed sheet. "And I'm so sorry to tell you that. I will always be here for you though."

Rose loosened her grasp of his hands. "That's okay," she finally said with a whisper and a forced smile. She quickly wiped away several tears.

"But just like you, I'm going to move on with my life one way or another. I'm going to have my home in East Horsley cleared out and I'll sell it. I'll sell that and my Wanstead house and I'll buy somewhere new. Somewhere without any memories."

"That sounds sensible. Are you keeping the apartment then?"

David let out a soft smile. "I have other plans for that. But first things first, we're gonna find your family and make sure you're taken care of. I'm sure the police will want to speak to you later, but it's nothing to worry about."

Rose nodded.

David glanced to the curtains that were still drawn around her bed. "Now why are these closed?"

"I was scared, and I'm used to being by myself."

"You don't need to be scared anymore, Rose."

She shrugged.

"I've got a few things I need to do, but I'll be able to come back and see you this afternoon," David said, glancing at the bedside table next to her. "Do you need me to get you anything?"

"I'm fine, I've got water and my phone."

"Perhaps try and make conversation with the women next to you. A normal, everyday chat is what you need."

"What are you going to do?"

"I need to check in with Kristian and see how Bev is. Then I've got a bit of work that I want to catch up on before I come and see you again."

The corners of Rose's mouth slightly pointed up.

"Now concentrate on getting better. You have a completely new life to lead."

Rose's smile broke out as she looked up at David.

He stood up and took hold of the curtains. "Shall I?"

She gave a delicate nod.

David pushed the curtains back to the wall, bringing Rose into full view of the other women in the same ward. Several pairs of eyes flicked over in their direction. "Say hello, ask how they are," he whispered. "This is the start of your new life."

David left the ward and walked down the corridor. He dug out his mobile and tapped into his list of contacts, initiating a phone call.

The other line answered. "David! How are you? Are you out of the hospital?"

"Hi, Kristian. I'm okay, and I'll be leaving the hospital shortly. How are you?"

"Christ, never mind me. I can't believe what happened. I'm so thankful you're okay, you're bloody lucky."

"I think it's all still sinking in, but we can put all of this behind us now. How are things with Down Dream?"

"Crazy. We thought things picked up after what happened to Stu and Bev, but after the media got hold of everything that went down with you and Quentin yesterday, it's all just got out of hand. I actually think we might have just become one of the biggest charities in the country."

David felt a wave of pride sweep over him. "Whoa."

"Honestly, I need you back to the office as soon as you're ready. I can't keep track of everything."

"I'm sorry. I'll drop by the office in a bit, but I have a few things to sort out first. I'll start looking into hiring a few new members of staff to help take on the extra workload."

"Whatever number of staff you were just thinking of hiring, double it. Seriously."

David laughed. "Wow, ok. Leave it with me. Thank you, Kristian. You've been a major help in all of this, I couldn't have done it without you."

"Hey, don't worry about it. I'm just sorry I couldn't have done more."

"You've done more than you realise."

A moment of silence filled the phone.

"Oh, by the way," Kristian said, his voice softer, "Stu's family have organised his funeral for a week on Monday. It'll be the first of

March. I've already made sure the office and the shelter will be manned while we're out."

David bit his lip. "Okay, thanks, Kristian." He stopped walking down the corridor as he noticed a TV on the wall. "Listen, I've got to go, but I'll see you at the office later?"

"Yeah, that sounds good. I'll see you then."

"See you then," David said, clicking his phone off and shifting his attention to the TV as the midday news report was just starting. Unable to properly hear the television amongst the hive of activity within the hospital, David reached up and raised its volume.

"After journalist Alex Haynes's ground-breaking exposé was published in the early hours of this morning, exposing Eva Shields and the Shields Corporation as contributing associates to an underground criminal organisation, a Shields Corporation spokesperson has now confirmed the temporary closure of its headquarters whilst the police investigation gets underway. The corporation's stock price has plummeted fifty-six per cent as police have raided more of its premises up and down the country. CEO and founder of the corporation, Eva Shields, who has been accused of playing a lead role in the operation, is currently in police custody. Scotland Yard have also confirmed that they have now arrested a total of twenty-six people, including Junior Justice Minister Duncan Chiles and the Metropolitan Police Service's own Detective Superintendent Christopher Forrest on corruption charges. David Dale, the founder of charity Down Dream, is still said to be recovering in hospital after he was attacked for a second time yesterday. Alex Haynes has commented since the release of his publication to say that he is pleased that so much is being done in regard to the contents of his report. Mr Haynes has also stated that if it wasn't for Mr Dale's bravery throughout his ordeal, then he may not have been able to finish his detailed, ground-breaking report."

*

David peered around the open doorway, looking into the large room searchingly. He cast his eyes across each of the six beds, starting with the one closest to him on his left and moving clockwise around the room. First, David saw an elderly woman reading a newspaper, lying on her bed with her feet crossed. In the second bed, another elderly woman with her head resting on the pillow and her eyes closed, presumably concentrating on whatever she was listening to from the headphones resting on her ears. In the third bed, and in the furthest corner from him, David spotted her.

Resting her head on a pillow, with her body slumped to one side, Bev slept peacefully. Dressed in her hospital gown, it looked like the strain of her injuries had taken their toll. She had lost several pounds since her arrival at the hospital, but her face looked rosier and healthier, as if her recovery was in full swing. Her bedside table had two bouquets of fresh flowers, a half-eaten punnet of grapes, and several crossword books stacked on top of another.

David observed her face, looking for any sign of stress or worry. He could only find contentment. He moved around her bed, pulled up a chair, and sat down next to her, placing a hand on one of hers. He rested his other arm on his knee and held his face with his free hand, processing everything that had happened.

Bev's body stirred and her eyes flashed open, looking up at the ceiling. She turned her head, looking down at the hand on top of hers, soon realising whom it belonged to. Her eyes instantly glazed as a rush of blood filled her cheeks. "Oh, David," she whispered.

David only managed a timid smile. His eyes filled and the first tear soon fell.

She pushed herself up from her bed and brought round her free arm in an inviting gesture for a hug.

David remained in his seat, his face turned down. "I'm so sorry, Bev," he said as he sobbed. He looked up at her. "I'm so sorry I got you involved in all of this," he whispered with a cracking voice. "I didn't mean for you to get hurt. I'm just so thankful you're okay." He rubbed his eyes and wiped his nose.

Bev silently sighed, now sitting upright. She gripped his hand. "Look at me."

David wiped his nose once more and then looked up at her.

"If I knew what was goin' to happen before I signed up and joined Down Dream, I would still, every time, choose to do it."

David's eyes stared back into hers, his expression frozen.

"David, no amount of violence or threats to me or my life would stop me from helpin' ya. Those people who attacked me and Stu, they are mindless criminals who don't understand the consequences of their actions or the people that it affects. They have my sympathy. But ya cannot apologise to me for getting me involved. I got myself involved and I'd do it again." Bev's eyes welled up further, producing several small tears. "Ya mean so much to me, David, and I will always stand by ya."

David closed his open mouth as he swallowed. "You're an incredible lady, Miss Walcott."

Bev leaned forwards. "And don't ya forget it," she said, quickly forming a smile and laughing loudly.

David laughed with Bev, his eyes dried. "Why have they moved you to a shared ward? You were in a private room."

Bev smirked. "Ya know me, I like talkin' to people. We are social creatures remember. As soon as I came round, I wanted movin'." She looked over her shoulder at the elderly patient in the bed next to her with the headphones on. "Although some don't seem to be a fan of my talkin'!"

CHAPTER 39

With only a handful of thin, high-flying clouds in the sky, the sun was able to beat down onto the city of London with little resistance. Trees swayed gracefully in the modest breeze, dancing to the tune of chatting people as they passed by.

David drove to the edge of the city, observing the world around him in a different light. Everything seemed brighter, louder, and more real.

The radio in the car sounded as it began its short news segment. *"Police today have stated—"*

David switched the radio off, deciding to drive the rest of his journey in silence. He lowered the window next to him, enabling the summer-like air to infiltrate the car.

Almost twenty-five minutes later, David arrived at his destination and parked down a quiet side street next to a little café. He rolled up the window and jumped out of his car, walking around to its rear. Opening the car's boot with a click of his car key, he picked up a long, thin black bag and a cardboard box. He heaved the black bag over his shoulder, tucked the box under his arm, and closed the door, locking it. David then made his way to the café's entrance. As he stepped inside, it didn't take long for him to spot who he was searching for. He nudged through a small gap between two tables before reaching his target. He looked down at the man who was hunched over an old, stained newspaper.

Still with an overgrown beard and a neglected head of hair, John Fairburn looked up at David. "Mr Dale, hello," he said, standing up and offering his hand. "Jeez, you look like you've been through it."

"Thanks," David laughed. "It's been a journey." He quickly placed the cardboard box and the black bag onto the floor beside the wall and shook his hand. Glancing at John's clothes, David spotted the same waterproof jacket and khaki baggy pants full of dirt and holes. He quickly looked at his chair. "Sit down, sit down."

A young waitress approached the table with a pen poised on her miniature notepad. She raised her eyebrows silently.

David did the asking. "What would you like?"

"Er," John hesitated. "I'll have whatever you're having."

David looked to the waitress, said, "Two cappuccinos then, please."

The waitress scribbled the tiny order onto her notepad with lightning speed before giving a slight nod and walking away.

David settled into his chair and looked at John, now sat opposite him. "How are you doing, John? It's been a few days since I saw you at the shelter. Have you stayed with us since then?"

John slouched against the back of his chair as he crossed his legs under the table. "I'm just as I am the day we met. Not too bad, I guess. I've stayed twice now at your shelter. It really is a lovely, friendly place."

"That's great to hear. You're always more than welcome to stay with us. I hate the thought of people being out on the streets in the cold and rain. Please mention us to anyone else you meet that's in your situation."

John nodded. "I will."

David smiled, then allowed it to fade over several seconds. "Do you mind me asking how long you've been homeless?"

"Er, the best part of two, three years, I reckon."

David pursed his lips and shook his head.

"The first year is the worst as you just have no idea what to do or where to go. After that, you start picking things up and getting a bit clued up on where's all right to sleep and where's not safe."

"I remember you saying, when we last met, that you struggled with alcoholism, and that it cost you your job, your marriage, your home, and your relationship with your son."

John nodded with a downcast expression.

The waitress returned, planting two cappuccinos onto the table.

"Thank you," David said. He pushed one of the cups towards John and slid the other to himself. "How have you coped with drink whilst you've been homeless?"

John sipped on the foam at the top of his mug. "I haven't touched it since, and that's the God's honest truth."

David raised his eyebrows. "Wow, that's a massive achievement."

John put his cup back down onto the table. "It is, but what kind of achievement is it? It's just a consequence of my failings."

"Everybody makes mistakes of some degree. Some mistakes can be tiny in comparison to others, but they're mistakes nonetheless. By not touching alcohol since it all happened, you've proven to yourself that it was a blip that's cost you dearly, but that it can and has been rectified. You've made your mistake, but it isn't fair for you to currently live how you do, for so long, without real chances of bettering your life. Without being in your son's life."

"That's life, I guess. The local Councils are always overburdened with people needing temporary accommodation, they just don't have enough to go around. Women and children get priority, and rightly so. So people like me have to drift for longer than we'd like. It's no one's fault, just the system we have."

"But there's such a lack of support and assistance out there to help people like you. It's incredibly frustrating."

John smirked despite the reality. "What can you do?" he asked rhetorically.

"I've got you a job interview."

"What?" John asked, instantly leaning forward and against the table.

"It's for next Wednesday at ten thirty. It's not the best, but it's a start. It's for a position at a small estate agents, just outside of Holloway."

"Are you serious? But why would they want to interview me? I'm homeless, I don't have an address. Look at me. I mean, they haven't seen the state of me, never mind my CV."

"We're going to be piloting a new scheme where Down Dream works with small businesses around the country in getting people back to work, whatever their circumstances. This agency is our first partner and they're keen to take you on."

John raised his hands and flexed his fingers, an unmistakable smile across his face. "What the hell."

"And I couldn't let you go without some new clothes, could I?" David said with a grin as he leant down, picked up the long, thin black bag and passed it over the table.

John couldn't find the words as he rested the bag on the table, being careful not to knock the cappuccinos, and unzipped it. As the zip rolled down, John could see the contents inside, seemingly freshly ironed. A cotton, white shirt, encompassed by a black suit jacket with matching trousers.

"David, I'm, erm… I'm lost for words."

"And," he said, leaning down to pick up the cardboard box. He passed it to John.

John shook his head. "I can't."

"Yes, you can. Go on."

John took the box and rested it on the suit, pulling the lid off. Inside, he looked down at the polished black shoes. "David, why?" he asked, shaking his head. "What's all of this for?"

"You know why, John. You've had years of hell for a stupid mistake you made and you've now corrected. Down Dream wants to see you get back on your feet. To regain some sense of a normal life. To have a relationship with your son again."

At first, John was speechless, his jaw hung open. He finally found his words. "But how do you even know my shoe size? Or my chest or waist?"

David laughed. "You've got me there. I asked all of our volunteers at the shelter to best estimate your shoe and body measurements." He couldn't hold back another loud laugh. "I've had all thirteen of them report back with their estimates and I've gone from there. I hope they're okay for you, just let me know if they're not and I'll get them exchanged."

John looked back down at the shoes, checking their size. "I am a size nine! Jesus Christ," John said, shaking his head repeatedly. "Thank you so, so much. This is enormous, David."

"I was also hoping you'd do a favour for me," David said, taking his first sip of the cappuccino.

"Sure, of course. Anything."

"I'm planning on moving out of my apartment and into something a little different, maybe even somewhere out of London. I was thinking, though, that it'd be nice to keep hold of the apartment as a long-term investment, with house prices rising so quickly and all."

John nodded, resting his hands on the shoe box.

"I'd like you to live in it for me. Keep it clean and tidy and whatnot. Just take care of it, really."

John's breathing shortened. "You, what?"

"I want to keep hold of the apartment, and I know you'd look after it. So, could you move in? Just until you're in a position to get a place of your own."

John's face couldn't hide his bewilderment. "I don't even know what to say," he managed. "You want me to live in your apartment? On my own?"

David shrugged. "Well, once you're properly on your feet, I imagine you'll be able to reconnect with your ex and arrange some sort of visits with your son. Maybe even aim to have him stay with you at the apartment every now and then, whatever you can agree with his mum."

John froze for a silent moment before tears rolled from his eyes at the very thought. He couldn't hold back the sobs, quickly wiping his eyes, trying to regain his composure. "But I have no money. I can't pay you anything to stay there."

"Don't worry about rent for now. Find your feet first."

John shook his head. "This is all too much. I can't."

"Yes, you can. There's a huge lack of support for people who are in similar positions, so you can help me feel like I'm doing something to make this world a better place by accepting my offer. You deserve a break, John."

John sat motionless, his eyes a blurry red. "I don't know what to say. Thank you. Thank you so much."

"It's an honour to help," David said before taking another sip of his cappuccino. "There's a bit of paper in the shoebox that has the address of the estate agency and of your new apartment."

John wiped his eyes once more.

"Well," David started, "I better get going. There's so much to do at Down Dream."

John nodded, his eyes locked on David.

David climbed to his feet. "Best of luck on Wednesday, John. Smash the interview." He dug into his pocket, removed his wallet, and placed a £10 note on the table. He then took out a single key and offered it to John. "I'll be moving a few personal items out of the apartment later today and tomorrow, but the furniture is staying. Here's your key."

"Thanks," John said, hesitantly taking the key. "David," he said as he sobbed, "thank you so much. You've changed my life."

David offered his hand in a final handshake, which John accepted. "You are most certainly welcome. I'll see you soon, John," he said as he turned his back.

"Oh David," John said, looking up at him, clearing his throat.

David turned back around, his eyebrows raised.

"I almost forgot. Who was the guy hanging round the shelter yesterday?"

"What do you mean?"

"There was a man hanging around, talking to people. He wanted to ask me a few questions about the charity and about you, but I didn't have much to say."

"When was this?"

"It was early morning. You weren't around, but it was like he was looking for you."

David felt the heat emitting from his forehead and cheeks. "What did he look like?"

"Kind of slimy. He had his hair brushed all to one side and wore glasses."

"Did you get his name?"

"I heard him say Ben a few times, but at one point he rushed inside a room to answer his phone, and I could have sworn he said Richard."

David's breathing faltered as he only managed to take in a single short breath of air. "*Richard?*"

John nodded.

The name paced up and down David's mind. He thought of the very first time he met Richard back at Sam's cottage in Euxton, their relationship springing out of nowhere. He thought of Sam mentioning that Richard was recently working in London for the week, and anybody could have been the driver of the car that followed him to meet with Eva at the Chiltern Firehouse restaurant. The recollection of telling Sam his address in Wanstead sprang to mind, and her saying she'd speak to Richard because he, too, had been asking about him.

How else did they find out about my house in Wanstead?

"Is something wrong?" John asked.

David once again turned his back and ran for the door.

John watched as David left the building, following him with his eyes. He composed himself with several deep breaths, willing his hands to stop shaking. He looked down at the gift of the key, shoes, and suit. He shook his head and laughed to himself. "What the actual hell?" He lowered his head and looked at the fine detail on the suit, impressed by its intricate design and texture. He ran his fingers across the jacket, feeling the softness of the material, something he hadn't experienced in so long. As his fingers slid over a patch on the front of the suit, he felt the crunching of something underneath. John flipped one side of the suit over to reveal the inside jacket pocket and dug two fingers inside, pulling out a small, folded envelope. He glanced over at the café window where David had just walked past before focusing back on the envelope. Carefully, he tore away at the fringes before slipping two small pieces of paper out of the envelope.

He unfolded the first piece of paper and scanned the handwritten message.

John, accept this one final gift and turn your life around, for you and your son – DD.

He put the note down onto the suit jacket and shifted his focus back to the second small piece of paper. He unfolded it and inhaled sharply, feeling his stomach sink for the second time. In his hands, John held a cheque for £10,000.

David dialled Sam's number as he hurried around the café and down the side street.

No answer.

He approached his parked car, clicking on his key fob to unlock it as he searched for Rose's number. He pulled on the car door handle and opened it, but without hearing a sound, David found himself unable to move. He looked down, noticing a man's hairy arm had rapidly been thrown over his right shoulder, across his neck and down around his chest, holding his body in a locked position. An excruciating sharp pain struck his lower back. Despite the fear, the unknown, and the pain, David couldn't find the energy to resist, his forehead suddenly hot and sweaty. His phone dropped out of his hand, bouncing along the concrete.

The pain deepened, gradually worsening to a throbbing, stinging burn that echoed throughout his lower back. Another agonising sharp pain struck him again in the same area, this time David noticing the sound of metal slicing flesh. The world seemed to transition into slow-motion. Sounds were dampened, colours darkened, and his vision slow to process. David's breathing slowed as he felt the arm from around his chest recede, catching sight of the arm disappearing behind him.

An unnerving familiar voice whispered in David's ear. "Quentin's revenge is always cold."

David dropped his car's key fob and calmly moved his hand around his back, feeling the area that now burnt. As he brought his hand back around, he looked down and noticed the crimson blood covering his palm. He turned on his heels and stumbled against his car, grabbing hold of the door for support. His eyes looked down at the ground and then followed the concrete to the sound of the footsteps sprinting away from him. He slumped against the car and hit the floor; his eyes fixed on the running man with the bloodied knife. At the junction of the side street, the man paused in his escape and turned his head to look back at David. Recognising the face, panic ripped through David, overtaking the sensation of the unbearable pain as he fought for an intake of air. Just as his eyes started to phase into a fuzzy blur, David flopped onto the concrete from his seated position and reached for his phone, resting just inches away. He brought it closer to his face, its screen now covered in shallow cracks and scratches, and tapped it several times before pressing it against his ear.

The line rang twice before being picked up. "Hello you, how are things going?"

"Hello, Rose," he said in several drawn-out breaths.

"David? Are you okay?"

"I'm not sure if…" he stuttered, coughing softly, "I'm going to be able to see you this afternoon."

"What's happened? David, where are you?"

"They've got me, Rose," he said with a break in his voice. "He's got me."

"What? David, what do you mean? Where are you?"

He squirmed in pain on the floor. "I need you to tell," he winced, scrunching his eyes, "to tell my sister... Sam, that her boyfriend is involved." David's breathing was heavy and slow. "Richard's just stabbed me."

"Oh my god. David, where are you? I can call the police. I can get an ambulance."

"Go out and take your life back, Rose."

"David! David, where are you?"

The sun broke out from behind the café, shining its warmth onto David's face. Numbness consumed the pain.

"David!" Rose shouted down the line. "David!"

"Shine that light," he whispered.

"David!"

With her voice ringing in his ear and with her face flashing across his mind, David closed his eyes.

ACKNOWLEDGEMENTS

If *They'll Take Everything* made you feel something, whether good or bad, I kindly ask you to write an honest review on Amazon or Goodreads. It truly helps support my work and I'd be forever grateful. Thank you.

This book wouldn't be what it has become if it weren't for the work of my incredible editor, the wonderful Debz Hobbs-Wyatt. Thank you ever so much for your time and effort.

I'd like to thank my partner for the ever-encouraging words of comfort and support throughout this creative journey.

In everything that I will ever do in my life, I will always have my parents to give my biggest thanks to. For your unwavering and unquestionable love and support, I will never be able to repay you.

If you're interested in new book updates and bonus content, you can subscribe to my newsletter at www.chconnor.com.

In a world where you can be anything, be kind.